Having previously worked as a journalist and then a psychotherapist, Caroline Dunford enjoyed many years helping other people shape their personal life stories before taking the plunge and writing her own stories. She has now published almost thirty books in genres ranging from historical crime to thrillers and romance, including her much-loved Euphemia Martins mysteries and a brand-new series set around WWII featuring Euphemia's perceptive daughter Hope Stapleford. Caroline also teaches creative writing courses part-time at the University of Edinburgh.

Praise for Caroline Dunford:

'A sparkling and witty crime debut with a female protagonist to challenge Miss Marple' Lin Anderson

'Impeccable historical detail with a light touch' Lesley Cookman

'Euphemia Martins is feisty, funny and completely adorable' Colette McCormick

'A rattlingly good dose of Edwardian country house intrigue with plenty of twists and turns and clues to puzzle through' Booklore.co.uk

Also by Caroline Dunford

Euphemia Martins Mysteries:

A Death in the Family
A Death in the Highlands
A Death in the Asylum
A Death in the Wedding Party
The Mistletoe Mystery (a short story)
A Death in the Pavilion
A Death in the Loch
A Death for King and Country
A Death for a Cause
A Death by Arson
A Death Overseas
A Death at Crystal Palace
A Death at a Gentleman's Club
A Death at the Church
A Death at the Races

Hope Stapleford Series:

Hope for the Innocent

Others:

Highland Inheritance
Playing for Love
Burke's Last Witness

A DEATH
AT THE
RACES

A EUPHEMIA MARTINS MYSTERY

CAROLINE DUNFORD

ACCENT

First published in 2020 by Headline Accent
An imprint of HEADLINE PUBLISHING GROUP

3

Cataloguing in Publication Data is available from the British Library

ISBN 978 1 7861 5792 8

Typeset in 10.5/13pt Bembo Std by Jouve (UK), Milton Keynes

Printed and bound in Great Britain by Clays Ltd, Elcograf S.p.A.

Headline's policy is to use papers that are natural, renewable and recyclable
products and made from wood grown in well-managed forests and other
controlled sources. The logging and manufacturing processes are expected
to conform to the environmental regulations of the country of origin.

HEADLINE PUBLISHING GROUP
An Hachette UK Company
Carmelite House
50 Victoria Embankment
London EC4Y 0DZ

www.headline.co.uk
www.hachette.co.uk

For Clare and Bea for welcoming Euphemia so kindly to her new Headline Accent home and to Greg, my long suffering editor, who follows Euphemia wherever she goes.

Chapter One

In which my homecoming takes an unexpected turn

I closed Richenda's door quietly behind me. Hans, her husband, stood in the hall waiting. His handsome face was marred by creases across his forehead. 'How is she?'

'She's sleeping now. She seems content.'

'Not agitated?'

'Not at all,' I said. 'I think she was quite pleased to see me. She asked me about my honeymoon.'

Hans Muller exhaled a long, slow breath. 'That's good. That's good.' His expression relaxed, but even by the shaded electric light of the hall, I could see his face was considerably more aged than when I had last seen him, only some weeks previously. His gaze was focused beyond me, into the distance. I moved slightly to remind him of my presence. His attention snapped back to me.

'She has had some issues with her memory. The doctor says she has a long journey ahead of her. We will not know where it is to end,' he paused and shrugged, 'until it ends.'

I took a step towards him and laid a hand gently on his forearm. 'I am so very sorry, Hans. I wish I could have done more.'

He placed his hand over mine and shook his head. 'No. No. You mustn't feel like that. Bertram says without you she would have died, and you also saved our children.'

'Hardly that. It was Bertram's actions that saved the day. As for the children, I only told Fitzroy they were in danger.'

1

Hans looked puzzled for a moment. 'Fitzroy. Oh yes, that funny chap that had gone along with you as a chaperone. Do you still see him? I'd like to thank him myself.'

I smothered a smile at the thought of Fitzroy ever being a chaperone. 'No, I haven't seen him since, and I don't expect to for quite some time.' I felt relief merely being able to say this truthfully.

'Oh well,' said Hans. 'I expect I'll run into him. Especially as he's a friend of your mother.' I didn't correct my brother-in-law. He had no way of knowing that Fitzroy was a member of the British Intelligence Service and that, until recently, both my newly minted husband, Bertram Stapleford, and I had been assets of the Crown. This had changed of late, but I was in no hurry to remember that.

I drew my hand away gently. There had been a time when Hans and I were . . . closer . . . than we are now. I also knew he was not exactly the stand-up gentleman he appeared to be, and I, being newly married and freshly schooled in the ways of men and women, did not want to give him the slightest encouragement. I had no doubt he loved Richenda in his own way, but I also felt reasonably certain he would have already sought out a mistress, with Richenda so ill and unable to . . .

'Let us go down and rescue the children from Bertram,' I said quickly.

'It's more likely to be the other way around,' said Hans with the shadow of a smile.

We found Bertram in a large sunny room at the back, sitting on the floor, besieged by Hans and Richenda's twins, who were somewhere between one and two years old. I had lost count in all the recent mayhem. A small spotted dog with long floppy ears and a clearly mixed background had joined them. It was currently licking my husband's face and he was laughing. Of the nanny and the Mullers' older daughter, Amy, there was no sign.

'Good heavens,' said Hans, sweeping in and picking up the puppy. 'I do hope Spot has behaved himself. He is not yet allowed much in the house.' I saw his gaze sweep across the fine Persian rug that covered the area.

'He's a great little chap,' said Bertram. 'Normally don't go for anything less than a gundog myself, but that one's got a lot of spunk for his size.'

Hans held the dog slightly away from his jacket, which was, as usual, of the finest cloth and superbly tailored. 'Be that as it may, he should not be in the house at present in case he manages to get upstairs and disturb . . . I see Amy's hand in this. Where is my daughter?'

'Oh, she and Nanny had to do something or another,' said Bertram airily.

'Hmm,' said Hans. 'If you will excuse me a moment.' He walked out, frowning once more.

I held my hand out to Bertram, who took it gratefully and rose to his feet. It's true that the many fine breakfasts we had consumed while on our honeymoon had affected his figure slightly, but my husband is not an unfit man. Rather his health, ever since his episode of rheumatic fever as a child, has been compromised. His heart is delicate.

'That was rather splendid,' he said, looking down at the two cherubs who went back to playing with their wooden blocks. 'Do you think we will have children soon, Euphemia? I think I'd like two, or three, if that is all right with you. The twins have invented their own language that only they speak. Clever little things.' He smiled fondly.

I was about to scoff, but as I observed the children, they did seem to be communicating as they built their little towers. 'Possibly,' I said. 'I do not know that much about children, but these two are very pleasant.'

'We are going to have some, aren't we?' said Bertram, regarding me with wide brown eyes that would put the sweetest puppy to shame.

'Naturally,' I said. 'It's the normal way of things. But I do think I should remind you that we have little choice over what

3

kind of child or children we may have. They may not be as mild-mannered as these two.'

He met my eyes. 'You've guessed, haven't you?'

'Amy was taken away because she had another tantrum?'

Bertram nodded.

'She found adjusting to the twins difficult enough, and now with her mother unavailable . . . I do feel for her. I fear that Hans, without Richenda's influence, will be a stern father.'

'Well, she isn't his, is she?' said Bertram. 'He's bound to feel differently about her. Anyway, never mind that, how is the old girl.'

I shushed him as I heard Hans' footsteps in the hallway. Bertram had opened his mouth to ask me why I was shushing him, so I stepped on his foot. I felt resistance beneath my foot.

'Ah,' he said and smiled at me in a misty, soppy sort of way.

'Still stepping on your foot to make you behave, is she, Bertie?' asked Hans.

'It's become quite our thing,' said Bertram. He waggled one foot in the air. 'She even bought me these bespoke steel toe-capped shoes as a wedding present. They're quite smart, aren't they?'

Hans raised an eyebrow. 'Indeed.'

'We can't afford to buy fancy fitted shoes all the time, you know,' said Bertram, a slight edge to his voice.

'It has been a lovely visit,' I interjected, 'but if we are to have any chance of reaching home while it is still light, we must leave at once.'

Hans glanced out of the window. 'I think we have already missed that mark. The winter day is short here, and even shorter as you go further north. Will you not stay another night?'

'Thank you, but no. We are all packed, and Stone will have put our things in the car. We have had a lovely time, both here and on our travels, but it really is time for us to be going home.'

'Starting our new life together,' said Bertram, taking my hand and squeezing it.

'If you insist,' said Hans, smiling. He walked with us to the door. 'Enjoy your time together,' he called as we climbed into the car. 'You never know what's around the corner.'

We both smiled awkwardly, and Bertram drove away.

'Gods, that was painful,' said Bertram as we cleared the drive. 'I mean the children, the dog, the dinners were fine. But Hans lurched between being a perfect host and a depressing creature of doom. You were all right. You didn't have to sit with him after dinner, drinking port.'

'Neither did you,'

'Yes, well. He does keep a particularly fine cellar.'

I leaned my head carefully on Bertram's shoulder. 'He's had a bit of a time,' I said.

'Haven't we all?' said Bertram. 'Is my sister on the mend? Or has she turned into some sort of gibbering idiot?'

I punched him lightly on the arm. 'Honestly, she didn't want you to see, what with the bandages and everything. She's fine. Or will be.'

'She took an enormous blow to the head. And you know better than most that sanity is not my family's strongest trait.'

'She's quieter. More thoughtful. Her speech is slow and a little slurred at times. She has difficulty using one of her arms and the lid on her right eye droops slightly. But you'd only notice that if you looked closely.'

Bertram made a grunting noise. 'Sounds like a basket case to me.'

'Bertram! She is your sister, and while she might have been a little unkind to you when you were young, since she married Hans she has become a much better person.'

'That's largely due to you,' said my husband. 'Besides, she wasn't a little unkind, she was a hell-cat, cruel as a witch, and Richard's eager little helper in whatever nastiness he conjured up.'

I didn't respond. I knew Bertram cared for Richenda, and if he wanted to distance himself from his feelings for her until we knew she would survive, I could understand that.

'Goodness only knows how she landed Hans,' he finished.

'Despite being a bit moody at times, he's an all right chap. Must be the German half of him that gets the low moods.'

'I think it is best if we don't comment on his nationality to others,' I said.

'I know,' said Bertram. 'War is coming, so says everyone. Why they can't all sit down at a table and sort it out, I'll never know. I mean, if my family could manage to dine together when necessary, surely old Vicky's lot can?'

'Bertram! That is no way to talk of our late Queen and her relatives.'

'I mean . . . Kaiser Wilhelm is her grandson or something, isn't he? Our King's cousin, or some such?'

'I believe it to be somewhat bigger than that,' I said.

'Well, never mind. We don't have to bothered by all that anymore, do we?' said Bertram. 'You're married to me now and we will live happily together in the Fens for the rest of our days.'

'Of course,' I said, laying my head on his shoulder once more. I had my doubts about the Fens, but other than that, I was content. In time, I intended to persuade Bertram to spend some of the money I had inherited from my grandfather on a place in London, so we could split our time between there and Norfolk. I wasn't convinced that a cold, damp Norfolk winter would be good for Bertram's health, or my own sanity.

'At least *that man* is out of our lives,' said my husband with great finality. 'I cannot tell you how good that makes me feel.'

He shifted his shoulder under me. 'Bit uncomfortable that. Must be all those brains in your head. Settle back and try and get some sleep. I won't be driving fast, so it'll be some time before we're home. Hopefully those rugs and that hot brick will keep you warm enough.'

'If you're sure,' I said, snuggling down and making a pad of a second, smaller rug to rest my head against the door. 'Not driving fast, though . . . should I be worried about you?'

'My wife's in the car,' said Bertram. 'I need to get her home safely.'

'Wife's an awfully nice word,' I said.

'It is, isn't it? Almost as good as husband.'

It took me a little while to fall asleep. I turned my face away from Bertram so he wouldn't fret. Around us the dusk descended softly. The sky dissolved in a gentle greyness with wisps of white creeping in and out of the tree-lined road. Eerie, but pretty, I hoped that it didn't herald a complete fog. The area where White Orchards stood was much prone to mist and if it had already begun down here, I feared that it would be blanketed white out there.

True to his word, Bertram drove, uncharacteristically, with great caution. I didn't know if Hans' parting words had struck a chord, or if he was finally paying attention to the weather conditions. Normally, he simply protested that the road remained regardless of weather, and as he was short-sighted anyway, what did it matter? He claimed he drove by instinct. Once we were home, he would have no reason to use to the car to any great extent. This, I was looking forward to, but not much else. I was familiar with the house, having worked there for a short time as a housekeeper. Although in better repair than when Bertram bought it, the building still festered with issues brought on by careless contractors and agents. No sooner was one part fixed than another demanded urgent attention. The total collapse of the kitchen ceiling still remained the most dramatic.

But it wasn't simply the state of the house. My trust fund could stand that. It was the isolation of the place that I feared. My old friend Merry would be there, married to Bertram's chauffeur, Merrit, and expecting her first child. She lived in a small cottage on the estate. I had no idea how she felt about associating with the lady of the house. I would need to tread carefully. But apart from the other tenants, there was no society nearby. I didn't need the rush of daily entertainment, but the occasional family with whom we could share dinner, or even the odd exhibition to view, would have alleviated my doubts. Bertram would be happy with three cooked meals a day, a companion to play chess with, and a weekly delivery of new books from London. He needed little else.

I suspected this would not be enough for me. I loved him dearly, but I had discovered of late I was not made for a quiet life. My hope was that, now being an Agent of the Crown, I could have periods of adventure interspersed with the restful home life that Bertram longed for. Of course, I still had to tell him about my arrangement. Technically, as my husband, he could forbid my actions. Not that he would dare, but the last thing I wanted was to put him in conflict with my spymaster who, despite his charm, was deceptively ruthless.

Bertram hummed quietly to himself as he drove. I did a good job in mimicking sleep, but the reality of it evaded me. The temperature outside fell, as did that of the hot brick at my feet. If I fell asleep now, I thought, I might well catch a chill.

I felt the car slow and Bertram ceased all sounds. I peered out as much as I could without moving my head. There, in the headlights, stood a roe deer and behind her a fawn. She had stopped in front of the car to allow the little one to cross. Not the greatest of plans, but a motherly one, nonetheless. Beside me I heard Bertram inhale softly. I risked a glance and saw him looking at the animals with reverence.

The headlights picked out the soft brown hair on the doe's back, and her graceful, dignified face, with one ear twitching. Behind her the fawn trotted quickly across the road without even glancing in our direction. Perhaps, I thought, finally sliding towards sleep, Bertram and I could share a new interest in studying the wildlife of the Fens.

I awoke to the sound of my teeth chattering in my head. I felt cold through to my bones. The engine noise had disappeared. I opened my eyes and sat up, fearing we had broken down. My thoughts were still untangling from a dream in which Bertram and I had been driven to the edge of a quagmire by giant swans with razor-sharp beaks. We clung to each other as we descended into the murky depths. I don't think I had ever been more pleased to see the shadow of White Orchards rising up before me.

Bertram came around to my side of the car and opened the door. 'Careful, you'll be stiff with cold.'

'I'm fine,' I said, before discovering my legs no longer worked and, still tangled in a car rug, I fell straight in his arms. He caught and embraced me.

'I'm sorry, Euphemia. I should have got them to load more rugs. I didn't realise it would take so long to get back. I had to drive ever so slowly. The roads are swathed in fog.'

'We're here now,' I said. 'Let's go and sit in front a fire and thaw out.' At least that is what I meant to say, but my teeth were chattering too hard to speak clearly. Fortunately, Bertram was of the same mind. He helped me up the stairs to the entrance, where his new butler stood with the door wide open. A warming blast of heat washed over me.

'Welcome home, sir, madam.'

'Giles, I take it you have some fires burning?' said Bertram.

'In the main hall, the smaller saloon, the master bedroom, the library, and of course the kitchen, sir. I did not think that tonight was a night to worry over fuel.'

'Indeed not,' said Bertram. 'Once this place gets cold, it needs the fires of Hell itself to warm up the stone. Please ensure the fires in the servants' hall and the upper attics are also lit. We all need to keep warm. Did I imagine things or was there another car in the . . .?'

I slipped my hand off Bertram's arm and walked over to the hall fire. I still had a car blanket around me and I stood warming myself. The firelight danced across the panelled wooden walls, and the ebony table with its Tiffany lamp. The grandmother clock ticked faintly in a niche by an inset bookshelf. Large mirrors reflected the gentle glow from the hearth around the hall, eliminating the shadows and giving the place a most homely look. How could I ever have doubted that White Orchards would please me? I felt profoundly relieved to be home.

Bertram finally came in and Giles closed the big oak door. I remembered an old saying about all being safely gathered in for the night and gave a contented sigh. I looked up at Bertram to give my best welcoming smile. He knew full well I was not the greatest fan of White Orchards in general. However, the smile faded from my lips when I saw the frown on his face.

'What's wrong?'

'It appears we have a visitor,' said my new husband.

'Not tonight,' I said. 'Giles should have refused them.'

'Apparently he tried, but to no avail.' Bertram's upper lip was looking uncommonly stiff.

'Who on Earth is it?'

'He refused to give his name, but I rather suspect . . .'

As if waiting for his cue, our visitor erupted out of the library door. 'It's rather late, you know,' he said. 'Poor Giles was beginning to worry. You could have telephoned him. You do know I had a telephone put in, don't you? It's my wedding present to you. I'm sure you'll both find it very useful, living out in the middle of nowhere. May I kiss the bride?'

And with that, he darted towards me and, before I could step back, put a hand on each shoulder and placed a firm kiss on each cheek.

'Fitzroy,' I said wearily.

'Fitzroy!' cried Bertram. 'What the devil do you mean by showing up here. Tonight, of all nights?'

The spy smiled charmingly and tilted his head on one side. 'I don't suppose you would accept I merely happened to be passing?'

'On a filthy night like this, in the middle of nowhere?' said Bertram. By now I could see he had begun to quiver with rage.

'I wanted to give you my best wishes for your future happiness.'

'Fitzroy . . .' said Bertram in a low voice and through gritted teeth.

'Oh, very well,' said Fitzroy, shrugging. 'I needed to speak to Euphemia and as it happened, I was nearby. Can't tell you where or why.' He smiled again, perfectly at ease invading our home late in the night.

Bertram turned to me. 'I thought I had made it perfectly clear that we were to have no more dealings with this man?'

'Heavens, Euphemia,' said Fitzroy. 'You're barely married a moment and he's gone all dictatorial.'

Bertram flushed slightly red. 'I mean, I thought we had agreed this chapter of our lives had closed?'

Fitzroy looked from him to me, clearly enjoying the situation. 'I take it you haven't told him yet?'

'Told me what?' said Bertram, having been flushed, he suddenly paled. 'It was a real vicar that married us, wasn't it? It wasn't one of his ploys?'

'Honestly, Bertram,' I said, taking the higher ground while I could, 'we have been living as man and wife for over a week. Do you think I would . . .'

Bertram went back to being flushed. 'No, no, no, of course not,' he said. 'It's just with that dastardly fellow, one never knows where one stands.'

'The dastardly fellow is still here,' said Fitzroy. We both ignored him.

'You're quite correct in saying that I wanted to close this chapter of my life upon our marriage . . .' I said.

Fitzroy staggered dramatically as if shot, one hand pressed to his chest. We both continued to ignore him.

'However, that was before I was charged with murder.'

'Yes?' said Bertram. It may have been a trick of the firelight, but the loving look in his eyes appeared slightly diminished. His tone was certainly wary.

I looked over at Fitzroy. 'I take it I can tell him now?'

'As long as Giles isn't lurking in the shadows,' said the spy.

'He wouldn't let me tell you until we were married,' I said in a rush. 'I wanted to, but he made me promise, and I couldn't . . .'

Bertram held up his hand. 'This man has some hold over you?' he asked. 'You give your obedience to him over your own husband?'

'Oh no,' said Fitzroy. 'She's never been obedient with me.

11

Reluctantly compliant? Aggressively acquiescent? Contemptuous? Which is best applied, Euphemia?'

'If you could stop enjoying yourself for a minute, and let me explain,' I snapped. 'Go back into the library. I wish to speak to my husband alone.'

Fitzroy gave a mock bow. Then he threw me a wink behind Bertram's back that I interpreted as a sign he would be listening in.

'So?' said Bertram as the door closed behind the spy.

I sighed. 'So, when I was arrested for murder, Fitzroy offered me two ways out of the mess. One was to flee abroad—'

'What!' exploded Bertram.

'Oh, not like that,' I said. 'He doesn't think of me in any romantic way. I'm useful to him, that's all.'

'How?'

'As an asset,' I said, 'nothing more. Or, it *was* nothing more.'

'Euphemia, if you don't stop prevaricating and spit it out, I swear, I will take that umbrella over there and go into the library and thrash that man.'

I could almost hear the eavesdropper thinking, *you can try*. 'I joined the intelligence service,' I said, 'as an Agent of the Crown. I'm only allowed to tell one person, and Fitzroy said as I kept almost getting married, I shouldn't tell you until after we were. I agreed. I'd rather not have told you at all.'

'Is that all?' said Bertram.

'What do you mean?'

'You're a spy now? It always seemed to me you were doing the lion's share of the work whenever we were involved with him. I can't see how it would be different.'

'I took an oath,' I said, 'to protect King and Country.'

'Of course, I'd expect nothing less of you. We both tried to do our bit.'

'You don't understand. He's my superior now.' Bertram looked at me blankly. 'I have to follow his orders.'

At this point he strode over to the stand and lifted the umbrella.

'Thinks he can order my wife about; well, I'll damn well show him.'

I put out a hand to stop him. 'But he can. That was my Faustian bargain. It was the only way he could legally get me out of custody.'

Bertram paused. 'Since when has obeying the law mattered to that man?'

'I was publicly accused of murder. Short of spiriting me out of the country, there was nothing he could do to save me from being hanged. The evidence, although largely circumstantial, was compelling enough for most juries.'

'I'd never have let that happen,' said Bertram.

I walked up to him and gently took the umbrella from his grasp. 'I didn't do this without considerable thought,' I said. 'He explained in detail what it would mean for me and my future. If anything, he tried to talk me out of accepting.'

'No, he wanted you to run away with him.'

'How can you say that, after he saved your nephew and nieces? Not once, but twice. I don't always like the way he behaves, but he does good, in the end. You know that.'

Bertram made a gruff sound, like a bear that had hit its head on the roof of its own cave. 'But what does it mean?' he asked.

'It means, if I am required to do something for King and Country, then I must obey.'

Bertram gave a deep sigh, echoing my own earlier one. 'I suppose that's not so bad. I mean, on occasion, it was almost fun. And together . . .'

I shook my head. 'Only I took the oath.'

'Well, I'll take the damn thing too.'

I held out my hands to him. He took them. I raised his cold right hand to my lips and kissed them. 'You know I love you . . .'

'But?' said Bertram, his body taunt with tension.

'I asked Fitzroy at the time and he said because it was a military outfit you could not be admitted – due to your health.'

13

Bertram bristled like an indignant hedgehog. 'I am hardly ever ill. Besides, I cannot have my wife going into danger alone.'

'I won't be alone. At least not for my first few missions . . .' A heavy silence fell between us. I swallowed.

'You mean?' said Bertram.

I nodded. 'I'll be with Fitzroy.'

Bertram withdrew his hands from my grip. 'I see,' he said in a tight voice. 'Well, while you attend to your guest, I shall retire.'

I opened my mouth, but he held up his hand in a most aggressive manner. 'You have explained. There is nothing more to be said. I must accept the situation. I must accept that my wife dances to the tune of another man.' He went for the staircase without another word and mounted it swiftly.

I stood there, stunned. This was not the homecoming I had wished for.

Fitzroy poked his head around the edge of the library door. 'Well, I think we can say that went about as well as we expected.'

It was with great difficulty that I prevented myself from picking up the nearest vase and throwing it at his head.

Chapter Two

In which I learn of my first official mission

'Good restraint,' he said, continuing to be as infuriating as ever. 'Come into your library. We have much to discuss. You can also ring for some hot drinks and sandwiches. You'll need them after your trip, and I fear I may be coming down with a chill.'

I followed him through the door and into the warm, book-lined room with its leather armchairs, smelling of saddle soap, and Bertram's rather battered old desk that he loved and refused to replace. The spy threw himself down into a chair in front of the fire and gestured to me to take another beside it.

I rang the bell and ordered refreshments before joining him. 'Giles gave you a most disapproving look,' said Fitzroy. 'I hope he is going to welcome you properly as the new mistress of the house.'

'I believe that was more to do with the company I keep than my character,' I said. Fitzroy ignored my comment. We waited in silence for the servant to appear. I knew him well enough to know he wouldn't start explaining anything official until the room was secure from eavesdropping.

The tray arrived in good time. Fitzroy locked the library door and even stuffed his handkerchief in the keyhole. 'Haven't had the time to vet Bertram's – I mean your – staff yet.'

'This must be serious for you to be so rude to Bertram,' I said. 'I will have a trying time getting him out of his sulk.'

Fitzroy grimaced. 'Grown men shouldn't sulk. What will you do, feed him jelly and ice cream and tell him he's a good boy?'

'What do you want?' I asked, pouring the tea.

'You may want something stronger than that before I tell you.'

I passed him a teacup. 'I am very tired. Please state your business and leave so I may go to bed.'

'Lovely to see you too,' said the spy, setting his untasted tea down. 'There is an item in Germany that needs to be collected. It is of national importance. Right now, tourists are hardly welcome in the country. It's all a bit dicey.'

'You're going to get it?'

Fitzroy shook his head. '*We're* going to get it.'

'But I've only just arrived home!'

'You got your honeymoon. Isn't that supposed to be the best bit of a marriage? All downhill from here on.'

'What on earth will Bertram say? He will be ever so upset. He might even try and forbid me to go.'

The spy made a huffing sound as he devoured a cold meat sandwich, making it clear that he didn't think much of that idea.

'Are you trying to ruin my marriage before it even starts?' I said. Fitzroy continued to make inroads through the food, as if his life depended on it. He appeared oblivious to my distress. 'Don't you see, this will make him think that our life is going to be such that you may appear at any moment and whisk his wife away?'

Fitzroy took another handkerchief out of his pocket and dabbed at his moustache. It was only then I realised he was not his usual clean-shaven self. He saw me looking.

'I've run into a few Germans before. I thought a slight change of features might be wise. And as to your comment about my taking Bertram's wife away whenever I wished, that is close to the truth. It will be whenever the service requires me to do so. It's nothing personal against the man. Are you forgetting, I stood up for him as his best man? This is what you signed up for, Alice.'

The introduction of my code name, I knew, was an indicator to let me know I was now speaking with a higher-ranking officer and not a friend, if ever I had considered Fitzroy to be a friend.

I nodded slowly and took a deep breath. Being angry with him would be to no avail. The oath I had taken was binding. That I suspected he had manoeuvred me into a corner so that I'd had to take it didn't matter.

'How long shall we be gone?'

Fitzroy shrugged. 'I really have no idea. The mission is to retrieve the item as soon as possible, but there are a few bumps along the road.'

'Other than the fact that we are on the brink of war with Germany?' I asked, trying to keep the sarcasm out of my tone.

'Yes, you'd think that would be enough, wouldn't you?' The spy's eyes sparkled. My heart sank. Knowing him, if he was this excited about the mission, it must be fraught with difficulties.

'What else?' I asked. The food, the firelight, and the warmth were having a strong effect on me. My sleep in the car must have been fitful for I suddenly felt bone weary. My eyelids felt heavier than stone.

'We don't quite know where the item is, or who has it.'

My eyes jerked open. 'We are to go to Germany and search it in its entirety?'

'Don't be silly, Alice, that would take far too long. No, I am reliably informed the person who has the item will come to us.'

'So, in the whole of Germany, they will find us and give us this item. Let us hope it will fit easily into our luggage. We wouldn't want to be conspicuous. Ah, but if we are not, how will they find us!'

Fitzroy helped himself to another cup of tea in a vulgar breach of social etiquette. 'You know, Alice, I had been doing this for some time before we even met. The service has been in play even longer than I have been alive. It's all muddled along quite nicely without your withering scorn.'

'I'm sorry. I'm tired, and this sounds so fantastical I could almost imagine it was a prank.'

'I never jest about such serious matters,' said Fitzroy. 'Enjoyable though it was to send your husband hot-footed and angry to bed, I really wouldn't waste the time and effort coming out here merely to amuse myself.'

'I am suitably chastised,' I said in as polite a tone as possible. 'Please tell me about the mission.'

'Good girl,' said Fitzroy, sitting back in his chair and stretching his feet out to the fire. 'Have you ever heard of the Monte Carlo Rally?'

'I assume it's an automobile race in Monte Carlo.'

'Oh, it's far more than that. Your husband will know all about it. Motor enthusiasts the world over enter their cars, and even more follow the race. In some places the streets are lined three people deep. Quite a spectacle.'

'Is this how the item is getting out of the country? Will we be intercepting it at the port?'

Fitzroy shook his head. 'I could easily do that alone. No, we will be taking part in this year's altogether unofficial rally. Whoever has the item will approach us as we travel through Germany, at which point something terrible will happen to our engine, or some such, and we will have to return home without finishing the rally. The race starts in one place and goes through a number of checkpoints, so it should be easy enough for our contact to find us. Has Bertram got any maps of Europe?'

I went to the shelves and managed to find one quite quickly. Bertram kept an ordered library. Fitzroy pushed everything on Bertram's desk to one side. I winced but managed not to protest. He laid out the map for me to see. He pointed to the cities as he named them, tracing his finger along the route.

'We start in Hamburg, go on to Bremen, and then Hanover, Dortmund, Cologne, Frankfurt, Stuttgart, and finally Zurich – which is the point you'll notice we leave Germany, so I anticipate this is the latest stage we will turn back. The race then goes on through Milan, Genoa, and ends in Monaco. It's a pity, I think you would have liked Milan.'

'It's still a fair journey,' I said.

18

Fitzroy nodded. 'That's why I need a navigator. How are you at reading maps?'

'Well, I know what one is,' I said, gesturing the one in front of us.'

'Let me guess, you can also read the names of the towns and cities?'

'So, that's good, isn't it?'

Fitzroy gave a groan that sounded all too genuine. 'I imagine I will have to teach you properly.'

'Now?'

'Good grief, no. I've far too much left to do tonight.' In the background the hall clock struck eleven.

'You said it was an unofficial race?'

'Ah, that. Yes, the official race has been called off due to political instability. A most wise decision. This lot is just a bunch of riffraff who are risking all for a rather large purse put up by some industry mogul.'

'So we won't be doing the whole thing?'

'Nor, I sincerely hope, going through the Alps. It's going to be cold enough as it is. Don't worry much about packing clothing. Just ordinary sensible stuff will do. I'll pick up the coats, woollen underwear, and whatnots.'

The thought of Fitzroy picking out my intimate garments made me feel slightly uncomfortable. The idea that Bertram might ever hear of such a thing brought me almost to the brink of nausea. I held on to the edge of the table tightly and tried not to sway. I swallowed several times, closing my eyes and willing myself not to be sick.

'. . . so, you see why, don't you?' Fitzroy had carried on speaking.

I glanced over at him. Like some magician's trick he produced a large pair of scissors and was flourishing these towards me.

'Sorry?' I said, blinking in a bemused manner.

'Oh, do pay attention, Alice. I said that while women have been known to take part in the Monte Carlo Rally, it is rare. As

19

we do not want to attract any attention, you will portray my much younger brother, acting as navigator.'

I looked from him to the scissors and back again. 'You can't be serious,' I said.

'Sorry, Alice. Take pride in knowing your vanity is being sacrificed in the national interest.'

Chapter Three

In which my new husband is exceedingly unhappy

Bertram woke up and stretched. I sat up and leaned over him, giving him my best smile. He screamed and half-scuttled, half-fell out of bed. 'Dear God, what did he do to you?'

I put my fingers up to my newly shorn hair. 'I think it looks rather nice,' I said. 'It's quite fashionable – at least that's what he said.'

Bertram uneasily approached the bed and sat on the edge. Fortunately, the maid had crept in and lit the fire while we slept. A job I remembered all too well having to do. Waking up in the warmth remained a luxury for me. Now fully sitting up in bed, I stretched, knowing full well Bertram rather liked the silk negligee I was wearing. (Fortunately, having decidedly strong seams, it had survived the rigours of our honeymoon.)

Instead of getting into bed as I had hoped, Bertram remained where he was, but was now doing a goldfish impression, with his mouth wide open. It did not look as if he was inviting me to kiss him.

'Darling?' I said, shifting my shoulders slightly in an attempt to make myself even more interesting to my groom.

'Did he have a reason for doing this to you?' Bertram straightened. 'Did he have some kind of a turn and attack you. I've never trusted the man, he's—'

'No, on our next mission I am to act as his younger brother.'

'Am I to take it that this is to happen soon?'

21

Fitzroy hadn't actually ordered me not to tell Bertram. It had taken time for him to finish with my hair – we had argued about exactly how short it should go and he had wanted it very much shorter. He had proved remarkably adept with the scissors, so the cut itself wasn't bad. The hour had grown very late by the time he had given me necessary instructions, so much so that when he had finished, he promptly ran from the room and out to his car. When I followed, more slowly, I saw the night was woollen-thick with mist and freezing cold. He had resisted my entreaties to stop for the night and driven off at quite a spit, leaving me to face the even colder stony visage of Giles, who, by expression alone, had made it clear what he thought of his new mistress chasing after men into the night and bidding them to stay. I wondered when, if ever, I would be able to look Giles in the face again.

Because of this, because of the lack of orders, I told Bertram everything. As I carefully went through the whole plan, Bertram's face got sterner and sterner. He ended up gritting his teeth so hard I feared his jaw would crack.

I faltered in my tale. 'It cannot be that you do not trust me with Fitzroy. I know much more about the relations between a man and woman since our marriage. He will not be able to trick me into indiscretion. Not,' I added, feeling slightly peeved, 'that he has ever tried to do so.'

Bertram unclenched his jaw with obvious difficulty. He spoke slowly, as if under the pressure of great emotion. 'For once, it is not the spy's morals that concern me.'

'Oh, good,' I said, smiling brightly. 'I know the timing positively stinks, but at least I will have got the first mission over with. I have been worrying about what it might be like.'

'Do you have any idea of how dangerous it will be in Germany at this time for an English gentlewoman?'

'It's not where I'd choose to go for a picnic,' I said.

Bertram stood up and marched over to the hearth. 'You sound as flippant as he does.'

'I don't have an awful lot of choice, Bertie. I have to make the best of it,' I said, realising for the first time that was exactly what Fitzroy did.

'Leaving aside the fact that you will be in a foreign country, without your husband, and leaving aside the fact that you don't speak German, and even leaving aside the fact that you're with a man who would leave you dead in a ditch without a second thought if his mission required it—'

'I do think I would get a second, perhaps even a third thought before he did away with me. He likes me far more than that.'

Bertram would not be stopped, he raised his voice louder, 'Leaving aside all these credible, distinct, and excellent reasons for you not to go on this ruddy mission, do you have the slightest idea of how cold it will be? The Stapleford House attics in winter would seem tropical compared to this.'

'Maybe we should go down to breakfast? You're always a little out of sorts when you're hungry.'

'Toast, eggs, and bacon are not going to change my mind over this, Euphemia. This is a damned bad idea and you shouldn't be going with him.'

'Are you forbidding me to go?'

Bertram thrust his arms through his dressing gown and wrapped it tightly around him. 'Most husbands would,' he said.

I got out the other side of the bed. I took my own dressing gown from its hanger and put it on. The silk felt soft against my skin, and for a tiny moment I thought about simply acquiescing to Bertram. I had lost my father, spent a long time living the hard life of a servant, been involved in more murders than any non-police person should, and laid my life on the line for King and Country (despite not being an agent then). Didn't I deserve to return to a normal life? After all, what could Fitzroy do if I said my husband, who under the law was my lord and master, forbade me to go with him?

Quite a lot, said a little voice in my head, and you wouldn't like any of it.

My reflections must have shown on my face as Bertram's rigid

23

stature relaxed slightly and he took a pace towards me. This was the moment for me to capitulate.

I said, 'Then you will have to decide if you are "most husbands".' Then I flounced out the door to my own room. Bertram had retired to his after his sulk last night and I had followed to appease him. As he had slept soundly through the night, there had been no need.

Once in my own chamber I rang the bell and ordered the maid to bring me tea and draw me a bath. I had no idea if Bertram would head straight down to breakfast, but I needed time to get my thoughts in order.

A little under forty-five minutes later I faced my husband across the breakfast table. He was forlornly dipping soldiers in his eggs and wearing the expression of a beagle that has been kicked by its master for no good reason. He looked up at me, not with ire, but with a pathetic sorrowfulness. I steeled myself. A rant from Bertram would solidify my determination to go, but I was not immune to his obvious misery.

I reached out a hand. 'Rightly or wrongly, I did take an oath. You would never ask another male to go back on his word, would you?'

Bertram took my hand. 'Of course not, but you're a female.'

'I don't believe Fitzroy was making that distinction when he swore me in.'

Bertram withdrew his hand abruptly. 'I don't want to talk about that man. You can go if you wish. I am only fearful for your safety. I daresay he knows a thing or two about keeping out of trouble, but he can't change the weather. You'll come back with pneumonia.'

After this cheerful prediction, I rang for some more hot toast, which I buttered for him and cut into pieces so he could dip them in his egg. I passed the plate across to him and it was accepted with a grunt. I decided the best thing to do was to have as normal a day as possible. Bertram had not enquired when I was going so I saw no reason to tell him. Instead we spent the day looking over our home and making minor adjustments so what was once a bachelor's abode became our married home. This consisted of no more than adding vases of cut flowers, re-arranging a few knick-knacks, and having some pictures brought down from the attic and hung about the long plain walls. We took a short walk after lunch and spent the afternoon playing chess (I let Bertram win) and reading. I took a short rest before dinner, during which time I packed a few necessities.

I was extremely attentive during dinner. Bertram's mood had brightened considerably. He remained happy and full of affection towards me until halfway through the dessert course, when the doorbell clanged through the house.

Bertram paused with a piece of apple tartine wobbling on the end of his fork. He looked me directly in the eye. No mean feat when I was doing my best to look anywhere but at him.

'No,' he said. 'No.'

Before I could answer we heard Fitzroy's voice from the hall loudly telling Giles not to bother showing him the way, but that an extra portion of everything sent up by cook would not go amiss.

'Tonight?' said Bertram.

I nodded. 'I didn't tell you because I didn't want to spoil our first day at home.'

His face softened slightly when I called White Orchards home. Then the door opened, and Fitzroy entered, casting off coat, scarf, hat, and goggles in a grand trail behind him. Giles followed, picking up the cast-offs. 'Sir?' he said to Bertram. In that one word a myriad of emotions and questions echoed around the room.

'Yes, yes,' said Bertram, waving his hand. 'Take our guest's apparel away and bring him some food.'

'Very good, sir,' said Giles. The butler kept his voice level, but his disdain cut through the atmosphere like a knife.

After he had closed the door, Fitzroy, who had already pulled up a chair, remarked, 'Very fine butler, that. Disapproves of me immensely. Always good to have senior servants who are sound judges of character. What kind of soup is it?'

Bertram turned a light puce. 'I don't know where to start,' he said.

Fitzroy helped himself to a bread roll and began to tear it to bits. 'Then, my good fellow, why not leave well alone. Your ire will not change the facts.'

Bertram went a slightly darker puce. 'You had the damned audacity to cut my wife's hair.'

The spy tilted his head on one side to make it clear he was considering me. 'Should have let me cut it shorter, Euphemia. You still look too damn pretty to be a boy.'

Bertram made a series of sounds somewhere between puffs and growls. 'Bertram, please,' I said. 'Be calm. You'll make yourself ill. It's only hair. It will grow again.'

'It's the intimacy of the thing,' said Bertram. 'Touching your hair.' He struggled to find the right words. Fitzroy watched silently. I tried to kick him under the table, but the spy had placed himself just out of my reach. Wretch!

'In the spirit of owning up to things, I should mention I also touched the nape of her neck and the top of her forehead. Your wife is very bad at sitting still. No patience at all.'

At this point I stood up. 'If you do not treat my husband with some respect in his own home, you and your service can go hang,' I said. 'Bertram has suffered far more than most husbands would have put up with when it comes to my working with you. So, let me assure you, any further attempts to damage my relationship with my husband will be met with expulsion. I may not be able to throw you out of this house alone, but I have servants to hand, and I will call the whole bloody pack of them on you if I need to. Your manners are execrable and your attempts to amuse yourself at our expense despicable.'

Fitzroy slid back his chair but did not stand. 'If you remember, it was you who was going to hang,' he said, quietly but with menace.

'And I'd have rather I had than you continue to make Bertram so unhappy,' I responded in a flash. By now I was blinking rapidly as tears threatened to overwhelm me.

'Oh, sit down, Euphemia,' said Fitzroy. 'Bertram, I apologise unreservedly for my behaviour. I am always at my most disgraceful when I am worried. I quite agree, I shouldn't take your wife with me, and if I had another option, please believe me, I would take it.'

Bertram, who had been regarding me with a slack jaw, stood, and came behind me to help me back into my seat. He squeezed my shoulder as he returned to his own. For him, this was a very public and unusual display of affection.

'My wife,' said Bertram, 'as you have witnessed, is a remarkable woman of great courage and wits. So why the hell she ever allowed herself to become involved with you, I have no idea. But as she has, I respect her decision. I doubt there will ever be anything about you, Fitzroy, that I will ever respect.'

To my surprise the spy inclined his head slightly as if he agreed.

The rest of the food then arrived and he, at least, ceased to talk while he ate an enormous amount.

An hour later, and having said my tearful goodbyes, I sat in Fitzroy's car, while Bertram hopped from one foot to another waiting to see us off.

'So, you're going to travel through the night?' he said.

'Less likely to be spotted,' said Fitzroy. 'I'll hire a room at the coast tomorrow so Euphemia can change and then we'll get right on the boat. There isn't a lot of time to spare if we're to catch the other members of the British contingency.'

'And they're doing all this for money?' said Bertram in a slightly disgusted voice.

'A lot of people might know about this race, but it's strictly unofficial. I expect the genuine car-lovers will reclaim it after the war and it will once again be a thing of true sportsmanship.' He climbed up into his seat. 'I trust you feel your wife is adequately wrapped up and has enough hot bricks that she will stay warm? I have flasks of coffee in the boot too.'

Bertram came up and took my gloved hand. 'Try and sleep, my dear. You'll need all your strength in the days ahead.' He kissed my hand. 'If she so much as loses another hair, Fitzroy, your life is forfeit.'

'I hear and obey,' said the spy. 'I will treat her like – like something fragile.' He gave a cheery wave and drove off.

In the past I had been as excited as I was apprehensive of starting a new adventure. Tonight, I felt miserable. We drove in silence for several miles.

'Alice,' said Fitzroy finally, 'I do hope you're not going to be such a wet blanket for the whole journey. The job's going to be difficult enough without you moping.'

'I am not moping.'

'Then you're doing the best damned impression I've ever seen.'

'You were horrible to Bertram.'

'Yes, I thought that worked rather well, don't you?'

I gasped.

The spy continued, 'I thought I was utterly loathsome. Such is my dedication to this partnership, I was quite prepared to let him attempt to deck me.'

'But why?'

'You mean you didn't follow? I *am* disappointed. There was I thinking how nicely you were playing along.'

'You wanted me to cross you and defend Bertram to show him my loyalty,' I said, sighing.

'I do hope this doesn't mean you meant the ghastly things you said of me. Otherwise, as your ranking officer, I'd have to take you to task.'

'What does that mean?'

'Never mind, Alice. I daresay you believed that drivel about driving through the night too?'

'Well, yes. Why not. It's the kind of thing you do.'

'I haven't slept in around fifty hours. We will be stopping in about an hour at an inn where I have reserved rooms. We need to talk about how I am going to usher you inside as a lady and out tomorrow as a boy.' I saw his teeth flash in the darkness. 'This is where the fun begins, so forget about your lace and jam-making, we're on a mission for the King!'

Chapter Four

In which Fitzroy barely contains
his temper

We drove for what felt much longer than an hour. The night sky, inky dark above us, showed the stars clearly enough that I managed to pick out a couple of constellations my father had taught me. I didn't share my observations with Fitzroy who, for once, was not driving as if the Hounds of Hell were at his heels. I glanced askance. The luminous half moon lit his face a ghastly white. He studied the road with intensity, yet with a stillness that reminded me of the statuary to be found outside Grecian-influenced court houses. I couldn't deny his stark profile showed him to be of above average handsomeness, but at the same time something about him filled me with unease. I might mock him from time to time, but I knew him to be a killer and a deceiver who could challenge the father of lies in a battle. That he treated me well often allowed me to forget what sort of man he really was. When he spoke suddenly, my heart quickened.

'Alice, will you stop staring at my profile. I know it's a particularly fine one, but your unwavering gaze is unnerving me.'

'You, unnerved?'

'Go to sleep. I'll be driving a while yet. You'll need all your strength in the days ahead.' He looked at me briefly and frowned. 'I wish you understood what you'd got yourself into.'

On which reassuring note I settled down in my seat and closed my eyes. I had no expectation of falling asleep, but the recent excitements must have taken their toll for I drifted off almost at once.

I awoke to the shuddering of the engine as the car stopped. I stirred. The spy jumped out of his seat and went to retrieve his luggage. I unwrapped myself carefully from my rugs. I knew better than to wait for him to help me. I stumbled a little as I got out. I felt remarkably stiff for such a short drive.

We were parked behind a large building on an unlit, grassy plot. Fitzroy handed me a bag. 'You'll find your new outfit in there. Come and find me before you go down to breakfast. We need to work on your voice. You sound like a girl.'

'Really?' I raised an eyebrow, but my sarcasm fell off him like snow off a hot grate. He hefted a larger bag out and walked towards the dark building.

I didn't ask. I followed. He opened a door and we walked into a hot and busy kitchen. People in white chef's outfits bustled to and fro among steaming pots of and pans. A glorious smell of tomatoes and garlic filled the air. 'We've come in the wrong—' I began, when a stout, sallow-skinned woman of about forty, in a bright peasant skirt and a scarlet top, spotted the spy and cried out, 'It is the Fitzy-roy. Husband, the Fitzy-roy is here.' Then, to my immense surprise, she embraced the spy and kissed him soundly on both cheeks. She had to stand on tiptoes to do so.

Fitzroy dropped his bag and bent down to return her greeting. 'Consuela, lovely as ever.'

The woman blushed and said something in a foreign language. Without hesitation Fitzroy answered her fluently in the same tongue. I stood in the background and tried to avoid getting in everyone's way. Fitzroy beckoned me forward, continuing to talk in the woman's language. She looked me up and down swiftly and said something to him. He laughed and shook his head. They went through to the main part of the building with me trailing like an unwanted chaperone. We came into a hotel reception area. Consuela took a key from the board, then another, and handed

30

them to Fitzroy. Then she embraced him again and retired back to the kitchen.

Obviously very much at home, the spy walked over to the large oak staircase that dominated the hall and began to climb without even checking to see I was following. I was.

At the first landing he went to one of the rooms and unlocked the door, ushering me in. If ever someone had designed a romantic boudoir and taken the concept too far, this was it. At the centre of the room stood a four-poster bed, complete with red velvet curtains. Two chairs and a chaise longue were similarly upholstered, and the large window even had curtains made of the same material. The wallpaper shouted with vividly red peonies. I stood uncomfortably as the spy sat down on the bed, dropping his bag at his feet.

'Pull up a chair,' he said. By the warm glow of the room's lamps, I could see he was sheet white.

I sat down. 'Your friend likes red,' I commented.

Fitzroy frowned briefly. 'Oh, Consuela. She's not a friend. She's an asset. She and her husband are in my debt. There's always a room or two here if I need them. No questions asked.'

'She seemed fond of you.'

Fitzroy shrugged. 'I expect she is. I may fall asleep at any moment, so let me say what I must. I drove much further than I thought I would. We're two-thirds of the way to the coast. Your new costume is in that bag. Pack your current clothes in it and Consuela will keep it until we come back. I'm afraid you'll have to remove your wedding ring. Your character is too young to be married. Do you want to leave it here or would you rather I took it?'

I tugged at my finger. 'I've hardly had it five minutes.'

'You'll be wearing it again before you know it,' he said as I passed the ring to him.

'You keep it. That way it'll be near me even if it's not on my finger.'

'So sentimental, Alice?'

I didn't bother to reply. He passed me another key. 'Your room is next door. A maid will bring you tea in the morning to wake you. Don't talk to her. I'll likely be down before you, but knock on my door and check, will you please? I haven't been this weary for a long time.'

I must have looked relieved for he said, 'Did you think I had romantic designs on you? I assure you, Alice, if I had I would have acted on them long ago. I am not a patient man when it comes to matters of the heart. Besides, I hope you'd know I would take any love interest of mine to somewhere less . . .' he looked around, 'obvious. You're quite safe.'

'I'm sorry. It's just the four-poster . . .'

The ends of his mouth lifted slightly. 'I rather think Consuela likes imagining me in it. You're right, of course, she has a soft spot for me.' He brushed his moustache in an obviously preening manner. I laughed.

'But seriously, Alice. We're a team. It would be inappropriate and distracting if I had romantic feelings for you. I treat you as I would any other fellow agent.'

'I know. That's why you never help me out of the car.'

'Do you need help? You seem able-bodied enough. But, no, I won't treat you like a lady, if that's what you mean. We don't have the time for niceties, I'm afraid, but your virtue is quite safe with me.'

For a moment I felt a small pang of disappointment. I had no desire to be intimate with the spy, but on the other hand, no woman likes an attractive man explaining quite so plainly that he is entirely uninterested in her.

Something of this thought must have showed on my face as the spy gave another little laugh. 'If it's any consolation, Alice, I do count you as a friend – which is terribly unprofessional of me, I know. I generally work solo because I don't, on the whole, like many people. You are different.'

'Thank you,' I said. 'I'll let you get some sleep.'

He nodded. As I closed the door behind me, I heard the sound of a body collapsing back onto the bed.

My room, it transpired, was less vibrant, in shades of muted blues with a large but uncanopied bed. I unpacked the bag Fitzroy had given me and laid out the attire. Although I had now seen first-hand what males wore as underwear, it felt very strange to think I would be wearing the same. I packed my own clothes away in the bag as instructed. Naked, I stood in front of the long mirror and considered my reflection. It wasn't only my voice I would need to change; my form and mannerisms were clearly those of a woman. I could play an effete boy, but if Fitzroy was determined not to attract any attention, that wouldn't work. I tried a few poses in front of the mirror and considered the way I walked. I had seen the spy appear to change his entire personality merely by changing his gait and his table manners (which were usually atrocious). It would be a long time before I was quite that good, but by the time I went to bed I thought I had cultivated a few stances and mannerisms that made me appear more boyish.

Then I climbed into bed, and despite my rest in the car, and the thought of the dangers ahead, I fell asleep.

Fitzroy had it right. I did feel safe with him. Not that I had any intention of telling him that.

The next morning, after a brief but excellent breakfast with plenty of hot coffee, we were on our way before the sky had time to fully lighten. 'I'd like to catch today's ferry,' said the spy as he hustled me out. He wore a long thick driving coat, gauntlet-style gloves, goggles, and a leather cap. I had no urge to laugh. My attention was focused on managing my own overly large greatcoat and the difficulty of walking in what felt like rather constricting trousers. As I struggled into the passenger seat, the spy said, 'I may have to drive a bit faster than yesterday, but at least I have daylight.'

'Oh, good,' I said without relish. The spy laughed.

As soon as we left, he began to build up speed. 'Lovely clear morning,' he remarked and put his foot down harder.

I resisted hanging on to the sides of the seat. 'Are you going to drive like this during the race?' I asked.

'Lord, no,' said Fitzroy, 'I'll have to go much faster than this.'

'It may be time for me to take up praying again,' I said.

'Heavens, Alice, and you a vicar's daughter. I'm counting on your prayers to keep us safe. The good Lord wouldn't listen to the likes of me. I'm far too wicked.'

I smiled. 'Too many Consuelas in your past?'

'I can categorically state that I have never trifled with Consuela. I was merely instrumental in reuniting her with her fiancé, now her husband.'

'I suppose they think that you did it for the sake of love.'

'Consuela maybe. Not her better half.'

'I almost laughed out loud when she threw her arms round your neck. I wish I could have seen your face.'

'She does that every time I see her. Believe me, I have suffered far worse indignities for my country. As you should know.'

I recalled the state he had been in when I had found him on the German's farm. 'Yes,' I said in more subdued voice.

'Cheer up,' said the spy, 'this time tomorrow we'll be on the Continent. You've never been to France, have you?'

I shook my head.

'Ah, France. If it wasn't for our mission, I'd show you the sights.' He then began to tell more and more outrageous stories of his exploits in the country when he was younger. I didn't believe the half of them, but they made me laugh.

We stopped for a quick luncheon in a wayside inn. I practised being a little brother. I scowled at Fitzroy when he ordered for me and scuffed my heels on the floor. I even managed to utter an, 'I say,' when he ordered lemonade for me and beer for himself.

When our luncheon arrived, I looked at the golden crust, with juices and carrots spilling out from underneath. 'So, *this* is shepherd's pie,' I said.

'Keep your voice down, Alan,' said Fitzroy. 'Someone of your class and gender would have eaten this before.'

'Oh, I have,' I said, suitably lowering it, 'Mrs Deighton called it minced ends and tatters.'

'You mean taters. Otherwise known as potatoes.'

'Oh, that explains it,' I said. 'I always wondered what was tattered about it.'

Fitzroy gave a slight sigh and tucked into his pie. He ate solidly all the way through. I didn't disturb him but dedicated myself to my own meal. It was nowhere near as nasty as it looked. As Richenda's housekeeper, I had always avoided serving anything but whole meats, although I knew the cook sometimes minced leftover meat for the servants. As I ate the same as the family, that particular indignity had passed over me.

Fitzroy wiped his mouth with his napkin and laid his cutlery neatly on his plate. I half expected it to be warm from the frenetic speed at which he ate. 'I daresay you've never eaten eel,' he said.

'A water snake?'

He nodded.

'Why would I want to do that?'

'Cockles? Mussels? Beef heart? Sweetbreads?'

I shook my head repeatedly.

'Then I won't ask you about liver and lights. You are rather spoiled, aren't you? Especially for a vicar's daughter. I would have thought circumstances might have forced your mother to lower her standards.'

I could tell by his voice he meant only to tease, but I felt a wave of sadness all the same. It must have shown on my face.

'What's the matter,' he asked sharply.

I shook my head again. 'Nothing of any import. You're quite correct that mother was overly particular in her menus for the family, but then, we had a small farm along with the vicarage which made the acquiring of meat a cheaper proposition. Plus,

35

we had a great many hens, so there was always one on hand for the pot.'

'You're not sad about a chicken, are you?'

'Of course not. On more than one occasion I was the one who had to wring their necks. The kitchen maid was far too squeamish. She did it so softly it took ages for the poor creature to die. I couldn't abide that.'

'No, quite right. Death when it comes is better swift, for beast and man.'

I tried to suppress a sniff.

'You're not missing Bertram, are you? Because if you're already getting homesick on me, I don't—'

I looked up from studying my plate. 'If you recall, my father died eating liver. You later discovered it had been poisoned. As you did not inform my mother for some years, she firmly believed the eating of lowly fare was responsible and made me promise never to eat any.'

'Oh,' said the spy. He wrinkled his nose slightly and shuffled back in his seat. He had clearly forgotten the details of the incident. I knew, due to his workload, this was not that offensive, but I felt offended all the same.

'I'll pay the bill. You'd better make use of the facilities. Be careful.' He nodded very slightly towards the gentleman's restroom.

Fortunately, it was unoccupied when I entered.

Afterwards I went out to the car. The spy had left it open, so I got in, hoping he would have mentioned any booby traps that he might have left. I was staring out into the distance when I was startled by Fitzroy's sudden appearance at the car door. 'Budge over,' he said. 'You can drive for a bit.'

My jaw slackened with astonishment. The spy jerked impatiently with his hand to indicate I was to assume the driver's seat. 'I've made up a fair bit of time for you to have a go. Don't waste the opportunity.'

'I don't know how to drive,' I said.

'I know,' said the spy, starting the car for me. 'I said I'd teach you. Better this side of the Channel and on some quiet country lanes. I hope to God you don't have to drive during the race, but it's best to prepare for the worst.'

'Like you getting shot?' I asked.

'Like you getting the map reading so wrong I have to take over until we're back on known territory.'

'I am not that bad,' I exclaimed.

'Hmm, you should have heard what your service instructor said about you.'

'But he was so nice . . .'

'How did it go . . . something about you being unable to find your own backside in a well-lit room?'

'It's a wonder you asked me to accompany you at all.'

'Don't sulk, little Alan,' he said and ruffled my hair. 'Now, listen carefully . . .'

It quickly transpired that accelerating a vehicle along a road was nowhere as complicated as I had feared. I leaned back in my seat and began to enjoy the ride. This was far more comfortable than riding a horse. Although there was some slight jostling, one was not bounced up and down in that slightly nausea-inducing way that generally occurs in a postprandial ride.

I glanced at the spy to see why he had not praised my efforts.

I gave him a big smile. He opened his mouth to speak, when out of the corner of my eye I spied a bend in the road. I looked away from him and turned the wheel hard. The back of the car slewed out behind us. I, with an alacrity that surprised even myself, found I could not fight this metal horse, so let it have its head and only swung the wheel back the other way when shrubbery at the side of the road touched the car's side panel.

Beside me, Fitzroy made a choking sound. Then he reached across and seized the brake. We screeched to a halt amid his coughing. The engine stalled.

'Are you all right?' I said. 'Did you swallow a fly? You should keep your mouth shut when we're driving.'

Fitzroy spat something over the side of the car. I suspect it was indeed a small insect of some sort. Then he turned to look at me. I was about to suggest we should move out of the middle of the road so as not to hinder any other traffic, but the words died in my mouth. His eyes fairly blazed and his lips were set in a thin, pinched line. He sat perfectly upright, the stiffness of his frame and the coldness of his expression projecting an anger I had never seen enacted towards me.

'Get out,' he said in a tight clipped tone.

'I apologise for whatever I—'

'GET OUT!'

The words were roared at me with such force I found myself practically toppling from my seat and onto the ground. To my horror I found myself trying not to weep. I kept my face turned away from him.

Fitzroy climbed into the driver's seat. 'By God, I swear, if you were a man, I'd give you a scar to remember your stupidity.'

I stood on the road and waited for him to drive off, leaving me behind.

He restarted the car, avoiding looking at me. Once back in the driver's seat, he readjusted his goggles. Then glanced at me.

'What the hell are you standing around for? Get in before I decide to leave you behind.'

As I had no idea where I was, and had no money with me, I climbed back into the car. I knew better than to say anything further. Fitzroy drove straight to the coast with no further stops and no words to me.

I tasted the salt in the air before I saw the coast, and even now the wind whipped against my face and threatened to steal my breath. I had previously travelled by ship with the Mullers, so the sight of the sea did not affect me as powerfully as it had once done. All the same, the heavy rumble of the great rolling waves as they smashed on the shore, foaming with power, was something to behold.

Rather than driving down to the harbour, Fitzroy pulled up at an inn, The Seafarer's Rest, which stood high up, overlooking the sea. From the inn's yard, we could see down to the shore. It did not bode well for a fair crossing. I shivered. Fitzroy got out of the car. This time he offered his ungloved hand to help me down.

'Your hand is cold,' he said in his normal voice. 'I do have further items of warmth for you, and we can get coffee here and ask about the sea crossing. I have something of a bad feeling.'

'Have you forgiven me yet?' The words were out before I could stop them.

'I have forgiven neither of us,' said the spy crisply. 'Though the time lost will have made no difference.'

I followed his gaze and saw the channel clouded with grey in the distance. Nearer to the British coast it was choppy, as evidenced by a myriad of white crests. The boats I could see from our vantage point bobbed up and down alarmingly.

'You think today's crossing has been cancelled?'

'Maybe not just today's. I didn't check the weather forecast, I had no reason to think the Channel would be so formidable at this time of year. Besides, we need to get across as fast as possible or we'll miss the starting point. I may need to hire a boat for us.' He pulled off his cap and ran his fingers through his hair. 'It'd have to be a damned big one though, to take the car, or we'd risk losing it over the side.'

'We could always acquire another car on the other side?'

Fitzroy looked down at me. 'I don't know whether to praise you for your lateral approach or laugh at your naivety as to what the department can afford.'

'You never seem to be out of funds,' I said.

'That's me. Not the department. Besides, I'd rather not leave my own car here at the seaside where the salty air would work in its corrosive effects on it for a few weeks.'

Then the expression on his face softened. He smiled slightly and reached out a hand to ruffle my hair. 'Bugger,' he said under his breath. Then in a louder voice, 'Never fear, little brother, we will find a way.' His eyes flicked over to my left. I followed his gaze and saw the figures of two men watching us.

'Are you going to do that often?' I asked, smoothing down my hair as best I could.

'Oh, I think quite often, little brother. I am, after all, quite fond of Alan. Alice is quite another matter.'

'Do you think they saw you help me out of the car?'

'I hope to God they didn't. You're not so bad at playing the little brother but you need to age yourself up a bit. You're not Joe.'

'It's not easy, but I'm trying.'

'Oh, it's a role made for you to play,' said the spy. 'The single main trait of any younger male sibling is to be annoying. You excel at that.'

I took from that rejoinder I was yet to be forgiven. Fitzroy quickened his pace and left me behind. As he walked up to the hotel, one of the watchers approached him, his voice carried high and sharp on the wind.

'I say, is that your motor? It's rather fine.'

Chapter Five

In which a gentleman installs himself in my bedroom

This is how we met the second, and only other, British team. Fitzroy sent me up to see if I could secure a room at the desk and when I returned, I found him laughing loudly with three men. I hovered in the background watching Fitzroy and waiting to interject. The personality he now exhibited was brash, boastful, and extremely derogatory about women wishing to vote, let alone drive. Not only was he louder, but his gestures were broader. He stood in front of the inn fire with his legs placed so far apart I could have easily crawled through then.

His audience, on the whole, seemed to be taking to him. The gentleman who had approached him outside was of a slender frame, wearing a country-style jacket with plus-fours, brogues, and a flat checked cap, which currently sat in his lap. He sported a fine, narrow moustache and, while not bald, his hair was thin and lank, slightly longer than the norm. Next to the braying Fitzroy, he appeared a rather a poor specimen of a man.

A quieter man sat next to him. Nearing middle age, he was dressed with the assured confidence of a gentleman who wore his clothing without any unnecessary ostentatiousness. Occasionally he looked across with a frown at his moustached companion, or up at Fitzroy. I got the impression he cared for neither.

The fourth member of this group almost entirely escaped my attention. He had pushed his chair further back from the glow of the firelight and lamps and sat in partial shadow. I guessed he was in his thirties. He wore a plain dark suit. One ankle caught the light and the shoe he wore was scuffed and of the cheaper variety.

'Ah, little brother. Did you manage to scare us up a room or two?' the spy called out to me.

I nodded, expecting him to come over to me to converse.

'See what I mean, gentlemen,' said Fitzroy to his small crowd. 'You'd never know we were related. Got the manner of a pigeon that just sighted a cat. Like that all the time. Pater thought the trip might bring him out of himself a bit.' He took a swig from his glass. 'Can't see it happening myself. If we'd had the time, we could have done something in Paris that might have brought him on a bit.' He laughed heartily. It took me a few moments to realise he was talking of taking his fictional brother to a brothel. Heat swarmed into my face. Fitzroy laughed again and gestured at me with his glass. 'Can't help wondering if dear, late Mama didn't always drive a straight road.'

He laughed again and I saw the middle-aged gentleman glance down at his shoes as if unwilling to be part of this conversation. 'Come over here, Alan,' Fitzroy said, beckoning me. I did as I was told, keeping my head down, so as not to meet the pairs of enquiring eyes that were assessing me. He turned me round by my shoulders to face the group, keeping a firm grasp on them, as if I might bolt. 'Gentlemen, may I present my little brother, Alan Charles Fitzroy, newly released from Eton College.'

There was a beery and unintelligible response.

Fitzroy pointed to the man in plus-fours. 'The Honourable Neville Crawford, a newly elected member of the King's Parliament, ex-professional racing driver, Mr Mark Crabtree, and finally, Mr Fred Hartmann.'

'Fred'll do,' came a low voice from the corner. The speaker stood up and stepped into the light. Only Fitzroy's fingers pinching into my shoulders kept me from flinching away. He had the ugliest face I had ever seen. From his bulbous nose to his frown-laden forehead, his face was dotted with small dark indentations.

As if that wasn't enough, his ears stood out as if his mother had repeatedly picked him up by them when he was a baby. 'I'm off to bed, gents, on the off chance we're moving in the morning.'

Fitzroy manoeuvred me into the vacant seat. 'What's this? Do you have information the fog is clearing?'

'Not at all,' said Crawford. 'Indeed, the outlook is bad for several days.' He had a curiously light way of speaking and gestured with his hands most gracefully.

'Damn it! If we're held up for two days, we'll never make the starting point. Not even with the way I drive,' said Fitzroy and huffed into his moustache. 'Damn. Damn. Damn. I don't mind telling you that disgruntles me. Wretched ferry owners. They know nothing about taking risks. I bet it's as calm as a mirror when you get away from the shore.'

'You a sailor yourself?' asked Crawford.

'Done some travelling in my time. Been round the Cape. Cape of Good Hope.' He laughed. 'If those waters didn't get me, I doubt these will, what?'

Crabtree opened his mouth to speak, but no sound came out. His jaw shuddered. 'I-I-I say—' he managed, but Crawford spoke over him.

'Fred is very keen. Very keen indeed. Wants to see what the others are putting up against us more than anything. I mean, with his sort, you'd think it was all about the money, but no. The man loves motors.'

Fitzroy regarded Crawford for a moment and then turned his attention to Crabtree, indicating with blunt clarity how uninterested he was in Fred's proclivities. 'You trying to say something, old man?' For the first time he didn't bark his question.

Crabtree nodded.

'I don't think—' interjected Crawford, but Fitzroy held his hand up.

'W-w-want to hire a boat. W-w-would help to have another in on it.'

Fitzroy nodded. 'Not a bad idea.' He turned to Crawford.

43

'I understand you wanted to keep any advantage to yourself, but if two teams were attempting to cross, you'd be able to afford a bigger and better boat. Much more likely you'd find a captain with enough spunk to go out there if he has a bigger ship. Very important to a man, a big ship.' He laughed again, and I shrank back into my corner.

Crawford took his time to answer. 'Bit delicate, but do you have the funds?'

Fitzroy shrugged. 'Not a problem. Might need to send a couple of wires, but my backers will pay.'

'Backers?'

Fitzroy touched the side of his nose. 'All you need to know is I can get the money if you can get the boat. It's hardly going to cost more than the purse, or you wouldn't be thinking of it, now would you?'

'Maybe we should discuss this somewhere quieter?' said Crawford.

Fitzroy nodded. 'Get the key, little brother, and go to bed. It's way past your bedtime as it is.'

I didn't need to be told twice.

The key the innkeeper gave me opened the door to a comfortable room, if not as exotic as the one at Consuela's property. It was clean, with two twin beds, a single shuttered window and pleasantly floral rugs scattered across a well scrubbed floor. A small fire had been lit in the grate. It felt cosy without the fuggy nature of downstairs. My bag had been left at the end of the bed. In it I found only male accessories, but in my size. I rather gingerly put on a pair of striped blue pyjamas. The soft cotton against my lower half felt very odd to one accustomed to wearing a nightdress. And since marriage, I had rather scandalously decided I preferred not to wear clothing in bed. Bertram was in a continual state of fear that our servants would talk about it.

I found a small bookshelf with a few popular mysteries of the day. Not feeling at all tired, I took one to bed with me and read by the technological marvel of an electric light by the bed.

I must have fallen asleep while reading an exciting bit as I was dreaming of running through some twisting underground passageways, being chased by smugglers, when I was woken with a start as the chair that I had placed beneath the door handle crashed to the floor.

My light was still on, so I saw Fitzroy in the doorway. He picked up the chair in one hand and dumped it to one side. 'Really?' he said. 'Who else did you fear would appear?' I watched open-mouthed as he walked across the room, with a slight stagger, and fell dramatically onto the other bed.

I waited. He neither said anything nor moved.

'Is there a reason you have burst into my room?' I said at last. The spy rolled over and propped himself up on one arm to look at me. His gaze focused on the bedsheet clutched to my chest.

'We've shared quarters before,' he remarked calmly.

'You slept in the bath.'

He rolled back onto his back. 'Well, you were quite the innocent then. You're a woman of the world now. I doubt my snores will offend your virtue. And before you say anything else, apparently you were so convincing as my little brother they gave us a twin room. Rather a lot of people have been caught out by the weather.'

'So, you're going to stay here?'

'I thought I had made that clear. I've been driving for hours and I need some sleep.'

'Aren't you going to undress for bed?'

'Wouldn't that frighten you? Although I do believe myself to be a rather fine specimen of a young man.'

'You're drunk,' I said accusingly.

'How remarkably perceptive of you. I repeat, I've been running on very little sleep for the last several days and not had nearly enough to eat. Of course I'm ruddy well drunk.' He sat up and took off his jacket. He looked at the spare chair but seemed to decide it was too far away and slung the garment over the foot-post of his bed. I saw he was carrying a gun. Quite casually, as if he was stowing a watch or some other valuable, he took this off and put it under his pillow.

'You were vile tonight,' I said.

'Thank you. I was aiming for boorish, but vile will do. I'm not on this mission to make friends.'

'Oh.'

He stopped in the process of fishing his watch out of his waistcoat and looked at me, eyebrows raised. 'Good heavens, girl, you don't think this is the way I normally behave when I've been drinking, do you? I suppose it would explain why you're mangling the linen.'

'I haven't seen you drink much before,' I said.

He frowned. 'No, I suppose not. I don't tend to drink when I'm working.' He retrieved his watch and began to awkwardly wind it. I suddenly remembered the previous injury to his hands and how it had happened.

'Would you like me to do that?'

He leant over and passed me the timepiece. 'Never really got my fine motor skills back,' he said with a tilted smile.

'I'm sorry.'

'Don't be,' he said bending down to untie his shoes, so I could no longer see his face and had to address the back of his head. 'If it hadn't been for you and yours, I would have ended up as pig feed.' He sat up and pulled off his shoes one by one, sighing after each one. 'I couldn't wear my own shoes,' he said to me. 'Someone might have spotted they were handmade, and as I have just let slip I'm doing the race because I'm being paid to test a new carburettor, it wouldn't fit. Hence my backers being very keen on me getting across the Channel.'

'Will it be safe?' I handed the watch back.

'Thank you. No, not at all. That's why I will be leaving you here. Sorry to abort your first serious mission. I'd have liked you to see France, and even Germany, before they blow it all up.'

'Hang on, you can't leave me here.'

'Don't worry, I'll wire someone to come and pick you up. Lots of deskbound souls in London just waiting for an excuse for a field trip. One of 'em will be only too happy to come and get you. I believe you are something of a talking point in the department.'

'I am an agent, aren't I?'

Fitzroy tucked his shoes under the bed and began peeling off his socks. 'You're a trainee.'

'I swore the oath.'

He didn't reply but got up and pulled out a small suitcase that had been placed on the other side of the bed. He began to rifle through it. 'I prefer to sleep naked,' he said. 'but, to save your matronly blushes, I'll wear pyjamas. I'm sure I have some in here.'

'So do . . .' I stopped and felt heat flush my face. 'Well, that's neither here nor there. You told me when I joined that there would be dangers and I agreed to them. Besides, what would you do without a navigator?'

'Read the damned maps myself. Ah, here they are.' He held up a pair of fine, bright blue pyjamas.

'Are they silk?' I demanded. 'These are rough cotton.'

'Yes, well, they fit my image of being a ladies' man. Can't seduce a woman in flannel.'

'Are you planning on seducing any women?'

Fitzroy put the offending items down on the bed. 'You really are the most difficult female of my acquaintance. Asking things like that. How do I know if I'm going to be seducing someone on this mission? I don't have anyone in mind, but you never know what might come up. Besides, it fits the character.'

'The boorish character,' I said.

'Oh, for heaven's sake, think! The louder and more boorish my character, the less attention is paid to my shy little brother.'

I hung my head. 'Yes, of course. I should have thought of that myself. Thank you. It does make playing my part easier.'

Fitzroy gave a wobbly bow. Then he began to unbutton his waistcoat.

47

'But you can't read the maps yourself, it will slow you down too much.'

He started to speak, but I cut him off. 'I know you'll say you'll find someone on the other side, but you're on a secret mission, having a civilian tag along will be awkward. They might even find out what you're doing – and then you'd have to dispose of them.'

Fitzroy smiled. 'Dispose? Don't you mean kill? Murder?'

'I don't see what there is to smile about. But how else could you assure their silence?'

'My dear Alice, I don't even shoot grouse. I abhor the taking of life . . .'

I scoffed.

'Yes, I know you've seen me kill people, but it has only been when absolutely necessary. I happen to rather value life. Odd in my profession, you might think, but there it is.'

'Yes, I do know that. So, you're not going to risk having to kill an innocent map-reader, are you? And you can't possibly manage to read and drive, so you will have to take me with you.'

The spy took off his waistcoat and begun to unbutton his shirt. I could see he was gritting his teeth.

'You know I'm right,' I said.

'I've wired for assistance. If they can get someone down here in time, I'll take them instead.'

'You're making me look a fool!' I protested, kneeling up in bed and quite forgetting the bedclothes. 'People will think I'm not up to the task!'

Fitzroy stopped unbuttoning his shirt and squared up to me. I looked him in the eye – although I was quite curious to see what colour his chest hair was. After all, I knew he dyed his red hair, but . . .

'I would far rather have the department think you foolish than have to face Bertram and tell him his new bride is drowned.'

'Well, then you had better make sure you drown too!' I said angrily.

'If you don't want to see more of me than you already have, you'd better look away. I am continuing to disrobe.'

I slumped back down on the bed and turned away from him. 'At least take me with you if there is no one else available.'

I heard a heavy sigh. 'If there isn't, I am afraid I may well have to. But I'm counting on one of the desk jockeys to get themselves down here in time.'

'If they don't . . .'

'If they don't, we'll discuss it again in the morning.'

'You won't just leave?' I said.

'Gods, you're worse than having a wife. No, I won't just leave.'

'Promise?'

'What, are you eight years old?' said the spy. 'Besides, my promise isn't worth—'

'You said you never lied to me.'

'I never said anything so ridiculous,' said the spy. 'I never tell anyone everything. Not even myself.'

'I didn't say that. You said you often omitted things, but you didn't lie to me.'

I heard a grumbling sound and thought about turning around, but then I heard the faint swish of trousers descending. I stayed put.

'Tell me you won't leave without talking to me.'

'Very well,' said Fitzroy. 'And it's red. I only dye the hair on my head. I saw you trying to peek.'

I buried my face under the sheet as I felt it flame.

I heard the other bedclothes being pulled back as the spy climbed into his own bed. 'I should have brought the dog for company.'

I turned around at that. 'You have a dog?'

'A pit bull called Jack. He's going to be very cross with you if you get me drowned.' Then he turned away from me and within moments was snoring lightly.

Chapter Six

In which Fitzroy finds himself praying

The next morning came all too soon. Groggy-minded and sleepy I sat up in bed. The bed next to me was neatly made. I took me a moment to remember what was going on. Then a fury filled me. I shot out of bed. As I did so, the door opened, and a dressed Fitzroy walked in. He carried a tray with food on it.

'Nice to see you awake. Although you'll need to wear more than that. It's a horrible day outside.'

He put the tray down on my bed. 'Tea, toast, eggs, and bacon. I thought I'd spare you breakfast in the communal area. The others we met yesterday are currently infesting it.'

I sat back on the bed and picked up the tea. 'Am I coming with you?'

He sighed. 'I overestimated the willingness of less experienced field officers to leave the security blanket of London. In short, yes, and I am very unhappy about it. Don't you dare drown.'

I took a bite of toast. 'Why are you fixated on my drowning?'

'Wait till you see the boat. I'll meet you downstairs. A porter will load our luggage. Hurry up and eat, we leave in twenty minutes.'

'I had hoped for a bath,' I said.

Fitzroy laughed at me and walked off. He paused for a moment by the door. 'Sorry if I was a bit out of order last night. I don't normally get tipsy, but I'd had a hell of a day.'

'Sorry about nearly killing us in the car,' I said.

His face darkened. 'I've not forgiven you for that yet.'

'You have to,' I said. 'I can't drown without being forgiven.' But I was speaking to empty air. 'Only has a sense of humour when it suits him,' I muttered to myself. He really was the most infuriating man.

I came down to find him paying the bill and braying about something or another. I also saw him stash a number of what looked like telegrams in his pocket. But I only saw because I was watching him closely. Despite the injuries, his sleight of hand remained good.

I stood behind, waiting quietly, head down, in the manner of a shy gentleman who is ashamed of his loud older brother. He didn't look around at me, but I saw him spot me in the mirror behind the reception area. He set off for the car and I followed. Once we were seated in it, a porter put our bags in the back.

'A short drive to the docks and we'll be on our way,' the spy said. I took the cue and hunkered down in my seat. The drive down to the seashore took less than fifteen minutes. Fitzroy and I, along with the other team, were ushered into what was little more than a shack on the shoreline.

The wind clawed at the thin walls, stirring tarpaulins and sacking lying on the floor. I found a damp corner to lean against and watched Fitzroy. This struck me as exactly the kind of place one might choose to murder boorish individuals, steal their expensive cars, and hire dock hands to toss their corpses into the sea.

'So how long till we can get on the boat?' Fitzroy asked.

'They wanted us out of the way while they loaded the cars,' said Crabtree carefully. 'Too much wind—'

Fitzroy interrupted. 'Hang on a minute. Surely we can just drive the motors on? What kind of a boat did you get?' He whirled to face Crawford, who gave a shrug.

'It took a lot to even get this captain to agree,' he said. 'Beggars can't be choosers.'

Fitzroy's face lost some of its colour. 'You don't mean they are using a crane, do you?'

Crabtree nodded.

The spy was through the door before I realised. The gust of wind he let in would have pushed me off my feet if I hadn't been standing in the corner. As it was, it took several moments for me to find my breath. When I had, I followed him.

I found him on the quay, one hand holding onto his driving cap as he looked up. I came up beside him and followed his gaze. There, high above us, hung his car, swinging like a child's conker in the wind as the crane operator tried, and retried, to land the car on the deck of a rusty steamship.

'Euphemia, if you ever prayed,' he said in a very low voice, 'pray now. Our whole mission is literally up in the air.'

He moved very slightly, and I realised he had put himself between me and worst of the wind. I stayed beside him to watch the attempt. I rather think if we hadn't been undercover, he might have held my hand. For his comfort, not mine. He loved his car.

Ocean spray. The term sounds so romantic, but here it felt more like tiny daggers of salt attacking our faces in their thousands. The wind roared and I wondered how any boat could possibly make sail today. A dockhand yelled something at us and gestured we should leave the quay. Wind stole the meaning of the words and left only the angry concern of his face. Fitzroy turned to look at him. I didn't see the expression on the spy's face, but it was enough for the dockhand to retreat.

Still watching the car swaying wildly, he leaned down to speak to me. His lips brushed my ear. 'You should go back to the shed. You're too small. You may literally get blown off the quay.'

I turned my head to speak. 'I wouldn't rate my chances getting back safely. Besides, I don't trust any of the men in there.'

Fitzroy finally tore his gaze away from his car. 'Damn it,' he said. He opened his coat, so he could half wrap it around me. It gave him the ability to place his arm around my waist without it being seen by others. The wind was now so raw and angry I was unclear if he was anchoring me or if I was merely providing extra ballast for him while he helplessly watched his beloved car in peril. He certainly hadn't offered to escort me back to the shed.

Then, with a clang that I heard even above the devilish weather, the car landed on the deck. Fitzroy didn't move. I watched as men scurried across the deck securing it. When they finally released the crane hook, Fitzroy let go of me. 'Come on,' he said. 'But be careful. Don't slip.'

I followed him down the quay towards the ship. If I had been able to, I would have tartly told him I had no intention of slipping, but that this swelling ocean might have other ideas. But he kept a fast pace and we were quickly alongside it. A plank without railings connected the ship to the shore.

'Wait,' roared Fitzroy in my ear. He raced unerringly across the thin walkway. I watched in horror. Even on a good day I doubted my ability to walk across such a flimsy walkway. The ship did not so much bob up and down as seem to plummet towards the seabed only to be lifted at the last minute by an incoming wave. Fitzroy had crossed at a moment when the waves had only been dropping a few feet. Now it seemed like ten or more. Spray stung my eyes and if Bertram had appeared at that moment, I might have turned tail and gone home. Frankly, I was terrified.

I saw Fitzroy reappear on the deck at the railing on the other side. In one hand he held a coiled rope. He held up his free hand to indicate I should stay where I was. Easier said than done. The wind already pushed at my back, urging me towards the foaming edge. I found a rock to half-shelter behind, and a handhold – a rusty remnant of an old railing that remained lodged in the rock and held on for dear life.

When the waves eased a little, Fitzroy came back across. He didn't exactly run, but he moved quickly. The rope trailed out behind him. When he reached me, he undid the rope at his waist and pulling me up, tying it around me. 'It'll only take the weight of one of us at a time,' he said. 'It's calmer now. I'll go back across and you follow. The rope will steady you.' He didn't say that it would stop my body being washed away. If I fell from the plank, I would be hurled against either the side of the quay or the side of the boat. Either would be sufficient to badly injure or even kill me.

'Don't come over until I've picked up the slack of the rope,' he said.

'I don't think I can do this,' I said.

'No choice,' said Fitzroy.

He headed off up that plank back to the ship. This time he stopped on the way as the boat dipped alarmingly. I saw him stretch out his arms for balance. I didn't think he would make it, but he suddenly broke into a run and leapt the last third of the distance. He caught the railing and pulled himself up before the deckhands could reach him.

From this distance I couldn't see his expression, but I don't believe he would have asked me to cross if he had known that had been the last lull the weather would offer. We waited on either side for what seemed like for ever. The wind pulled and pushed at me. I knew that making my way back up the rocky path would present its own dangers. For the first time I truly appreciated the old adage of being caught between a rock and a hard place.

I made my mind up. I would not wait for the wind to push me into the sea, nor would I allow myself to be smashed to bits while attempting a cowardly retreat. I tugged on the rope and set my foot on the plank.

Whatever I had been imagining, it was infinitely worse. The very fibre of it seemed to give beneath my feet and it bucked like an angry horse that hadn't been broken. I either had to move forward or fall. The land beneath my other foot felt as if it was moving away. I knew this was the action of the sea. I stepped forward and, for a moment, just stood there. I looked down at the eddies around the rocky shore beneath me. I could not move. I willed myself to go forward, but a very real mortal terror held me motionless. The plank bucked beneath me once more. My footing shifted and touched the edge of something. Looking down through the spray, I saw that every foot or so, the plank had raised wooden straps nailed across it. It wasn't much, but it was something to set my shoes against. If not actually a decent grip, a nod towards one. I took a deep breath of water and salty air, coughed, and willed my foot forward. This time it moved. I looked up and through the spray I could see the outline of Fitzroy's figure. I told myself it wasn't that far away. He yelled something, but I only caught the word 'me', which struck me as hysterically funny. I was about to die and yet Fitzroy continued to talk about himself. I took one step and then another. I didn't think about how far I had to go.

'Keep looking at me,' yelled Fitzroy. He was trying to stop me looking down – and of course as soon as I realised that, I did.

Below me the water roiled and swirled in eddies. Caught in the water between the boat and the shore, dead seaweed gave off a rank, sickening smell. The water itself frothed inky black, with hints of green slime, more like the contents of a witch's cauldron than the bright blue of the English Channel I had anticipated. As I watched, it seemed to rise up to greet me. I was to be the next ingredient in the sea witch's brew. I felt myself swaying. The water rose and fell, and I knew any moment I would fall. I'd been stupid; there had never been any way I could have made this crossing. I thought about Bertram and hoped he would find someone else. I closed my eyes and hoped it wouldn't hurt too much.

Three sharp tugs at my waist snapped me back to wakefulness. Fitzroy roared, 'Move yourself now!' I hurried to obey and, somehow, I ran and fell onto the ship. Fitzroy caught me and placed me firmly behind him - away from the edge. He untied the rope and shoved me towards a hatch. I went down the steep little stairs and found myself in a small common crew area. A table took up much of the space. Benches lined the walls and tucked in the corner was a small kitchen – or galley, as I believe they call them on boats.

'What the hell were you doing out there?' yelled Fitzroy. 'Composing poetry?'

'Sorry,' I said. 'Thank you. You were right, I shouldn't have come on this mission.'

'There's no going back now.'

'I know. I hope I won't be more trouble than I'm worth,' I said, trying a small smile.

'I hope so too,' said the spy. 'Stay below decks.'

Then he left me. The boat pitched and fell. At first, I felt terrified and nauseous. The fear gave way to the sickness, but by dint of closing my eyes and breathing deeply, I managed to get that to pass. After that I began to get bored and wished I'd brought a book with me. I must remember on my next mission to ensure I had reading material with me, I thought.

What seemed like hours later Fitzroy came back down the ladder. He thrust a life jacket at me. 'We'll be moving off soon. Put this on.'

'You mean we're still moored in England?'

My face must have shown real shock as he gave a crack of laughter. 'Yes, Alice. It'll get rougher than this when we're at sea. Been sick yet?'

'No, I was wishing I had a book.'

He smiled slightly. 'Welcome to my world. Moments of intense terror followed by interminable boredom. Of such are most missions made.'

'Where are the others?'

'Sadly, up top. They insisted on still coming and it took a while to load their car. They're staying up top while we leave port. Something about the fresh air making them less seasick. I hope they all get swept over the side.'

And with that, he wedged himself into a corner and closed his eyes, taking advantage of a moment of rest. Maybe ten minutes later I felt the first pulls as the steamer forced its way out into the Channel. The movement of the boat changed. It yawed as much as it pitched, so that one was locked into a seeming eternal circle of movement, rather like being on a carousel. I copied Fitzroy and wedged myself into the opposite corner. It made the movement seem less. The spy opened one eye. 'This is the worst bit. Once we're away from the shore it will either get much better or much worse.'

'Much worse?'

'If it does, it won't last for long. We'll capsize. Remember where the hatch is. It's likely we'll be upside down if that happens. There'll be some air left at the top of the cabin, so we'll get to form a plan before we swim out. You can swim, can't you?'

I nodded. 'A bit.'

'All you need in a storm like this. No one swims in it. You keep your head aloft as much as you can and go where the water takes you. Hopefully to shore.'

'Has that ever happened to you?'

'Once. But not here.'

The boat pitched violently. I suppressed a cry. Fitzroy had closed his eyes again. 'We're out in the Channel now. Won't be long before we find out what's going to happen.'

I heard the thudding of footsteps. Crawford and Crabtree entered the cabin, soaked to the skin and shaking themselves like dogs. 'We've made it out into the Channel,' said Crawford. 'Looks like we might actually do it.' He gave a little, high-pitched laugh.

Crabtree sank down onto the bench opposite me. 'It is w-w-wild out there,' he said. 'This boat must have a g-g-grand engine, despite her appearance. She fought like a lion to break free of the shore.' He took a handkerchief from his pocket and wiped his face. 'It was actually quite exciting. Reminded me of my old racing days. Bit wetter, of course.' He gave a genuine-sounding laugh. 'How are you bearing up, Alan?'

'I'm doing all right, sir,' I said. 'Feels rather odd, but I'm hopeful we'll make it—'

'Has your brother fainted?' said Crawford, breaking in.

'No sir. I believe he is asleep.' I didn't think any such thing. It was more likely Fitzroy was sparing himself from conversation with these two. I owed him enough to be more than ready to pick up that slack. 'He's not particularly bothered by rough seas. He's been shipwrecked a couple of times, so . . .' I shrugged.

'He is a fatalist,' said Crabtree, whose stammer appeared to have entirely vanished. 'Like myself. There are times when we are in the hands of the gods. There is no point wasting energy on fear or losing your reason to panic, you merely await the time when you may again act.'

I nodded. 'That sounds like him.'

Crawford took the last corner, putting his feet against the table. 'Where is the other man?' I asked. 'Did he decide not to come?'

'No,' said Crabtree, 'he wanted to stay with the cars.'

'Idiot,' said Crawford. 'As if he could do anything if one came loose. It's hardly as if he could swim out and pull it back.'

'Is that likely?' I asked.

Crabtree shook his head. 'Whatever the reasons these seamen have for risking their necks, they know what they're doing. Everything on deck is well secured.'

'As tight as a nun's knickers,' said Crawford.

It was at this point we heard the sound of feet rushing down the ladder. 'You'd better come,' said Fred. 'The man's car has lost one of its tethers.'

Fitzroy's eyes flew open. 'My car?' He cried shooting to his feet.

Fred nodded. 'It's lashing across the deck like a wild thing. Captain's talking of cutting the car free if we can't get it locked down. Says it's too much of risk to his men.'

Fitzroy slid along the table on his side, jumped off, pushed roughly past Fred, and was up the ladder before any of us could draw another breath.

Chapter Seven

In which Young Fitzroy is rather brave

'That's going to be a two–man job. If it's possible at all,' said Crawford. 'Fred, you'd better go and help him.'

Fred looked as cheerful as one might expect at this request. Nevertheless, he headed back up the ladder.

'I should help,' I said, rising to my feet.

Crawford shook his head. 'You're too light. You'd be over the side in a moment. Even if we could turn back, we'd never find you. Better you stay here with us.'

I sat back down, nodding agreement. But there was something in his manner I didn't like. He sounded almost avuncular. Last night he'd taken no interest in me at all. Crabtree wore a fierce frown and stared at the hatch. Crawford, though, lounged back in his seat. Concern for me, but not for Fitzroy, and his man? It felt off. I gave him a nervous little smile and watched his response closely. The muscles around his eyes didn't change. It wasn't a real smile, but what did that tell me? Any man in his right senses would not be smiling at our situation, however much he was trying to reassure a colleague's younger brother.

I glanced over at Crabtree. He stood suddenly. 'I'm going up to help.'

Crawford caught his sleeve. 'I don't think that is wise,' he said.

'I weigh a lot more than young Fitzroy over there.' I realised with some shock he referred to me.

'Yes, you do,' said Crawford. A tinge of impatience sounded in

59

his voice. 'But you don't want to get yourself into a place where you might have one of your episodes. Hesitation up there could cost lives.'

I frowned. Crabtree flushed dark red and sank back into his seat. 'If they're not back soon I'm going up,' he said.

It was the look of satisfaction on Crawford's face that decided me. He looked exactly like the old Richenda when she'd managed to finesse the last piece of cake away from other diners. Without a word, I got up and copied Fitzroy's action by sliding along the table. I didn't have his weight, and I hadn't leapt with his alacrity, so I only made it three-quarters of the way down. I scrambled the last bit and Crawford made a grab for my left leg. I kicked him off and managed to get my feet on the floor. All around us the boat pitched and yawed. Crabtree appeared frozen in surprise. Crawford got in front of me. 'I can't let you go up there,' he said, catching my arm.

I had little space to manoeuvre, so I merely twisted my arm towards his thumb, breaking his grip, but, at the same time, pulling him closer. I then kneed him in a part of the anatomy that, as a woman, I do not share. He folded over in pain very nicely and even fell sideways onto the floor. I had kneed him with some force. Before Crabtree could act, I was up the ladder and out the hatch.

The wind hit me full force and knocked me onto my backside. Fortunately, the hatch had closed, so I did not tumble ignobly down the ladder. Instead, I came to rest against a structure. Possibly the wheelhouse. I didn't stop to look. I started to crawl up the deck. Keeping low down, and using various shrouded tarpaulins and barrels as handholds, I managed to edge my way towards the end of the boat where the vehicles were.

As low down as I was, the wind whipped at my hair and the coat on my back, but did little to impede my progress as long as I kept myself almost flat against the deck. Beneath me the boat rose and fell, but holding on to objects around me, I found the wooden deck of considerable reassurance. My stomach might be rising and falling too, but by managing to keep most of my body in physical contact with the deck, I could trick my mind into thinking the movement was an illusion. If nothing else, if the boat broke up, I would be clinging to a part that floated and not trapped beneath the waves in an upturned cabin, which I feared would quickly become a watery grave.

As I made my way forward, I didn't especially think of the danger Fitzroy might be in. It was only a vague suspicion. One I felt I had to act upon – the consequences of ignoring it, and it being true, were unthinkable.

He'd lashed himself to the deck, which was just as well, as he was very nearly hanging off the edge. As I came closer, I saw he was attaching a rope that held our car in place. Clearly bone-weary, his fingers numbed with cold, I saw him fumbling with the knot. Across his face showed more than one stripe of purple. Fred had meant it when he said the rope had gone wild in the wind. It must have lashed Fitzroy in the face more than once. He was fortunate it had not caught one or both of his eyes.

But where was Fred? It struck me as strange that I hadn't seen a single sailor on deck. It might be foul, but surely they would still have duties to attend to up top? Where were they? I turned my head back and forth, checking for lifeboats. Could they have abandoned us to our fate? No, the small, and I feared largely useless, lifeboats were still secured.

I twisted carefully, so as not to lose my grip, and checked to see if Fitzroy was in any danger. I couldn't help hoping he was. Nothing deadly, perhaps – but enough to justify my appearance. I neither fancied crawling back without help, nor facing the spy's anger if nothing was amiss.

At that moment I saw Fred making his way over to our car. He was out of Fitzroy's line of sight; a pathway that took him close to the edge. He hadn't bothered to lash himself to the deck, but was rather moving in a crouch, going from secured item to item, finding handholds, much as I had done, although he leaned more into the wind and managed to stay upright.

The boat dipped suddenly, and the edge of a wave washed across the deck. The force of the icy water took my breath away. It swept across me, soaking me to the skin and shocking the breath from me. And it was strong, like several brawny men trying to push me across the deck. I managed to get my feet caught in a tarp, as well as hanging on for dear life to a rope, or I would have been over the side.

I looked across at the spy to cry out for help – his anger be damned – when I saw that during the last swell, Fred had somehow managed to close the gap between him and Fitzroy. He held a large spanner above the spy's head. Fitzroy remained intent on securing his knot, completely unaware of the danger he was in. I knew there was no way I could reach him in time. I tried to shout, but my body still struggled with the shock of the cold and little sound came out.

I did the only think I could think of. I pulled free a small crate that had already been partly loosened by the movement of the boat and slid it across the deck in the direction of Fred. Fortune was with me, for at that very moment, the boat rolled in such a way that the small object sped at a satisfyingly high rate across the slippery deck. I, on the other hand, had to contend with not going overboard myself. I pressed my face against the deck and clung on, as yet another wave crashed over me.

I really had no idea any human being could be quite this cold and survive. I felt my fingers loosening. Any moment now and I would be swept overboard. I daren't even lift my head to see what was happening. I had to hold on. Wave after wave soaked me as the boat pitched and yawed in the most vicious manner, almost as if it resented us being on its deck and was trying to rid itself of us.

Then someone was kneeling over me. Binding a rope around me. I looked up into Fitzroy's face. His eyes blazed and the purple marks of the rope, along with the blue hue of his cold skin, made him look like some kind of sea-devil. As he finished lashing us together, he bent his head close to me. 'What the devil are you doing out here?'

'Fred. Fred was trying to kill you.'

'Nonsense.' Fitzroy gave me a filthy look, all flinty-eyed and thin lipped, and hauled me to my knees. 'Do what I do,' he said.

I glanced around as he steadied himself for the return to the cabin. I could see no sign of Fred. Had I just sent an innocent man to his watery death? Or had he avoided the crate and was now lurking somewhere, ready to strike us both down. A sharp tug on the rope brought me back to my current plight. Fitzroy mimed my looking at him and scowled. I nodded. Although he must have been exhausted, he continued to pull us forward. He took only handholds I could reach, so I could literally do as he did. He kept himself in a half-crouched position, but more than any-thing, he seemed to have a sixth sense of when the waves would wash over the deck. Before each one did, he hunkered down behind shelter and, if I was near enough, also held on to me by rope, arm or waist – whatever he could reach. Close beside him, I could feel his body shivering. I had no idea if it was the cold or his rage doing this.

It took us what seemed like for ever before he abruptly pushed me down the little hatch, so hard I tumbled down the ladder. I managed to put my arms up to protect my head, but other parts of me bounced hard off the metal. I was too cold to feel anything, but I suspected I would be black and blue tomorrow. Fitzroy fol-lowed by jumping down into the small space.

Crabtree and Crawford stood in front of us. Shock clearly written across their faces.

Crabtree moved first. He began to stoke the small fire at the back of the room. 'Where's your man?' said Fitzroy to Crawford.

'He was with you.'

'He went to fetch a tool to fasten the bindings on the car. I didn't see him after that,' said the spy. 'I hoped he'd changed his mind and come back in.'

Crawford reached for an oil-slicked mackintosh that hung on

the wall (my powers of observation clearly needed more work). 'I will go up and look for him.'

'I'll come with you,' said Fitzroy.

'No,' said Crabtree. 'Your younger brother will catch his death if you do not help him out of his clothes. His fingers are bright blue and he's swaying on his feet. Besides, you almost look done in yourself. Let us do it. He is our companion.'

Fitzroy grunted but stepped aside. The two men made their way up on deck.

'Explain yourself,' he demanded, towing me across to the stove and the blissful warmth. I felt him pulling at my coat as he undid the buttons. I tried to tell him not to bother. The fire was so lovely, all I needed to do was slouch down beside it and I would dry out. The thought occurred to me that my mother would have died on the spot if she saw me slouch. What a lovely word, slouch, and what a lovely thing to do. Being male was so enticing, you could throw your body into any old position and not be judged for it. How glorious. Fitzroy shook me. Somehow my eyes had closed, I opened them. 'I really wish you'd stop that,' I said, or tried to say, only the words came out somewhat slurred. I closed my eyes. If he wanted to hold me up like a rag doll rather than just let me lie down, then that was his problem. Sleep beckoned.

He slapped me so hard, my teeth rattled. I gasped and opened my eyes.

'We need to get out of these wet clothes before we succumb to hypothermia. You remember that from training, don't you? Or do I have to slap you again?'

Never, not even when I had deeply loathed the spy, had I imagined him hitting me. I touched my cheek, and despite the cold, it stung. He had struck me quite hard.

He watched me closely. I began to take off my outer garments. He did the same. I could see his fingers fumbling, both with his disability, and with the cold, but he managed. Finally, we were both standing there in damp long johns. The others had yet to return.

'Damn it,' he said, 'You can hardly take those off.'

'It's one layer. It'll dry by the fire.'

'Hypothermia,' repeated Fitzroy. 'We need blankets, and distance from the fire. A gentle warmth, or the centre of the body grows too cold to sustain life. Remember your training!'

He pulled at the benches and the top of one of them rose. Rummaging through, he pulled out some foul-looking blankets. He threw one to me and gestured to me to secure myself once more in my corner. The blanket smelled horrible.

'I saw him lift a tool above your head,' I said. 'I was sure he meant to kill you.'

'Well, he didn't, did he?' snapped the spy. 'Besides, how could you have possibly known?'

'The others didn't want me to go up on deck.'

'That's sheer bloody common sense. Something you seem to lack.'

'No, there was something off about it,' I said. I could feel my eyelids getting heavy.

'Keep your eyes open or I'll slap you again.'

My face still throbbed, so I did my best to obey. 'I saw him,' I persisted.

'And yet, here I am, saving you once again.'

'Only because I slid a crate across the deck at him.'

'What!'

'I didn't see what happened because another wave came across, but he wasn't lashed to the deck like you. I think he went overboard.'

A myriad of emotions crossed the spy's face, so fast I couldn't follow them. Then we heard the hatch listening. 'Keep your mouth shut,' commanded Fitzroy.

Crabtree and Crawford half slid; half fell down from the deck. 'I fear he is lost,' said Crabtree, as he began to strip off his wet outer clothing. Neither of them was as soaked as Fitzroy and I had been, so I was relieved to see they removed less clothing.

'I am sorry,' said Fitzroy. 'If that is the case, there is nothing we can do. Even if we did turn back, we'd never find him in this storm.'

'No,' said Crawford sitting down. 'We must accept the loss.' He sighed and dug a flask out of the wet coat that lay beside him. He took a sip. 'To Fred. The best mechanic I ever had.'

He passed the flask among us. I only pretended to drink, as I believe did Fitzroy. At the very least, I had remembered that, contrary to popular opinion, alcohol was not the best thing to give a half-frozen person.

After this the weather abated slightly, and by the time we reached the coast, the movement of the boat was hardly noticeable. Fitzroy engaged the men in talk of cars and memories of Fred. It turned out Crawford had known him the longest. Crabtree had only just met him on this trip.

Every now and then I caught Fitzroy watching me, a very curious expression on his face. For once I couldn't read it. From wishing every moment to be off this boat, I went to fearing our landing and being alone with the spy once more.

Chapter Eight

In which we endeavour to analyse things

Fortunately, Crawford and Crabtree were eager to get to their car, so Fitzroy and I were left alone to dress. My long johns had dried, and while my other clothing remained slightly damp, it was dry enough to wear. I realised I was ravenously hungry.

'Fitzroy . . .' I began when the others had left.

He shook his head at me. 'We'll talk later. Get up to the deck.' There was no warmth in his voice and his eyes were cold and hard. The stripes on his face were now developing into splendid bruises. If we had been on good terms, I might have told him he looked rather like a tiger. As it was, I was rather afraid of how angry this tiger might be. What could be worse than him leaving me at the port? I thought I could cope with that. I went up the ladder into the clean fresh air. Would he do worse? I wracked my brain to think of something. I couldn't. But then I would never have thought, even at his angriest, he would have hurt me. I briefly touched my throbbing cheek. Hours later, it still hurt enough that I had to bite my lip to hold back the tears.

Getting the vehicles off the deck proved to be far less dramatic. On the French side the sun shone, and while the temperature remained low, the day sparkled with a cheerful intensity. Fitzroy dealt with payments and I sat on the harbour wall looking around me. I had been to the United States with the Mullers, and on a mission to Ghent, but never to our closest neighbours in Europe. I am not sure what I was expecting, especially as I knew war was in the air, but the people I saw seemed ordinary and friendly. There was a feel to the place that was different. It wasn't simply that people carried narrow, elongated loaves of bread, or that the men wore berets, or that small dogs wandered without their owners, chasing seabirds bigger than themselves, it was something else. Down by the harbour I could see an eating establishment where some very old men sat outside, drinking wine. The boats and yachts that bobbed in the harbour veered towards brighter colours than you might see in an English harbour. The water glistened with a thousand tiny suns, looking beautiful and so different from the horror of yesterday. Other, bigger ships, seemed to congregate further along the harbour. The steamer had slunk into a side that was mostly full of small boats.

The wall I sat on was made of a sandy stone, tan in colour, and far less grim that the port we had left behind. It occurred to me then that we must have arrived very late at night and slept on the boat. I peered out across the Channel and faintly saw, or imagined I saw, the other side. The storm had swept away during the night, gone as if it had never been there. Fishermen were cleaning out their boats, their catches having already gone ashore. There seemed to be a good-natured rivalry going on between the crews, but I was only guessing. I couldn't understand a word they said.

Our car stood on the shore. I didn't want to make Fitzroy seek me out, so I went and waited in it. He joined me not long after. 'You look a total mess,' he said and passed me a comb. 'For God's sake, at least get the knots out of your hair if you can't be bothered to wash your face.'

The spy wasn't at his best, but somehow since I had left him, he had managed to shave and change his clothing. He looked bright, alert and respectable. I suspected I did not. I could have retorted by saying that no one had told me there was anywhere I could clean up, but I knew he would simply say I needed to show initiative.

He started the car and drove off. 'I need to get to a post office,' he said and that was it. I said nothing. I looked out the car as we went at a reasonable pace, passing through villages small enough that young children came out to see and wave at the car as it passed. The flora here was different. Tall, slender trees lined the roads – cypresses, I think. After the winding road of the villages, the route would suddenly stretch out in a straight line into the distance, the scenery flat, but vibrant with evergreens and heather-like plants.

We passed through three villages before the spy found a post office he was prepared to use. 'Stay here,' he said. He came back a while later, during which time I wondered if it was possible for one's stomach to eat itself. Mine rumbled and gurgled in a most unladylike manner, but then, I suppose it all added to my disguise.

When Fitzroy returned, I gave him back his comb. I hadn't wanted to distract him from driving. He took it and tucked it in his inside pocket. As he did so, I saw the edges of a number of telegrams. Without warning he grasped my chin and turned my face towards him, and then from side to side. 'Hmm,' he said. 'Nasty bruise. I don't believe either of us look remotely respectable. However, the weather has been so vile they've delayed the start of the race. We will have a couple of days to recuperate. At least time enough for me to show you how to cover that up with make-up. It's only going to get worse before it gets better.'

'You hit me hard.'

The spy frowned. 'For what it's worth, I may have been more heavy-handed than I intended. I was wet through and numb myself. You do understand why I did it though, don't you?'

I looked down at my feet.

'Oh, for heaven's sake, you know I am not the kind of man who strikes women in anger.'

I brought my gaze up to meet his. 'And yet you did this. It still hurts, by the way.'

'Alice, you were going into hypothermic shock. If I'd let you fall asleep, you would have died. I tried shaking you, but you were already too far gone. I really thought I was going to lose you. Accordingly, I may have been a little overzealous, but I assure you I only struck you in the hopes of keeping you alive. Not out of anger.'

'You were angry. Even if I was sleepy, I could tell that.'

Fitzroy started the car. 'Of course I bloody was. You'd followed me out on deck, against my orders, and recklessly endangered your life, and the mission, for nothing. Anyone else would be in deep trouble when we got back to England.'

'So why won't I be?'

'Because I have no intention of reporting you. However, I am seriously considering whether I should take you any further.'

'That's rich,' I said, as anger welled up inside me, 'considering I only went on deck to warn you. Not only did I save your life, I had to kill a man in the process.'

Fitzroy threw me a sidelong glance. 'I thought you were delirious. Do you still stand by what you said?'

'That I saw Fred raise a makeshift weapon above your head? Yes. I tried to call out, but the waves had knocked the breath out of me. The only thing I could think of doing was to slide something along the deck, to knock him off balance.'

'You're telling me, quite calmly, that you committed murder?'

I hesitated for a moment, thinking it over. 'I hadn't thought of it like that. I was only thinking of keeping you alive.'

'You're admitting to having killed a man – and have no remorse over having done so?'

I cast about for a negative feeling and could find nothing. 'It's not as if I knew him,' I said.

'And that makes it all right?'

'Well, of course I didn't want to kill anyone, but neither did I want anyone to kill you.'

'Despite me slapping you?'

'Yes, well, you keep telling me how important you are to the service. I must have started to believe you.'

Fitzroy made a sound that could almost have been the start of a laugh. 'Tell me again, in detail, what happened to make you think I might have been in danger.' I repeated, as exactly as I could, the events as they had happened. Fitzroy listened without interruption. When I had finished, he said, 'The bit about Crabtree makes sense. Took me a while to remember. He was a top-notch racing driver but crashed during his last professional race. After that, he found he couldn't get into a racing car again. He'd walk right up to the vehicle and freeze. Simply couldn't open the door. Press was rather hard on him and he disappeared for a while.'

'If he can't drive . . .'

'He can't drive on a racetrack. Maybe ordinary roads feel different to him. It's not as if he'd be vying neck and neck with other drivers. This kind of race takes skill, but it's not the same as track racing.'

'I suppose this could be a way back into his old career.'

'I imagine he's more likely to be doing it for the money. He'd have lost all his patrons, and it wouldn't be easy for him to gain employment without someone finding out who he was. As I recall, he spoke to one newspaper of his shame at his fear. I suppose he thought it might help people understand.'

'It didn't?'

'No, they called him a coward. Nasty business.'

'So Crawford had cause to believe he might freeze on deck, and be swept away?'

Fitzroy nodded.

'No, it wasn't that. It was if he was threatening Crabtree.'

'Threatening to spread his story, or remove him from the team?' I nodded.

'But – let me guess, this is when your intuition came into play?'

'Hasn't yours ever?'

'Of course,' said the spy, 'but I'm somewhat more experienced at this game than you are.'

'You have to admit, I've had more than my fair share of life-threatening experiences,' I said. 'My intuition may have developed beyond the average too.'

'You certainly have no difficulty finding trouble.'

'Is it possible they knew about our mission and were trying to stop us? Not that I know a lot about the mission,' I grumbled.

Fitzroy smiled. 'I'll tell you more as we go along. But no, I can't see how they would have any idea who we really were. We met

71

them entirely by chance. No one could have anticipated the schedule I decided to take. I stopped on impulse to make it so. I suppose it's possible they thought they had an opportunity to take out a rival, but most people don't go straight for killing someone in the first instance.' He frowned. 'Not unless they're truly desperate.'

'I told you there wasn't anything else I could do.'

The spy shook his head. 'I didn't mean you. Even with fortunate circumstances like a storm at sea presenting a suitable opportunity, it takes quite a leap to think of murder – unless you're already into the way of it.'

'Like you.'

'I wouldn't describe it as a hobby of mine, but when it's necessary, when I can't think of another option, yes, as you well know, I have to take lives. I'm not the least bit proud of it, and while I may morally regret it, I've never been able to practically regret it, given the relevant circumstances.'

'That's what I said.'

'No, it isn't. You showed no moral regret, which I do find a little concerning.'

'Oh, for heaven's sake,' I snapped. 'He was our enemy. He was trying to kill you. I'll be damned if I will regret saving your life. Now, when are we going to get something to eat? I am starved.'

Fitzroy laughed. 'You almost sound like me.'

'They were calling me young Fitzroy,' I growled.

Fitzroy laughed even harder. 'I'm not convinced you were right about Fred, Alice. But I accept you were doing what you thought was right. Rather bravely, as it happens. I very much regret slapping you so hard. Do you accept my apology?'

'If it is followed by luncheon.'

'We're going to stay with some people I know. The ones I told you about when we discussed your options that night at the police cell. I know a lovely place to eat that's on the way. And before you ask, yes, we are almost there.'

'You're not going to leave me there, are you?'

'No, I believe I won't. You may be damned reckless at

times – and I need to curb that in you – but I have never doubted your loyalty to me. Which is odd, really, as I know full well there are times when you cannot stand me. I suppose it's the Office of the Crown that I represent that you are loyal towards.'

He said the last bit more to himself than me. 'No, it's you,' I said. 'I appear to be able to both loathe you and feel loyal to you. It's extremely annoying.'

'I feel much the same about you – although I don't believe I have ever loathed you. It's more a sense of exasperation.' He turned to look at me. 'Look, I really am sorry about the bruise. I don't think you realise how much you frighten me when you put your life at risk.'

'I thought that was the job?'

'No, the job is to get the mission done as swiftly and as trouble-free as possible.'

'Does that ever happen – the trouble-free bit.'

Fitzroy gave me a face-splitting grin. 'Not in my experience. That's what makes it fun.'

For once, as good as his promise, we stopped twenty minutes later at a café. Fitzroy kept ordering and I kept eating. The food was simple, but good. Slices of cold meat, pickles, a rich golden butter, olives, a variety of cheeses I had never seen before, and fresh bread, warm from the oven, all washed down with two glasses of a deep, fruity red wine and then water. Fitzroy wouldn't let me drink any more than that, although he had three glasses himself. Around us local people came and went. Conversation buzzed and the room fogged up with cigarette smoke. Fitzroy didn't skimp on his eating either. When I finally sat back, fully sated, he continued a while longer. 'I take it you enjoyed that?' he said at last. 'Always best to eat where the locals do.'

I nodded, slightly tipsy from the wine. 'You know you look like a tiger, don't you?'

The spy regarded his image in his wineglass.

'Grr,' he said, validating my statement.

Chapter Nine

Meeting Fitzroy's French family

The Girauds clearly held Fitzroy in high esteem. They welcomed him with open arms, and even accepted me without question. Fitzroy told me to spend the time here in my true gender. Madame Giraud unquestioningly lent me some clothes but remained very cold towards me. When I offered to help her prepare the evening meal, she shooed me from her kitchen with no apparent sign of gratitude. Both their children, a boy of ten and a girl of seven, were fascinated by me and tried to talk to me in their school-level English. From them I learned that the farmstead was up in the hills, behind a small village, and that no one ever came here, and their parents rarely left. Only the two children went out daily to the village school, but they always had to come straight home. The children managed to tell me they grew vegetables and had a plentiful supply of fruit trees. They also had chickens that roamed free and two goats, called Bête and Noire, which ate anything within their reach. Then, without warning, their mother descended and shepherded them off. I was left alone. Monsieur Giraud and Fitzroy were off somewhere together, so I decided to take a short walk before dinner.

Stepping outside the back door, I was grateful for the scarf and woollen coat I had been lent. The air still had the bite of winter, although it already felt warmer than England. I took a well-trodden path that lay alongside the chicken coop - a black-tarred, rough, hand-built box on stilts. The sun had set, but the moon waxed bright. I could see enough to walk to the forest line, at the bottom of the cultivated patch, and back. I smelled herbs on the air, that and the rich, loamy smell of the forest as it waited for Spring to return. It reminded me of the Fens while remaining alluringly exotic.

I'd kept my boy's boots on; besides, I was used to walking in the country. I came to the forest edge before I knew it. The forest stretched off into the dark. I could see between the irregular gaps of the many trees, and I heard the distinctive calls of two different night owls. I stopped at the treeline, though I wouldn't have minded venturing further. Although the tree canopy did not shut out all the moonlight, it obscured it enough that I feared I might lose my way. I didn't want to bother Madame Giraud, who so clearly disliked me, by asking for a lantern. Besides, for all I knew, lamp oil might be an extremely valued commodity in a household that seemed to want to isolate itself.

I found a tree stump that wasn't too damp and sat on it. This way I could keep my eye on both the forest and remain within sight of the house. When I stopped, the night air came alive with the sounds of insects, little scurrying noises among the underground, the settling noises of the chickens, and the occasional echo of a faint cry from one of the children in the house. The setting was as peaceful and as unthreatening as any I have ever had the privilege to witness.

I sat for a while, simply listening. The stiller and quieter I became the more I heard and saw. I caught a glimpse of a white streak between the trees, close to the forest floor. I had no idea if they had badgers in France, but that seemed the most likely. The memory of my father and I camping out one night to see badgers and their cubs at a sett near the vicarage came back to me all at once. I recalled the scent of the English summer countryside at night and my father's gentle reminders to keep as still as possible as the badgers were wisely scared of humankind. He'd convinced our maid to make toffee. My mother was quite against children having sweets. I must have been nine or ten as Joe was a mere baby and Mother was preoccupied with him. Thus, Father and I had snuck out together. As we waited, he talked of the connections between all life, of the value of wild animals, even the animals we used as food. He spoke of how all must be treated kindly, because if man could not value life that was below him, how would he ever truly come to value the life of his fellow man. In appreciating nature, he said, we saw into the heart of God's great creation, where he cared for one and all, man and beast. My father really was the gentlest of men.

The tears took me quite by surprise. One moment I was lost in a happy memory and the next I was sobbing as if my heart had broken. I turned away from the house and covered my face as much as I could to muffle any sound. It was the first time in my life that I wept until I had no more tears to give.

I was mopping myself up as much as I could when I felt a light touch on my shoulder. I turned to see Fitzroy standing in the shadows behind me. He nodded forward and I looked in that direction. Perhaps twelve feet away from us, a pair of yellow eyes regarded us in the darkness. I would have left at once, but Fitzroy's hand grew heavy on my shoulder. I did as I was bid and waited. I could see the outline of a four-legged animal with a bushy tail. It was quite the largest fox I had ever seen. Then my breath caught in my throat as I realised it was a wolf.

As if it knew I had recognised it, the wolf took a few paces forward. It seemed as curious about us as we were about it. I shivered with excitement. I knew Fitzroy always carried a gun, so we were in no real danger. The moonlight caught the wolf's grey fur and made it shine. 'Beautiful, isn't he?' said the spy very quietly.

'How do you know it's a him?'

'Dog wolves are larger than the females. Besides, the females tend to be less brave around humans. They have more sense than the males.'

'Will he come closer? Is he dangerous?'

'You've been crying.'

'I was thinking—'

'Good,' said the spy, cutting me off. 'It's what you needed. I've got Madame to prepare a bath for you.' Then he took two steps forward. The wolf turned tail and fled. 'He was hunting for his supper,' said Fitzroy. 'Chickens,' he added jerking his head back towards the hen house. 'No, he wouldn't have harmed us. Wolves only attack when completely necessary, to defend themselves or to eat. Rather like us.' Then he turned and started walking back to the house. I caught up with him. Before I could say anything, he said, 'Don't tell the family what you saw. Monsieur Giraud would be out after him with a gun. Not everyone understands the nature of how things must be.'

He held the back door open for me and I went straight upstairs to find the bath. I doubted I would be bathing in front of the kitchen fire, as the family might. There, in my bedroom, was a tin bath, full of steaming water. I had never been so happy to scald my skin.

Later I came downstairs, feeling much better in body and soul. I found Fitzroy and both Monsieur and Madame Giraud sitting around the kitchen table studying maps.

'You're still damp, Alice,' said the spy. 'Go and sit by the fire in the other room.'

I put my fingers up to my hair. 'Oh, that's all right. Now it's so short, it dries in a trice.'

The spy gave a sigh as I came over to the table. 'Are you getting help with the . . .' I glanced down at the maps. Even my rudimentary knowledge of navigation told me these were maps heading to the coast, not inland to Germany.

Monsieur Giraud leapt to his feet and said something loud and angry. He glowered at me, and if I hadn't known him to be a country farmer, I might have thought he had adopted a fighting position, such was his stance.

Fitzroy made a sitting gesture to him and spoke calmly.

'It doesn't matter if she has no French,' said Giraud, breaking into rather good but accented English. 'She has seen our maps.'

'You can trust her. I do.'

Giraud made a 'Pfft' noise, a syllable I came to hear often in

French. 'Just because you trust your *bonne amie*, does not mean we must. You are not thinking with your head, Fitzroy. This is our lives. No, you must deal with her.'

'Does *bonne amie* mean your girlfriend?' I asked.

'Lover,' said Fitzroy.

'How dare you!' I said standing to face the man and adopting a fighting stance of my own. 'As I would ever consider . . . sleeping with Fitzroy! That is not the way of it at all.'

Real indignation must have sounded in my voice as the two men gave very different reactions. Fitzroy winced and Giraud laughed. 'That kind of dislike cannot be faked,' he said. 'I think she knows you well. She is a fighter too. Is she one of your agents? I did not think the English had the sense to recruit women.'

For the first time Madame Giraud smiled at me. 'I have always fought beside my husband,' she said in perfect English. 'So many men underestimate our sex. I am pleased to see our friend does not.'

'You're not French, are you?' I asked.

'We have been here many years. I was six months pregnant with Jean when we arrived.'

'I take it Fitzroy helped you find—' I asked, realising halfway through that was none of my business.

'He was in our country during the revolution,' began the husband. 'He fought with us.'

'I think we can dispense with reminiscing,' said Fitzroy sharply. 'The question before you now is, are you going to leave, and if so, how.'

'You think we should go?' said Madame Giraud. 'You are sure the war will reach here?'

'There are never certainties in war,' said the spy. 'But if my family were here, I would go now. Perhaps if you didn't have children you could wait and see how things transpire, but . . .'

'It is not worth it,' said Monsieur Giraud.

'It will mean giving everything up. I cannot bear to think that, once again, raiders will savage my home,' said Madame Giraud. 'I will burn my belongings before I let the enemy rob me again.'

Giraud put his hand on his wife's arm. 'You know what Fitzroy will say, we should not draw attention to ourselves before we leave. We must act as if everything is normal. People will only realise we are gone when the children do not turn up for school.'

'A school holiday, or a weekend at the very least, is the best time for you to go. But you must go on foot and not carry more than is necessary. I will arrange for someone to meet you at Ville de Leon. It is only a few miles; can the children manage?'

'They are wild creatures of the woods,' said Madame Giraud with a smile. 'Even Yvette can manage.'

'My contact will take you to a crossing point. When you reach England, you go the nearest post office and reverse the charges to the usual number. I doubt I myself will answer, but if you give the password to whoever does, you will be provided for.'

'Ah, so we must lose everything again,' said Madame Giraud.

'They are only things,' said Monsieur Giraud.

Fitzroy smiled. 'I have said you will be provided for, and you will be.'

'Your government is so generous to all refugees?'

'No, but I am to people who saved my life.'

Giraud put out his hand to grasp Fitzroy's forearm. 'My friend, we saved each other's lives in those dark times, more often than I can count.'

'Perhaps, but the information you have provided me over the years has been invaluable to our planning. Besides, I always told you I was a rich man. I have few calls on my pocketbook. I can afford to give you a decent start in your new country. If you must, you can pay me back in ten years or so. I would say five, but the way things are going, war will disrupt commerce for some time.'

'He is an English Lord, isn't he?' said Madame to me in a mock undertone. 'Related to the King himself?'

'Honestly, I don't know. But when it comes to Fitzroy, very little surprises me,' I said. The children came in to set the table for dinner and the maps vanished as quickly as they had appeared.

Chapter Ten

In which I get to drive again, and we finally reach Germany

We left after the lunch the next day, and still barely escaped taking live chickens with us. Madame Giraud seemed determined for us to take much of what she had to leave behind. Fitzroy repeatedly explained we were in a race, but even he could not stop us being loaded down with several crock pots of food to be reheated later, as well as enough filled baguettes to feed a small army.

My parting from the Girauds couldn't have been more different from our initial meeting. They kissed me on both cheeks and made me promise that when Fitzroy allowed it, I would meet up with them in their new country.

As we drove off, I could no longer contain my questions. 'Where did you fight with them?' I asked when we barely out of the village.

'During a revolution in the Balkans,' he said. 'I was meant to be on an observation-only mission – my first ever mission. I got too involved. It is not a time I care to remember.'

'But you remembered them?'

Fitzroy frowned heavily. 'I could do little among the massacres that were occurring. That I managed to get two decent people out of it at all does little to my credit. I should have done more, as should the service. They knew the Black Hand were attempting to operate in the area, and yet they adopted a "wait and see" approach. They sent me in to watch the slaughter.'

'I'm sorry. I didn't know.'

'I have only told you this much to stop you asking more. I don't want to speak about it again. Ever. Do you understand?'

'Yes.'

'For once, no caveat? Thank you. I suppose I should try teaching you to drive again. Heaven help us both.'

I cannot say my driving lessons went smoothly, or without argument. However, something had changed between us – or in one of us. I don't know. But since the ship, I didn't look at life in quite the same way, and I don't think Fitzroy thought of me in quite the same way either. Perhaps if we had been in some foreign tribe, I might have been considered blooded, but I think it more likely that we understood we worked under orders and by necessity. And that took a toll on us. I had seen Fitzroy shrug off many a dangerous situation as if it were nothing, but for a moment, he had let me see he didn't always agree with his orders and disliked at least some of what he must do. I had once told him I thought he was a good man who had to do bad things for the sake of the general good. It wasn't until then I truly understood what that meant – and he knew I understood now. It marked a subtle change between us, so when I barely avoided trees and he yelled at me, I took it on the chin. I comprehended that his anger was less with me and more with the circumstances that forced him to teach me to drive in so little a time. That, and of course, he dearly loved his car and my treatment of it left a lot to be desired.

As we travelled through France, I accordingly paid little attention to our surrounds, and spent my time focusing on co-ordinating my hands and feet and staying on the road. Fitzroy, eventually, managed to sit back and relax a little. He even looked around at the scenery. He made no comment, allowing me to divert all my attention to driving.

One evening, when we drew up to a local pension, I nearly drove straight into a wall as Fitzroy surprised me by fingering one of curls and saying, 'Very pretty.'

'Thank you,' I said, somewhat taken aback. 'I didn't expect my hair to grow back so quickly, nor with a wave.'

'No,' he said. 'It wasn't a compliment. You're a boy, remember. We can't have you too pretty.' At reception it transpired that, yet again, Fitzroy and young Fitzroy would have to share a room. Fitzroy sighed as he took the key. 'You must promise me you will never mention this aspect of our journey to Bertram,' he said as we made our way up the stairs.

'Why?' I said smiling. 'Do you think he would take a swing at you?'

Fitzroy waited until we had entered our room before answering. 'Possibly, though I don't doubt I could easily dodge it, being more used to fighting than your husband. It was more that I thought it would distress him, which would put a strain, not only on your marriage, but also on his heart.'

I dumped my bag at the end of my bed. I was growing quite accustomed to doing things for myself rather than letting a porter, or my escort, do so. But then, I suppose my time as a maid, and later a housekeeper, had shown me I was more than capable of doing things for myself.

'It is most disconcerting when you turn all wise and avuncular,' I said. 'It does not fit my image of you.'

'It doesn't fit with my image of myself,' growled the spy, stretching out, fully clothed on the bed.

By now we had worked out a way of sharing rooms when necessary that preserved both our modesties. It did rely on closed eyes and trust. I certainly never peeked – although my curiosity urged me to do so on more than one occasion. But then I thought doing so would open up new areas of our relationship which were really much better kept firmly shut. I already knew Fitzroy had no moral objections with romancing married women, but as a married woman myself, I had no intention of straying, and did not wish to signal in any way that I might. Besides, I did not find him attractive in what might be called a baser sense. Nor, do I believe he thought of me in that way. Other men had found me beautiful, but Fitzroy made it clear that he mostly found me annoying.

'I could cut your hair again,' said the supine spy. 'But it would get tedious as it appears to grow out so fast. I think as long as it doesn't reach an unmanly length, I should show you how to use oil to slick it back. It will add to the masculine impression.'

'Like you? Do you feel as if it adds to your manly charms?'

Fitzroy turned his head and scowled at me. 'I have exceptionally curly hair. I prefer it to be neat.'

'Gosh, red *and* curly hair. You really weren't born to be a spy, were you?'

'No,' said the spy. He got up and went over to the mirror. 'Come over here. You need to work on applying your make-up too. I can see the bruise.'

It didn't help that I had found, and continued to find, these make-up sessions remarkably funny. Fitzroy still had bruises to cover, so he had demonstrated on his own face how to obscure them. He'd also shown me some subtle, but simple, shading techniques that could change the contours of the face. This, in addition to his make-up case and brushes, brought out the devil in me. I tried hard to repress my laughter, but really, he was the last man I expected to see applying foundation to his face. Fortunately, he had taken this well. I suppose it reflected well on his masculinity. As long as I paid attention, he didn't appear to mind my giggles. Or so I had thought. Today he had his revenge. He was showing me how to apply the oil to my hands before putting it through my hair.

'Yes,' I said vaguely. 'I see.' I mean, how hard could this be? I was seating on a high enough stool that I could see out of the window and the rather beautiful scenery below. It was now late February. Not my favourite time of year, but France wore it well.

'I'll show you,' said the spy.

'Hmm,' I said, watching small birds in the trees outside. The next moment I felt his fingers running through my hair. I flinched slightly but composed myself. Fitzroy rarely touched me, except by the shoulder, or if he had to stop me falling off or out of something (which he claimed he had to do far too frequently). However, I knew this was a professional skill he was imparting, so I said nothing. I did however start thinking about supper and continued watching the birds. I felt concerned that were I to watch him too closely in the mirror doing my hair – the whole point of the exercise – I would be embarrassed and blush.

'There,' he said.

He stepped back and I finally looked in the mirror. All over my head were protrusions of tight-set curls. I looked like a hedgehog that had been caught in a tornado. 'Perhaps, next time you will pay attention to what I am teaching you. Time to do down to dinner.'

'I can't go down like this!'

'You're a young man, dressed without much taste – unlike myself.' He smoothed down his waistcoat. 'You clearly don't care very much how you look, so it won't bother you.'

'Can't we order dinner in the room as usual?'

'No, we can't. You should have objected before. It you try to brush it out now you'll look like you've been using curling tongs. Better to leave it as it is.'

'But I will be red with shame.'

'My point is that Alan would not be. Let's see how much in character you can stay.'

I can honestly say that after this dinner of shame, where ladies of a certain age whispered behind their hands about me, and small children giggled, I can now carry my head high no matter what I am wearing.

Fitzroy enjoyed every inch of my discomfort. When we finally returned to our room, he found a basin of water and helped me wash it out. If he hadn't, I think he knew I would have done my best to drive us into a ditch the next day.

Bremen was a surprise to me. As we had drawn nearer to Germany, I had been aware of more and more soldiers in the streets, both in France and later as we crossed the German border. I had been quite on edge as we crossed over, but Fitzroy, an old hand at travelling from country to country, didn't turn a hair. 'It's only a stretch of road,' was his comment. 'There's no real difference on one side or the other as far as Mother Nature is concerned. It's merely us, opting to speak in different languages, that makes this awkward and proprietorial.'

'You would hardly say that about England.'

'The Kingdom is two islands.'

'Yes, but you wouldn't say it was the same as France or Germany except for the language spoken.'

'Of course not, it's the King's Domain. We have different standards to the continentals.'

'You confuse me. You have such conflicting opinions.'

'I'm an enigma,' said the spy. 'What do you think of Bremen?'

He had insisted on driving, so for once I could look about. 'Too many soldiers,' was my first reply.

He nodded. 'For once we agree. Otherwise?'

'It's rather like something from a fairy tale,' I said. 'Pointy towers and quaintness. Not gothic. Something else. And there's a factory – the long, low building with a smoking stack, that's one, isn't it? Lots of wide flat barges on a—'

'On a wide flat river. But how does it *feel* to you?'

'Tense. People look up when they hear the car, but they don't stand and stare, they retreat into their shops or houses. It feels like they're all waiting for something, but I don't know what.'

'I'm not sure they do either,' said Fitzroy. 'They'll know of the war of words between Germany and Belgium – that's the one at the top of the list right now, but a war between Europeans seems unthinkable to them.'

'I take it they don't remember Napoleon,' I said.

'Probably not personally,' said the spy with a wry smile. 'But if your point is ordinary people rarely trouble themselves with history then you are perfectly correct. You may also note that Bremen appears prosperous. The buildings are in good repair and we have yet to see beggars on the street.'

'It is very tidy,' I said.

'The German mind,' said Fitzroy. 'Even their grammar is tidy. Much more so than other tongues. Their language is precise and not littered with hyperbolic idioms like ours. It sounds harsher too.' He spoke a couple of sentences quietly in fluent German (or at least I assumed it was German). 'The French have a softer lilt to their mother tongue. Much like as in France they drink wine, but in Germany they drink beer. None of this waiting around for wine to age. Hops, water, yeast, sugar, and as soon as possible in one's *stein* – that's a large beer mug.'

'A get–things–done sort of people?' I offered. 'Sort of like London, but without the rain holding up play?'

He laughed at that. 'I think we are straying a little too far into the imaginative now. They have an aerodrome here. The Town Hall and the Theater am Goetheplatz are only recently built. This is a city for merchants, a hub of industry, and a suitable city for a proud Germany.'

'Which sounds good, but not when you say it.'

'There are around a quarter of a million people living here, yet everything runs well – from trams to water traffic. The efficiency of a potential enemy is always concerning, but it isn't just that . . .'

'The place feels ambitious?'

'Why do you say that?'

'The new buildings, the efficiency . . . what else has it left to do?'

'This is the real issue with Germany. It is doing well, but it wants more. Very human. But very concerning when it's on your doorstep . . .'

'You mean we might be the more?'

'Either family connections with Good Queen Vic mean something positive to the Kaiser or they give him licence, in his mind, to covet London's riches. We don't know yet. As I said, Belgium is feared to be the front line. The first place they will cross. But that's not for general discussion. You won't find it in any papers back home. That's just what the service thinks. And we're not always right – just usually.'

'So, we must take care.'

'Always, considering what we are. But be aware, most Germans have more than a smattering of English. We cannot allow ourselves to be overheard. Talking in the car is the best place – engine noise can be an advantage.'

'Then is this the time to ask about our mission?'

Fitzroy edged carefully past a cart pulled by a skittish young horse. 'There isn't an awful lot to tell,' he said. 'At some point during the rally, an unidentified contact will pass to us the only blueprints of a new weapon that has been developed by a German pacifist.'

'You know that doesn't make sense – the latter part.'

Fitzroy grunted. 'That is the intelligence handed to us. For all we know, they may have threatened his family if he didn't come up with the goods. I'll extend him the grace to believe he doesn't generally design such things, which makes whatever this is particularly interesting. Anyway, from what has been left unsaid, we can assume this weapon is somehow critical to the way the war will be waged. The plans may have been stolen by a colleague, or more likely a member of the inventor's family, and that person is keen to pass them on. There are an awful lot of families tied up with both sides – including your own.'

'Mine? Oh, you mean Hans. He's my husband's half-sister's husband. No one could think I have German loyalties.'

'It *was* questioned. I vouched for you.'

'Oh. Thank you,' I said. 'That's . . .'

'Surprising? I find, in general, people get very touchy about patriotism and foreigners around wars. We're an aggressive, isolationist species at heart.'

'Except for the British.'

'That goes without saying,' said the spy with no trace of sarcasm in his voice. 'No, if I had to guess, I imagine it's a relative who is passing on the blueprints.'

I thought for a moment. 'You mean the inventor is dead? After all, if the Germans have him, they can simply get him to redraw the plans.'

'I doubt it would be quite that simple, but yes, I've been thinking along those lines. He could have asked for asylum in exchange for the information, but there's been no mention of that.'

'Any chance we might be being double-crossed?' I asked. 'Your knowledge would be worth a lot to Germany. Or am I being melodramatic?'

From the side I saw an ear-splitting grin cross the spy's face. 'Not at all. After all, they've tried to nab me before. The whole thing could be one giant set-up. Another reason this is so interesting.'

I swallowed. Fitzroy's concept of 'interesting' was close to the average person's 'incredibly dangerous'. 'So, someone, we don't know who, is going to pass us the information during the race. And then we head home, carry on, what happens?'

'It's a rally, not a race. It depends when we get it. Turning for home at once would look suspicious, but it's not unheard of for difficulties to knock teams out of the race. I'm sure we will be able to find a reason to slope off when necessary. Every moment we stay on foreign soil with the plans is a terrible risk, but we don't want to attract attention either.'

'I'm surprised you brought me with you.'

'I am too,' said Fitzroy with his normal discourtesy, 'but you have to learn sometime, and with a war coming, you've got a steep learning curve ahead of you. I've a good ten years' head start in this business. There will be times when, I am sorry to say, you will have to trust me.'

'I always trust you,' I said. 'I may be furious at you, dislike you strongly, but I always trust you to do the right thing for King and Country.'

Fitzroy finally turned to look at me briefly. 'Glad to see I've moved up from being loathed to merely disliked,' he said and winked at me.

'What's the difference between a rally and race?'

'Later, little brother. This, if I am not mistaken, is where the teams are meeting. Time to go to work.'

He pulled up outside a large inn. Unlike many of the domed or turreted modern buildings, this one had little ornamentation. It was functional with wooden panelled windows and stout oak doors. The only embellishment was the window boxes but it being February, these were flowerless and depressing. The inn was old enough that in its past life it must have catered to coaches with horses. Within moments a man directed us round the back of the building to what had been the old stables. I saw why the inn had been picked as a starting point. The stable yard was huge, and it was currently such a hive of activity my eyes didn't know where to look. If I had ever thought our engine loud, it was nothing compared to the din created by a half-dozen or more cars. Porters unloaded luggage. Men in long coats, with goggles pushed up on their foreheads, strode around shouting in foreign languages. Other men, in greasy tradesmen's clothes, hovered under opened bonnets prodding at engines, and somewhere a dog barked loudly. The whole place stank of car fumes. I could feel an acrid coating forming in my mouth when I spoke.

'How many other teams are in this race?' I shouted.

Fitzroy pulled into one of old stables that had a Union flag above it. The noise outside faded.

'Nine, I think,' said Fitzroy. 'The sign-up was on the informal side. Several of the usual participants refused, not only because it was unofficial, but it was in February rather than January. Less snow now. Less of a challenge.'

'Snow?'

'Hopefully, our mechanic will have been around a bit. It's a challenge to ensure we've the right tyres and all that.'

'We've a mechanic?'

'You're being most repetitive, do stop. It may fit the character of an annoying little brother, but it makes you seem rather dim.' With that he hopped out of the car. 'Hey, Gunther!' he called. 'We're here.'

'Coming,' responded a voice from above us, and I realised the hay loft remained. A man came quickly down a ladder in the far corner I hadn't noticed. The shed was deep enough that it ended in shadow. That shadow now crept further along the shed as Fitzroy pulled the doors almost closed. A streak of sunlight remained down the centre, splaying out slightly as it reached the car. Gunther stepped into the light, but I barely noticed him. A large white pit bull terrier ran full force at Fitzroy and jumped at him.

Fitzroy caught the dog with no apparent effort. 'You have to stop doing that,' he told the animal. 'People will talk.' The dog barked and licked his face. Fitzroy petted it and did his best to avoid its tongue, with no particular success. 'Gunther, you remember my little brother, Alan?'

'Of course, sir. How are you today, Mr Alan? I trust the drive here was pleasant,' said a man I had never seen before in my life. Taller than average, he stood a couple of inches short of Fitzroy's height. He had a mop of untidy blond hair, but clean, chiselled features. I could imagine him and Fitzroy, all spruced up, cutting quite a dash at a ball. I could only hope he didn't prove to be as annoying in temperament.

The deference he showed seemed too much for a mechanic. He had to be one of Fitzroy's colleagues, who was overplaying his hand. However, I couldn't count on it. It would be like the spy to put us both on the spot, to help ensure we remain in character.

'Oh, not too bad, you know,' I said climbing down from the car. 'France seemed rather nice, all trees and fields. A bit flat for my liking. But this city, it's bustling. Seems top notch.'

'And there you have it,' said Fitzroy, 'an in-depth comparison of two European countries, one flat, one busy. Honestly, Alan, the notice you take of the world around you is abysmal. I bring you on this trip as a favour to Father and all you can do is—'

'How did the car run, sir?'

'Here, take him,' said Fitzroy handing the dog to me. 'His name is Jack.' He then started talking about the engine with Gunther. I recognised they were both speaking English, but the conversation meant nothing to me. I took the dog over to one side and sat down on a crate. In my pocket I had the remains of a sandwich, filled with a cold meat that I had found rather nasty. Germans, it seemed, loved cold sausage in bread. I began to break it into bits and fed it to Jack, securing his friendship for life.

It was a while later, when I was teaching Jack to give me his paw for the last bit of food, when Fitzroy finally returned to me. 'What are you feeding that dog?' he demanded. 'I don't want Gunther to have to deal with him being sick.'

'He's hungry,' I said. 'And so am I. Isn't Gunther a German name?'

'German on his mother's cousin's side, or some such thing,' said Fitzroy. 'Come on then, we'll go and find our spot in the inn. I should imagine they are serving dinner by now. Then I think I might go for a nice walk. Seems ages since I've had an opportunity to stretch my legs. I take it I can leave you at the inn without you causing trouble. And don't think of troubling Gunther, he's got plenty of work to do. And leave the dog here. He's Gunther's.'

'No one will believe that,' I said. 'If they see him with you.'

'Exactly. Leave him here.'

I said goodbye to Jack. Gunther had to hold him by his collar to stop him from running after us. 'At last you've found total devotion,' I said quietly.

'Shut up, Alan,' said Fitzroy.

Chapter Eleven

In which Fitzroy and I dine in Germany and we meet some of the other teams

It wasn't surprising that Fitzroy sent me up to the room as soon as we got inside. He'd managed a fairly civil manner as we drove through Bremen and it had clearly worn itself out. Having not been told when the race officially started, I unpacked as few things as possible. Again, I found a small bookshelf in the room, and perhaps having been notified that an English team were renting this room, someone had left a selection of English detective novels.

I settled down with Baroness Orczy's *The Old Man in the Corner*, which I rather enjoyed. All he did really was sit in a café and unravel a ball of string while dissecting and uncovering mysteries where others had failed. I briefly wondered if Fitzroy's mood would be improved by buying him a ball of string. This had certainly entertained my kitten of my childhood days. Although someone less like a kitten it was hard to imagine. I should ask Bertram for a cat, if White Orchards didn't have a suitable one. There were doubtless outside ratters and mousers, but I didn't fancy being presented with dead, or worse still, half-dead creatures in the early morning. If Bertram could scream at my shortened hair, then how he would take a dead rat, I didn't want to know.

The thought of my husband threw me into a melancholy mood. I put the book aside, lay back on my bed and stared at the ceiling. Being white and blank, without so much as a crack, it offered no diversion and I was beginning to feel decidedly tearful when the door burst open and the spy strode into the room.

'What are you doing?' he demanded and walked over to inspect my book.

I sat up and took a deep breath. 'Thinking,' I said.

'Oh, dear me, no,' he said, 'quite out of character for Alan, and if you were thinking about this ridiculous book . . .'

'What do you need me to do?'

Fitzroy paused, looking a little nonplussed. 'What do you think you could do?' he countered.

'I could come down and get to know some of the other teams. I wouldn't mind some supper either.'

'This pre-occupation with eating,' he said, totally oblivious to his own hypocrisy, 'it won't do. You have to be ready to go without food for days in this career.'

'Not, surely, when one is staying in an inn.'

'Well, no, not usually.'

'Even if you do not choose to join me, having supper gives me a reason to be in the room with the others, and I can observe them while I eat. Have you already dined?'

'Not exactly,' said the spy. 'I have made arrangements though.' He paused. 'I am afraid they don't include you.'

'Well, then I can eat alone. If I am quiet and stay in the shadows, I may learn a lot. If nothing else, I may put my people-watching skills into practice.'

'Wouldn't you rather continue thinking and just eat here in the room?'

It was exactly what I would rather do, but the fact Fitzroy was so keen on me doing this made me quite contrary. 'No,' I said, standing. 'I'll come down with you.'

'Actually, I'm about to have a bath and a shave. Might be better if you headed down now. If you wait for me there might only be sausages left.'

'They appear to only eat sausages in Germany,' I said coldly.

'I take it I will see you later tonight, when you return from your postprandial exercise.'

'My what?' said Fitzroy.

I regarded him curiously. 'You're blushing.'

'Nonsense, I never blush. It would be completely unprofessional of me.'

'If you say so. I meant, when you had finished your walk around Bremen. I presume you hope to run into someone?'

'Oh, that. Yes, maybe. It has occurred to me that it might be someone among the teams and we should investigate them first.'

I must have looked confused, because he added, 'Don't worry about it. The first leg of the rally begins in two days. It'll give Gunther a chance to look over the car. The day before, I'll go over the maps with you. We should mark up the course together, so we're both speaking the same language.'

'And tomorrow?'

'A day of rest, I think. We've been travelling a long time. It'll give us a chance to find our footing around the others of the rally folk. Now, if you are indeed going downstairs, I shall direct them to bring my bath in here rather than the draughty little room they offered me as an alternative when I thought I would have to spare your blushes.'

'I thought it unlikely we could get baths as we arrived so late,' I said.

'Offer to pay extra,' said Fitzroy. 'Usually works.'

'Do they speak English?'

'Not a lot,' admitted Fitzroy. 'I'll arrange to have one brought up early tomorrow for you, if you let me bathe in here tonight.'

I nodded and opened the door to leave.

'The room will be free in about half an hour,' he said, 'I suggest you get an early night.'

I nodded again and left. I didn't feel especially sleepy and there was something about the way he phrased the suggestion that felt odd. I decided I would practise my shadowing and follow him on his walk after dinner. If he caught me then he could tell me where he slipped up, and if he didn't, all the better. I trusted Fitzroy not to harm me unless the mission left him no other choice, but in almost every other way I found him as trustworthy as your average snake.

However, I reflected as I went down the stairs to the open dining room below, he was only being what his job required of him.

Instead of the usual inn dining space, the serving area here was behind the reception area in a long cavernous chamber. From the roof hung what I first thought were cartwheels, but the objects had candles attached to the rim. Hoisted high above in the vaulted ceiling, there was no chance the revellers could knock the lit candles over. Perhaps that was the point. The light remained adequate, with the edges of the room sunk into the shadows. The tables were, for the most part, rectangular, lined with benches and the parties sitting at them consisting of six or more. I managed to find one of the very few smaller tables off to one side and took it. A menu sheet, which might have started out pristine this morning, lay, somewhat stained, on the table. I consulted it and could make no sense of the fare on offer.

A pretty waitress, in traditional plaits and a low-cut garment that would have scandalised my mother, appeared. I mimed that I needed something to eat and drink. I thought about trying to tell her of my aversion to sausages, but even as I began my attempt, I knew this was a mistake and stopped. There are really only a few ways one can mime a sausage, and in a foreign place with no mutually understood words, it can easily be taken in entirely the wrong manner. Beetroot red, I drew my room number on the table. She smiled kindly at me and nodded. I sat back and prayed. I am not fussy when it comes to British food, but as I looked over at the other tables, I saw more than one plate filled with an enormous sausage. We had hardly been in Germany any time and I already longed for something, anything, other than tubes of minced pig.

Very quickly a tankard of beer appeared at my table. I am about as fond of alcohol as it is of me. I succumb to its influences all too quickly. However, beer had to be better than spirits or wine. I sipped it and discovered that although the smell of hops remained strong (to be fair, the whole room stank of it) the beer had a light, nutty texture. I liked it much better than English beer but attempted to content myself with small sips.

Fitzroy had been vague about the other teams, even the numbers, let alone the individuals, so I had no idea if everyone here was in the rally. The room, being equipped with only the smallest of windows, which were shut, had become extremely warm, so no one wore driving coats. Perspiration formed at my hairline and my skin became sticky, like the feeling which is common on a summer's day and which real ladies never notice. I thought longingly of a bath. The spy had, by no means, been unhygienic, but his sudden desire for a bath before dinner surprised me. When I had complained of the lack of washing facilities before, he'd told me how he had gone for a fortnight without washing on one mission and that, by the end, he could repel others by the smell alone from a distance of four feet. As usual I took his stories with a pinch of salt, but . . . it was odd.

My train of thought was broken by a loud laugh. I glanced in the direction of it, rather than turning my head. Two men sat at one end of an otherwise empty bench. Both were remarkable for their extremely long beards, shaggy dark hair of longer than usual length, and weathered looks. I couldn't tell if they were actually twins, but they dressed alike, in white open-necked shirts, showing hirsute chests, and with trousers tucked into their boots. One of them had drawn a long, curved knife and the other one was the one laughing. The blade looked wicked and the light, such as it was, glinted off it, promising a deep and potentially fatal wound. My mouth went dry, and I clasped my beer mug so tightly my knuckles went white. I had taken a seat with my back to the wall from where I thought I would gain a good vantage point. However, I now realised there were far too many people between me and the only exit for comfort. I waited.

The knifeman plunged his weapon into his fellow's plate and

drew out a vegetable, held it aloft with a cry of triumph, then ate it from the point of his blade. His companion laughed even more heartily. The fellow then wiped his blade on his sleeve and tucked it back at his waist. The volume of noise in the room increased, and I let out a breath I had not realised I had been holding.

The waitress reappeared and planted a bowl of stew in front of me, along with a platter with several slices of a very dark bread. I thanked her. At least it wasn't sausages.

I took a tentative bite of something and identified that usual end-of-the-week-scraps stew that grand houses make for servants. It didn't taste bad, and I was hungry. If anything, it reminded me of my time at Stapleford Hall, below stairs. At the moment, in that large and crowded room, I suddenly felt extremely alone. Everyone I knew and cared about was hundreds of miles away. Fitzroy remained, but although we had declared ourselves friends of a sort, it was not the kind of companionability I had found with Merry, or even Rory Macleod, once. (Merry remained a good friend, but Rory, once a butler at Stapleford Hall, and I had become close and finally engaged. I jilted him, and while I am so much happier with Bertram, I hated the animosity that remained between Rory and me.)

I felt tears tremble on the edge of my eyelashes. This would never do! I did my best to pull myself together. I scanned the room and tried to pick out the teams. The two bearded men struck me as potential rally members. They stood out and didn't care a bit. They were almost oblivious to the people around them. They were clearly good friends if one could pull a knife and the other would only laugh. People avoided them - even more so now. So, they weren't locals and they weren't tourists. Their clothes were too nice to be used as napkins, so they must have been comfortably well off. They clearly had a joint pursuit. Their large frames also suggested a ruggedness that would stand them in good stead in the race.

I ate more stew, rather proud of my first piece of actual spying on my own. At another table I spotted two gentlemen, who

I thought at once had to be French. Neatly dressed, with exquisitely oiled locks, they frowned as they picked at their plates and took only tentative bites. A carafe of red wine stood at their elbow. They couldn't have been more French if they'd had the tricolour pinned to their backs. Both brown-haired, one, I observed during the course of my stew, had a thin moustache and a slightly bulbous nose, while the other had an extremely thin nose, larger eyes, and a goatee so small it looked like he had missed a bit shaving. They glanced around them but kept aloof from the other guests. The moustached one drank more freely than his fellow. I metaphorically patted myself on the back once more.

Who should I focus on next? It appeared to be the car teams only. The mechanics must eat in the garages. I swept the room.

I spotted another two pairs of men, who seemed very much at home, and who I presumed were German. Two more sat in the middle of the room, dark-haired with sallow skin, who were arguing loudly and quickly in a language I recognised for its similarity to Latin – Italians. There were another two who intrigued me, similar to the French, but beer drinkers and clearly happier with the food. I was deciding who to concentrate on next when two unpleasant things occurred at once.

I discovered my latest forkful to be a large piece of sausage, and Fitzroy entered the room. I might have been happier to see him if he hadn't had a tall, thin, glamorous blonde on his arm. She wore a silky, form-fitting gown more suited to a ballroom, or quite frankly a bedroom, than a German beer cellar. She glanced up at him, smiling, not sweetly, but rather knowingly. He bent his head for her to whisper in his ear, and whatever she said made him smile. Fitzroy had had the sense not to wear traditional evening dress, but he was dapper, a blue ascot at his throat, a crisp white shirt, and an excellent blazer – I didn't pay any attention to his trousers. I leaned back in my seat, as far into the shadows as I could get.

They swept past me with her still whispering in his ear. By

now the male-filled chamber had noticed them, and there wasn't a man who didn't drool as she slunk by in a dress that clung alluringly to her behind. Fitzroy found them a smaller table, similar to mine, but further away. At this point I should have got to my feet and left, but I didn't.

Instead, I stayed and watched them flirt throughout their entire meal. Fitzroy spoke fluent German (of course) and the lady, affected to be ever so impressed, pawed at his sleeve several times during the ordering of food and while they waited. I guessed her to be a little more than my age, but she had that gloss that makes it difficult to tell. Her curly blond hair appeared to be artlessly put up, but I saw the handiwork of a maid in it. Her make-up subtly highlighted her eyes and cheekbones, but in such a way that only another woman could tell those heightened tones were artificial, and she laughed melodiously, while pretending not to notice the attention she drew.

I knew my thoughts were unkind, but she was exactly the kind of vamp I had always despised. A man-trap on two legs. I don't suppose I would have cared except that my beautiful long hair had been shorn because I had been assured no women would be involved in the race, and because I had thought better of Fitzroy than to be so easily taken in. If nothing else, I'd thought he had better taste. Bertram would not have given such a woman a second glance, I reflected with satisfaction. He would have said, goodness me, that dress is a bit rich, isn't it, and taken me elsewhere. Rory would have been equally impolite, but more forthright in his description. Merry would have said that she was clearly no better than she should be (a strange expression, but it made sense this time).

How could I get out without drawing Fitzroy's attention? The last thing I wanted to do was let him know I had seen him with her. I didn't want to hear his excuses, or worse . . .

The waitress took my stew away and brought me, unasked, another mug of beer. I sipped at it and pushed my chair back against the wall. I now had room to escape and it was all about picking my moment. Hopefully the gentleman with the blade would start waving it around soon, or the Frenchmen would throw a tantrum over their food, or perhaps the Italians would break into a brawl. These were all options and if I could have brought any of them into being, I would have done so. What I must do was not watch Fitzroy and his companion, but again, I failed spectacularly at this. Against my will, my gaze kept being drawn back to their table, either by her laugh or his answering chuckle. Their chairs had moved closer together too. When their plates were removed, I saw Fitzroy slide his arm around the back of hers. The lady did not protest.

I couldn't watch any longer. The room had grown far too hot. Luck was with me. The Italians rose and one threw a punch at the other. I saw, briefly, beyond them, Fitzroy stand as if going to intervene. The woman reached up to him imploringly and he glanced down at her with an expression more tender than I had ever seen him use before, as he gently removed her hand and strode towards the battling Italians.

I took this opportunity to leave the room. I didn't doubt he could deal with them on his own, and if he couldn't, well, he could ask his escort to help him.

In a thoroughly foul mood, I dressed for bed and sat up, trying to read my book. I had abandoned all intention of attempting to follow the spy. I suspected his midnight walk would be delayed to tomorrow. I could not sustain interest in the book. I now found it boring and stupid. Eventually, I fell into a fitful sleep. I awoke to see Fitzroy crossing the room with his shoes in his hand. I sat bolt up right in bed.

'Ah, good, you're awake,' he said. 'I can put on a bit more light.' He turned his bedside light on. I did the same. He appeared happy and relaxed. I did my best to keep a poker face. Evidently, it didn't work.

'That is one sour look,' he said, taking off his blazer and hanging it carefully in the one wardrobe. 'Was the food that bad tonight?'

100

'You should know,' I said.

He raised an eyebrow and sat down on the bed. 'That was you in the shadows. I thought I was hallucinating. You should have been long gone by the time I came down.'

'Well, I wasn't. I was watching the room and trying to gather information on the teams,'

'Excellent,' said Fitzroy. 'How much did you learn?'

'I left when the brawl started, so it was observations only.'

'Still, that's something, and that fact that I wasn't sure it was you is even better. Your first piece of solo spying.' He smiled at me. If circumstances had been different, this would have made me happy. I might even have felt appreciated for the first time this mission. As it was, I couldn't keep the scowl from my face. My eyebrows lowered and only my mother's strict training prevented me from turning down the sides of my mouth (I could hear her in my head, *the lines, Euphemia, the lines. You will look like a washerwoman by twenty-five. Calm expression. Calm. A lady does not show her feelings.* Well, bother and blow that!).

Fitzroy leant back away from me. 'What is up with you? If I had milk that needed souring, you'd do a damn good job right now. Tell me what you observed.'

So, I did. I kept it as concise and neutral as possible. He nodded approvingly. 'Well done. I don't doubt if you'd had longer you would have learned more, but that is a good effort.' He was in a remarkably good mood, but the happier he became the angrier I got inside.

'I can tell you some more myself. Thin moustache is Monsieur Albert de la Flotte, the driver of the only French team. For reasons unknown, his navigator is referred to only as Monsieur Georges. They do indeed have something of a reputation of being finicky. They have their mechanic wash and polish their car at every available opportunity. They have become increasingly unhappy with many aspects of the impending rally and the general belief is they will not finish.

'The bearded men – I think are Cossacks, certainly Russians.

I am surprised they have entered. They are refusing to speak to anyone else and do their own mechanical work. I think the others are a little afraid of them and find them unpredictable. Personally, I think they behave exactly like Cossacks do. As long as we leave them alone – rather like wild bears – we will be fine.

'The duo who you thought weren't quite French are from Belgium. Monsieur Henri Mastiff and Monsieur Lawrence de Lyons – both seem rather unlikely names to me, but in general they are considered affable and are not above sharing supplies.

'I didn't get the Italians' names, not least because the Cossacks got to them before me.' He coughed. 'I was slightly detained.'

I briefly looked away to conceal my scorn.

'So, they both exited the room rather rapidly on the end of a large Russian boot,' he grinned. 'It was rather funny. Apparently, they are always arguing, rarely drink anything but strong black coffee – which may explain their bad tempers – and have the universally acclaimed best motor in the rally. However, they are so argumentative, there are side bets already as to when one of them will hospitalise the other! I have to say, it's all turning out a lot more jolly than I thought it would.'

'Yes, I saw that.'

Fitzroy narrowed his eyes and looked at me slightly askance. 'Anyway, there are two other teams from Germany. One, doubtless industrialists, they have what your mother would claim was the taint of the bourgeoisie. A Markus Winble and a Peter Housmann. Apart from the fact they are constantly retuning and refining their engine, there is nothing remarkable about them. I suspect, though I haven't seen it yet, that their motor is a prototype and they are trying to prove its worth, to gain investment, during the rally. If so, they will be very serious about winning and I doubt will have anything to do with our mission. Herr Claus Muller, the driver, and Herr Heinrich Mann are the other German team. Both clearly gentlemen, who speak perfect English. Perhaps the driver is related it your brother-in-law; do you know if he keeps up his German connections?'

'He is concentrating all his efforts on his family at present, but I believe he is keen to distance himself from Germany – especially as he is tied up with the City.'

'City? London? Yes, pity he didn't take my advice and change his name.'

'I didn't know you had spoken to him.'

'Oh, you know me,' said the spy, 'I get around.'

This was obvious bait, so I ignored it. 'Are there more teams?'

'An Austrian one, two older gentlemen – calling them middle-aged would be doing them a kindness, Herr Braun and Herr Milche. Names utterly transparent. They are obviously spies. Not, I think, our connection. Which worries me. I don't know what they are after – yet.'

'Don't other spies recognise your name?'

'No, I hardly ever use Fitzroy in the open. It's a service name, not a field one. You merely happen to be most familiar with that name, so I thought I'd use it this time. Being abroad for the first time in the field can be confusing enough without adding unnecessary levels of complication.' He smiled at me again, frowning slightly when I didn't smile back.

'Are there any other teams or can I go back to sleep?'

'You know Crabtree and Crawford.' He laughed softly. 'It's one huge gorgeous mess of greed, need, and . . .'

'Lust,' I said. Silently I berated myself. This habit I had of opening my mouth without consulting my brain needed to be overcome.

'Possibly,' said Fitzroy, now frowning more heavily at me. 'The final team is a divorcee. A British woman – notice I say woman and not lady – who married an American, divorced him and is virtually penniless. Her partner is a younger man, Luke. She didn't tell me his second name and I haven't spoken to him, but I rather think he is the younger son of a certain Viscount Marchant.'

'So, ten teams including us,' I said. 'I'm surprised it isn't a dozen.'

'There's certainly space for another team or two. I can only surmise this is all who would enter the unofficial race. There's already been some talk about anyone in this rally being banned from competing when the real rally returns. But everyone in this one seems to have a good reason to stay – most of which we now know.'

He stood up, 'If you'll excuse me, I should retire to my bed. We have a long day of ferreting out information tomorrow. Although I must say, between us, we have made an excellent start.'

'You do me too much credit,' I said. 'I take it you decided against the midnight stroll in case our contact was here and watching for us.'

'Too late now,' said Fitzroy. 'Besides I find myself somewhat fatigued after . . . everything.'

'I can believe it,' I said, half under my breath as I turned away to give him the privacy to change.

I felt a large mass drop down on my bed. 'Sit up and look at me,' he demanded. 'Now tell me what on Earth is the matter with you?'

I sat up but didn't look him in the eye. I didn't want him to misread me. 'Nothing,' I said. 'I'm tired.'

'You are behaving like a wife upset by her husband coming in late and smelling of another woman's perfume.' Heat poured into my face and my chin sank lower. 'It can't be Amaranth who has upset you. We – you and I – do not have a romantic connection, nor ever will.'

'I know that,' I said, gritting my teeth.

'Then why are you acting as if you are jealous? I've told you many times, I have no interest in marriage, but that doesn't mean I have to live like a monk. Especially when the woman concerned has information I need. Besides, I was flirting in the mildest manner in the dining room. No one could have found it objectionable. Anything that happened later is between her and me and no one else.'

I gave an involuntarily snort.

'If you have any reason to believe that my using her as an

asset is in some way compromising, you need to spit it out. Euphemia?'

'No,' I said. 'I'd never seen her before and know nothing about her.'

'Except her taste in evening wear, and her somewhat glamorous appearance,' he said. 'You are doing an awfully good impression of being jealous. I thought you loved Bertram.'

I jerked my head and snapped, 'Of course I do. He's worth twenty of you.'

'Probably many times more in the husband stakes,' said the spy coolly, 'although I am of more use to the Crown. The question is, are you going to be any use at all if you've fallen in love with me.'

I met his gaze, stuttering angrily for a response.

'Excellent,' he said. 'You look exactly like you did that time I let you slap me. I don't deserve it this time, so I have no intention of allowing you to do it again. Tell me what the matter is.'

'You were nice to her,' I managed to say and as I said it my eyes brimmed with tears, 'and you made me cut my hair.'

'Of course I was nice to her! I was flirting. You can't flirt without being nice. At least if you can, I don't know how one might go about it,' said the spy, sounding rather confused. 'I've been nice to you in the past when you were an asset and I wanted you to do things for me . . .' His voice trailed off. 'Did you think that was the real me? That I would be as nice to you on a mission? I'm sorry to disappoint you, but I have a terrible temper that I barely contain. If you'd seen the things I've seen one man do to another, you'd either suffer from terminal despair or never-ending rage. I choose rage. Generally, I keep it behind my teeth, but doing so can make me a grumpy companion, I admit.'

I gave what I hoped was a ladylike snort of agreement.

'I act a lot of roles, Euphemia. I'm a spy, as are you now. We do what we must to get the results our country needs.'

'I know that,' I said. 'And you haven't always been nice to me – sometimes you've been horrible.' Although, at that moment,

105

I couldn't remember when he had been unpleasant to me before I took the oath.

'I'm glad to hear it. You have seen at least a glimpse of the real me,' said Fitzroy. 'I got you to cut your hair, because in my experience there is only one kind of woman who comes on a rally, and she is as unlike you as I think it is possible to be.'

'You didn't think my acting skills were up to it?'

'Probably not, but that wasn't the point. I admit, it's a role I may need you to play one day, but I wanted to spare you it for now. I know there are many people in your life you care about, and that your affection for them is genuine. I didn't want you to have to start pretending that – not yet anyway. It's a hard-enough thing to do, when you're like me, and only have the one friend. But you have lots of people you value. It's going to be confusing for you to fake positive emotions for people you might inwardly despise. I would never ask you to cross a certain line, and I've ensured that's on your file. You're here because you're smart, not because of your looks, but all the same, it's not a very nice thing to have to do.'

'You despise this Amaranth?'

'Noxious creature. She's even adopted an American twang to her accent, if you can believe it.'

'But my hair!'

'It grows, Euphemia. Bringing you as a boy was the best way I could think of involving you, as well as the way least likely to upset Bertram. Did he react very badly to your shearing?'

'When he woke up and saw it, he screamed and fell out of bed.'

Fitzroy unsuccessfully tried to suppress a smile.

'It's not funny,' I said.

'I bet it was,' he said. 'Poor old Bertie. I can imagine his face. Even hear the high-pitched shriek.'

'What makes you think my husband doesn't have a deep, manly scream?'

Fitzroy tilted his head and looked at me.

'Oh, all right, maybe it was on the girlish side. But sudden shocks are bad for his heart!'

'It's only hair,' said Fitzroy. 'It's not like I'd stolen one of your arms, or both, like the Venus de Milo.'

The image of the ancient statue in nightclothes did finally make me smile.

'Go to sleep, Euphemia. I act all the time. You'll need to get used to it — and do it yourself. Don't let it get to you. None of it is real.'

'How do I know you're not acting with me?' I asked.

'I told you before, I never lie to you, and I give you my word, on my honour, that I will never do so.'

I did my best not to show my pleasure. 'Me and your one friend, I take it?'

'Idiot,' said Fitzroy, 'you are my one friend. Now go to sleep before I become too tired to get out of my clothes.'

Chapter Twelve

In which staying on course proves a problem

Fitzroy and I sat together at breakfast at one end of a bench. Crabtree and Crawford joined us. We responded in a very British way to the stacks of cold meats, black bread, and other strange comestibles that were provided for us. That is to say, we picked at it as cautiously, like the Frenchmen had the night before, and commented endlessly to one another on the breakfast's oddity. This ascended to another level when the Frenchmen themselves joined us: Monsieurs Albert de la Flotte (of the thin moustache and bulbous nose) and Georges (of the scanty goatee). Both, it transpired, spoke some English, and their arrival also had the fortunate side-effect of filling up our bench, so that when Amaranth entered, her young beau – he must have been all of nineteen – on her arm, there was no space to join us. Fitzroy, who alone of all of us, was tucking into the food without exclamation, pretended to miss her entrance and continued applying himself liberally to gobbling a cold sausage.

I say pretended, because although this time she didn't wear a ballgown, her riding jacket with its accompanying tight trousers drew the attention of many of the men in the room. The Italians on the other side of the room spoke so quickly it sounded like a river of words.

'Do you think,' said Monsieur Georges in a quiet and elegant voice, 'that there would be any point to ask for *du vin*?'

Crawford gave a bark of laughter. 'I think you'd have a better chance of getting a mare's eggs.'

Georges frowned and twittered to his friend in French. Then he spoke to us once more, 'I do not understand, we both thought a mare was a woman horse?'

Fitzroy, without looking up, let out a stream of French. Georges brightened. 'Ah, I see. A joke. A flying lady horse who lays eggs.' Then his expression fell. 'That means you also doubt the possibility of my obtaining wine for breakfast.' He sighed. 'But you, sir, speak the most excellent French.'

Fitzroy grunted.

'My brother also speaks in gruff noises,' I said, throwing Fitzroy a look of dislike. 'What are you two gentlemen planning to do today?'

'We make alterations to our motor,' said Albert, 'then we go for a test drive. Then we do more alterations.' He shrugged and made a 'pfft' noise. 'The Italians, their car is supreme, and Wimble and Housmann rebuild their engine all the time. Our poor *La Dame Sans Merci* is, more likely, to be at the mercy of others.'

Crabtree, whose vicinity to the rally and all its rank and file was obviously cheering, said, 'I know what, chaps! Let's have ourselves a little three-car race. A warm-up for tomorrow. It'll do both us and the motors good. Certainly better than hanging round here eating pickled goodness-knows-what. What?'

Albert and Georges exchanged glances and nodded. 'It is an idea most excellent,' said Albert. 'We had been intending to drive, but this will give the day a little more spice. A side bet too, perhaps?'

'Nothing too steep, if you please,' said Crabtree with a half-embarrassed laugh. 'I'm in this for the money.'

'Supper and the first round of drinks,' proposed Crawford.

'*Du vin?*' said Albert.

'We could forewarn the host,' I said. 'Let them know we will be wanting wine tonight.'

'Excellent idea, young Fitzroy,' said Crawford. 'What say you,

Fitzroy major? Will you race, or shall we let your younger sibling do the driving?'

Fitzroy drained his large beer mug. 'If you think I'm letting that scrawny mud-worm get his clammy little paws on any part of my car, you are much mistaken.' He paused for effect. 'I'll drive.'

The French team gave a little cry of 'hoorah' and Crabtree ran off to get a map so we could decide the course.

In my peripheral vision I saw Amaranth's boy, as I now thought of him, pull out her chair. Amaranth sashayed towards our table. Seemingly by coincidence, Fitzroy repositioned his chair to get a better view of the map and turned his back to her. Amaranth carried it off well. I doubt it anyone but I saw the slight wobble in her step as she redirected herself to the exit, as if that had been her plan all along. Only a faint blush on her cheeks betrayed that anything was wrong.

I bent down and whispered in his ear. 'That's a bit harsh.'

'But I'm a bit of a rotter,' he whispered back. 'Besides, when I am charming to her again this evening, she will be flattered and confused. The combination providing a useful vulnerability for me to exploit.'

'What do you intend to do?'

'Nothing that need concern you.'

'Fitzroy,' I hissed, slightly wetter than I had meant to.

'All right: for all her toxicity, the woman is a great observer of people. She and the others have been staying in the same inns while we made our way south and then doubled back, and she has yet more insights to offer me. I intend to squeeze them out of her.'

'I almost feel sorry for her.'

'You should,' said Fitzroy. 'I intend to exploit her with extreme thoroughness.'

'The Italians, they whisper, they plan,' complained Albert, 'but we have yet to agree the course.'

It took an hour, and several pots of eye-wateringly strong coffee, but at last a route and rules were agreed.

'*À la mechanique!*' cried Georges and charged out of the room.

Fitzroy folded up his copy of the map more slowly and passed it to me. 'I suppose I must now face Gunther and tell him his day of rest is no more.'

'I thought he was tuning the car?'

'He's had weeks to do that. Besides, he knows enough, but he's more manservant than mechanic.'

'Dog-sitter,' I said.

'That too,' said Fitzroy.

Less than half an hour later we wrapped up and were sitting in our vehicle ready to go. The others drew up alongside us. We had persuaded the mechanics to keep time both here and at the end of the leg. We would travel ten miles out, have luncheon at a supposedly Italian-owned restaurant, and drive back. As we were travelling on open public roads, we were setting off twenty minutes apart, our order determined by lot. We were going second. While we waited in the car, Fitzroy said, 'Right, you have the map. I've deliberately not memorised the route – which took some doing. You are in control of our direction. In the rally I won't be able to stop and help with the navigation, so it's all down to you. Remember, you have to give me directions in good time – clear directions. Not next left but left in twenty feet.'

'I've marked up the route as you taught me for the rally,' I said. 'But what if I get it wrong?'

'One, you almost certainly won't get any luncheon, two, you will have to face my wrath, and three, it will mean we are in a hell of a lot of trouble when it comes to the rally.'

'Is this meant to be a cheering speech?'

'It's meant to be you getting a chance to practise. Use it wisely.'

'All right,' I said, 'that sounds much better.'

'It's also a don't-raise-my-ire speech.'

'And there you go and ruin it,' I said.

A flag waved. 'We're off,' I cried, but Fitzroy already had us in motion.

'Be quicker,' he snapped.

I have to say, it was all going swimmingly. We had agreed to venture out of the town, for safety reasons, and were heading onto higher ground that had the first crunch of snow. Everywhere the trees were iced with white, but here the greenery was of a more chunky and sturdy nature and the snow fresh and powdery. It could not have been more unlike the wispy, wet nature of the Fens. The air knifed its way into our lungs, so cold it almost stole the breath. I had to put extra effort into yelling instructions, but from the off, Fitzroy and I worked harmoniously together. I have no idea why. I can only assume it was luck, but our timing coincided in the best way.

So, when I yelled at him to take a hard–right turn as we headed down a steep incline, having given fair warning and issued the relevant inclinations, I was confused when he didn't turn.

I turned to shout a query and saw how very white his face was. He pulled hard on the break, but nothing happened.

'How do you feel about jumping out into snow?' he asked.

'I don't mind the snow,' I said. 'It's the rocks underneath that worry me. What's wrong?'

'The brakes aren't working; I think a steering rod has snapped.'

'Ah,' I said, as we hurtled down the hill, gaining more and more speed.

'Masterful summation,' said Fitzroy. 'I really think you are going to have to jump.' Even with his driving gloves I could see how tightly he was gripping the wheel. His upper body was rigid with tension as he fought the car, trying to keep us on course.'

'What about you?'

'I need to try and save the car. It's needed for the mission.'

'No more than you are,' I exclaimed. 'We can always tune up Gunther's car.'

'Alice, you need to jump.'

'Only if you do.'

The car was now bouncing off bumps in the road and remaining airborne for a few seconds at a time. On each landing it shook from side to side as if it might break apart at any moment. What

112

had once been a cheery countryside was becoming a threatening wintry blur. Even if we jumped, I wasn't at all sure it wasn't too late. The road bore sharply to the left, but it seemed unlikely we would. Instead, it appeared that in a few minutes we would become far too intimate with a fence and a small copse of sturdy German trees.

'Jump, Alice. Protect your head. Remember how I taught you to roll. Now, that's an order.'

I didn't want to, not least because of what might lie beneath the snow, and the incredible speed with which the landscape roared by, but I had promised I would always obey an order. I have given an oath, so I jumped.

From when you exit a fast-moving vehicle to when you hit the ground, though incredibly rapid, is paradoxically long enough to allow numerous moments of regret, flashes of dear ones' faces, a great deal of mindless panic, and barely enough time to form into the necessary shape to land, if not well, then at least with a minimal chance of fatality.

The first time I met the ground I felt nothing. I thought, as the world turned upside down, this isn't too bad. Then I encountered something hard and every bone in my body shook. I tucked my head so far in a turtle would have been impressed. Snow and earth embraced me. I'm becoming an avalanche, I thought. How will I tell which way is up? I hit something that made me open my mouth to scream. It promptly filled with snow. I spluttered and choked. Far away I heard a bang that reverberated along the ground underneath me. An earthquake, was my first thought, but then I realised Fitzroy had not turned the car from the trees in time.

My limbs splayed out as I attempted to decrease my momentum. *He might still be alive. He could have been thrown free. He will need me*, and with a strength I didn't know I had, I waited for the hellish ride to end. I could feel myself slowing, and then a thunderclap went off in my head and everything went black.

★

113

I came to with a vision of the sky above me, the edge of a spade and Fitzroy's face. 'I've found her,' he shouted. The next moment a number of hands were scrabbling in the snow and multiple arms lifted me free. I lay on my back, pain whipping through my body like fire. I cried out.

'Careful, we don't know what he might have broken,' said Crabtree's voice.

'Let me through,' said Fitzroy. I heard the crunch of him kneeling down beside me. Then his hands went over every inch of me, testing and probing. Several times I couldn't help but whimper, and once I actually screamed.

'Some very bad bruising, maybe a sprain or two, but I don't think anything is broken.'

'C–c–c-concussion is the worst,' said Crabtree.

'Breaking your neck is the worst,' said Fitzroy. 'Sh . . . He's awake,' he corrected himself. 'That's good. Grab the blanket out of my boot and we'll put him in the back of your car. I'll have to ask you chaps to take us straight back.'

'Of course, old man,' said Crawford. 'Wouldn't think of doing anything else. The Frenchies will have to continue their little race on their own.'

'Talk to him,' said Crabtree. 'It's better if he stays awake.'

Getting me into the back of the car hurt. It hurt a lot in fact, but Fitzroy got in first, helping cradle my head and upper body. He shielded the light from my eyes with his hand. For the first time I noticed he had blood on his face. I pointed this out. 'Nothing,' he said, wiping it away with the back of his hand. 'A slight scratch. Mere carelessness. You got the worst of it. I'm sorry about that. It wasn't my intention.'

'I thought I'd had it,' I said, 'but then I thought you might still be alive and needed me to pull you from the car, and I tried ever so hard not to die.'

'Not the best reason,' he smiled down at me. 'But I'm glad you didn't die.'

'C and C?' I asked. Words seemed to become more of an effort.

114

'Oh, they rattled along a little while ago and found me trying to dig up half the bloody mountain. The snow got so churned up, I had no idea where you were. I was in a right state. Afraid you were running out of air. They were bloody decent about it. Worked with a will until we found you.'

'Do they know,' I said, lowering my voice. 'You said you'd found her.'

Fitzroy swore quietly and viciously. 'I didn't realise I'd done that. Bloody green error. What do you mean losing yourself inside a mountain like that?'

'We'll find out if they noticed.'

'Yes,' said Fitzroy, frowning.

'I'm sorry. I've messed things up a bit.'

'Nonsense, none of this is your fault. You need to rest, but not sleep. We'll work it all out.'

'Yes, I know. You always do,' I said as I drifted off into blissful sleep.

Fitzroy tapped repeatedly on my cheek with his other hand. I opened my eyes. 'That's so annoying. Worse than being slapped.'

'I shall keep doing this every time you appear to be falling asleep. You can sleep when we get you back to the inn and once you've seen a doctor.'

'But . . .'

'I am aware,' said Fitzroy. 'But most people have their price.'

'I don't,' I said grumpily.

'I know. Neither of us do.'

Then he continued tapping on my cheek all the way back to the inn. I got cross enough to try and bite him twice. Needless to say, I missed both times.

'By the way, Alan, you do realise, I am going to kill whoever did this to us, don't you? I trust you don't have a problem with that?'

'Not in the least,' I said, and failed to bite him again. 'Will you stop that infernal tapping?'

'No,' said Fitzroy, 'I'm beginning to enjoy it. You're pulling the most entertaining faces.'

For the first time I used one of his swear words back at him. Fitzroy recoiled in mock horror.

'Goodness, my little brother is growing up.'

Chapter Thirteen

In which suspicions abound

Back at the inn other people were summoned to help me into bed. I closed my eyes for the better part of it all. Fitzroy let me. There was no way I could have slept. When we got up to our room, a fire had already been lit, and the bed was turned down. Fitzroy turned everyone away.

'I'm going to take your outer clothing off, down to your underwear. I apologise in advance. It's going to hurt.'

'And be terribly embarrassing,' I said. 'If I wasn't so damn sore, I'd be mortified.'

'That's the ticket,' said Fitzroy. 'Look on the bright side. Besides . . .'

'Please don't say you're not going to see anything you haven't seen before. You haven't seen me.' I opened my eyes to see Fitzroy had gone a bright beetroot.

'I was going to say, I will be going no lower than your underclothes, and seeing as I supplied them, I know how covering they are.'

I couldn't suppress a smile at that. 'I didn't for a moment think you were taking advantage of me. However, it is not a predicament I would have willing placed either of us in!'

'Indeed not,' said Fitzroy. 'If you close your eyes, we could both pretend it isn't happening. I, however, need to see what I am doing.'

'I might be able to manage. It hurt a lot on the way back,

but I don't think there is much wrong with me, bar a lot of bruising.'

'I'm no doctor, but I believe they can be bad enough on their own. Besides, you might have a concussion. Although you can be ever so stubborn-headed at times, I wouldn't be surprised if your skull is extra thick.'

'I jumped the moment you made it an order,' I said.

Fitzroy nodded. 'Perhaps we should consider everything I say an order when we're in the field?'

'Wouldn't that be a gross abuse of rank?'

'Possibly,' said Fitzroy. He sat down at my feet and begun to undo my shoes. I shut my eyes and thought of home.

Not long after, I was all tucked up under the blankets and there came a knock at the door. Fitzroy opened the door, closed it, and took the visitor to one side. I heard a murmur of voices but couldn't make a word they were staying.

When the man came over, I could see he was carrying a doctor's bag. 'Sister, I have explained our situation to the doctor,' said Fitzroy. 'He wants to examine you. I shall remain as he speaks no English.' I nodded.

The German doctor preceded to poke and prod me in the most ungentle way. I squeaked with pain on more than one occasion. He even removed my top to examine the bruises on my lower back. Fitzroy tactfully looked away but continued to translate as the doctor repeatedly ask if it hurt. The whole ordeal made me feel physically sick and wretched.

By the time he had finished I was exhausted. He again retreated to talk with the spy and then left. Fitzroy came over and sat beside me. 'Well, he thinks you have a minor concussion, but as long as someone is with you, he's happy to let you sleep. He thinks you should have some strengthening soup and then bed rest for five days.'

'What!' I said, sitting bolt upright.

'I asked,' he continued calmly, 'what he would say if a man had the same injuries. He responded in much the same way except the bed rest would be reduced to a day or two. He explained that women, due to their fragile nature, needed far longer to get over the shock. So, I am uncertain if you can continue. I'm happy to accept that you, in resilience, are as strong as most men, but driving tomorrow is only one day away, and it will be bumpy. Mind you, Gunther might not have managed to fix the motor, so it could all be moot.'

'Gunther will fix it,' I said. 'He wouldn't dare to not do so.' I lay back down. 'Can we wait and see how I am tomorrow?'

'Thank you for being sensible.'

'If it was you, you'd drive anyway.'

'Yes, but I've been in the field for a good few years. I know my limits. I know how far I can push myself. Besides, it would be awkward to continue without you, but I could try and make do with Gunther as a navigator. He's not a field agent, so it would complicate things, but . . .'

'I presume you'd get me collected – like a parcel?'

Fitzroy got up and walked over to the window. 'This is where it gets difficult. While I have no reason to think that we will be at war with Germany tomorrow, I cannot vouch for next week with any certainty. We could put you in the back of the car and abandon the other vehicle.'

'And a good chunk of supplies?'

'Yes, mostly spare parts for the car, but . . .'

'You'd rather not. Can you order me my soup, please? Then I will sleep as soundly as I am able. If I can navigate tomorrow, I will tell you. I don't expect to feel well doing so, but if I think I will find it intolerable, I will say so. And you could always hire another driver for the second car.'

'I know,' said Fitzroy, 'but I don't want to be hiring anyone German at present. I think we'll go with your plan and hope for the best.' He turned back to me. 'I am sorry about this.'

'You did warn me what being an agent would be like.'

'Yes, but even I thought you wouldn't get into such a mess so early!'

119

'Then you don't know me very well,' I said, snuggling down. 'Soup, please. Then you should change out of those clothes. You've still wearing what you set out in this morning. You'll catch your death from damp clothes.'

Fitzroy shrugged. 'It's dry now. Besides, I don't get colds.'

This transpired not to be completely true. I was woken early the next morning by Fitzroy sneezing, violently, several times.

'Are you all right?'

'I'm fine,' said the spy, who was already dressed. He then sneezed several more times. 'Must be the dust from the garage. I went over to see how our car was. Slightly dented, but he's got the worse out, replaced the brakes and both steering rods.' He raised an eyebrow. 'You never asked, but I fishtailed it nicely down the hill, despite only having half the steering left, and slowed it enough that when the rear end collided with the fence, all that got damaged was the bodywork. She's not as pretty, but she'll run fine.' He sneezed again. 'How are you?'

I sat up slowly. 'Stiff,' I said. 'A little sore. Getting out of bed and getting dressed will be the real trial. Might you go down and order me a breakfast to be delivered? You could try drinking some strong, hot coffee for that sneeze too.'

For once he didn't argue and left. When he returned, I was fully dressed. 'I ache,' I told him, 'but I am a lot better. I think I can manage.'

'Your breakfast is on its way. Be certain, Alice. I won't be able to turn back.' He walked into the room. 'I'd get you out somehow, you know that. I'd never abandon you, but I can't abort the mission.'

'I know,' I said. 'And I wouldn't offer to continue if I thought my condition would undermine it. You have my word.'

'Right, want me to finish packing for you? We need to be off in an hour or less.

I felt a bit less confident as we drove off. The sun shone, but the air was bitter and nipped at my bruises. The passenger seat, which

I usually found more than comfortable, had grown mysterious lumps and bumps that dug viciously into me.

'Last chance, Alice,' said Fitzroy.

'I'm uncomfortable,' I said, 'but I will live. I know the first stage by heart, but where does it start?'

'It's all very civilised today,' said Fitzroy. 'We motor to another inn, have lunch, then set off on the leg, ending at the next stage point and convenient inn.'

'So, the only timed part is on the actual stage itself?'

'Exactly. The motoring in between isn't counted.' He glanced at me. 'We should get you some cushions.'

'I'm guessing that the main reason it's staged is that they have to close the roads to the public when the cars race. You're intending to go very fast, aren't you?'

'Not fast enough to win, but faster than you've ever seen me drive. There are goggles in the glove box for you. You'll need them. A bug in your eye at that speed really stings.'

'I hope you don't mind if I mention that this mission seems to be getting better and better,' I said. I had meant this sarcastically, but the spy chose to take my comment at face value.

'It is becoming more exciting by the moment,' said Fitzroy. 'I didn't think it would an easy one, but according to you, we've already had two assassination attempts. Although I am somewhat peeved that they injured you.'

'I'm not too happy about it myself,' I said, but the spy was already in full flow and didn't seem to hear me.

'You remain convinced that the mechanic for C & C tried to kill me?'

'I do.'

'Crawford said he recruited both the other men via an advertisement, so he doesn't know anything about our departed Fred. He tested the man by getting him to rebuild an engine. Thought seeing his skills in action would be a better indicator than a reference. I can see his point of view, but it does mean the man could have been anyone.'

121

'You mean a German spy?'

'Possibly, but I am – or, at least, was – confident our cover was secure. For someone to realise who and what we were so early in the race suggests a leak within the service. Likewise, that is not impossible, but a complete nightmare if true. I would prefer to think that it was someone employed to help another team win or skew the betting odds. But with the mechanic being a complete unknown . . .'

'And the possibility that there is a leak from HQ – you can hardly go sending telegrams back to ask. I mean, for one, they don't know he is dead, so they won't be—'

'Inclined to send anyone else after us yet? Exactly. Unless he had to report at regular points . . .'

'This seems rather a mess,' I said.

Fitzroy gave me a quick grin. 'Oh, missions often do before they come together. Part of the joy of it all is getting the pieces in place.'

'My joy will be sitting at home in front of the fire with a nice warming drink, thinking back on this mission.'

'Oh, yes, that's often the very best,' said Fitzroy. 'Brandy's my tipple for reminiscing.'

'I was thinking cocoa.'

'Well, as I never drink on duty . . .'

'I beg your pardon?' I said

'Yes, well, as you said, this mission is becoming exceedingly irregular.'

'We can't rule out that the danger from the C & C team is over, even with their mechanic dead. It might not have been a solo venture. Either C might want us dead. After all they suggested the race that almost killed us.'

'No, we can't. It could be revenge because they suspect one of us killed their mechanic. Although I have to say, they don't appear devastated by their loss. They picked up another with altogether too much ease.'

'You mean as if they had contacts here to help them?'

'Yes, again, but it doesn't make them spies. They could still be out simply to throw the race. They both admitted to being impoverished. The prize is sizeable. Crabtree is also desperate to regain his professional reputation.'

I nodded. 'But we can't forget the Frenchmen either.'

'No, I thought it was them who suggested the race anyway. It seems unlikely to me they would be German agents, but . . .'

'They're not beyond winning by sabotage. Shouldn't we watch the Italians? They've got the best car – no offence,' I said.

'Exactly what I was thinking,' said Fitzroy. 'It's a little disconcerting to have a partner who thinks so similarly to me.'

'Does it make us harmonious?'

'We're not a bally choir, Alice. Different perspectives can be helpful. Especially when you're trying to solve a mystery.'

'Well, it could have been Amaranth, upset that you snubbed her at breakfast.'

'I snubbed her at breakfast to keep you happy!' said Fitzroy. 'If this is all your fault . . .'

'To keep me happy? Why should I care who you sleep with?'

'Euphemia,' said Fitzroy, swerving barely in time to make the bend. 'My amorous adventures are not anything that I will ever discuss with you!'

'Even if it affects the mission?'

'I never let my affairs affect missions.' The spy's face suffused with red.

'Er, Amaranth?'

'She might be able to drive, but what goes on under the bonnet is as much a mystery to her as it is to you.'

'Are you sure of that? Or is that simply what she told you?'

'I haven't had the time to give her a full oral examination on mechanics, we were somewhat busy,' said the spy, still red-faced.

I took a moment to enjoy the cold wind on my face. For once, I was not the one at a disadvantage. 'I suppose it could be thought a bit of an overreaction to sabotage the car after so short an acquaintance, unless there was a reason I don't know about?'

'None,' growled Fitzroy.

'It could simply be that she too is after the prize money, and with her affections not engaged . . .' The spy growled and muttered something. I ignored him. 'I suppose it could have been her jealous lover, Luke? But by that logic it could have been anyone. We need to ask Gunther who had access to the garage to do the damage. Come to think of it, isn't it a part of his job to guard the vehicle?'

'I already asked him,' said Fitzroy.

We appeared to have speeded up somewhat. 'Look out,' I exclaimed.

Fitzroy swung the car to the far side of the road such that our outside wheels mounted the verge. The vehicle slipped sideways in the mud as he did so. The outside lamp scraped alongside the white wall of a tiny cottage, but we narrowly missed the horse and cart that was carrying milk churns. The horse gave a whinny as we passed it and shook its head, but it didn't rear. I had a momentary glimpse of the driver's alarmed pale face as he handled the reins, and then we were past.

I took several deep breaths to settle myself. There was no point chastising Fitzroy. He was already in a mood and pointing out he had spooked the horse would only make things worse. He knew what he had done, and from his gritted teeth I could tell he was as angry with himself as he was with me.

'I take it Gunther couldn't be helpful,' I said gently.

'He was off chasing the bloody dog,' said Fitzroy. 'The damn thing had managed to get out. Apparently, it led him a merry dance before he caught it.'

'But you're sure of him?'

Fitzroy turned to face me – an alarming thing for any driver to do. 'As we are considering there might even be a leak at HQ, I'm sure of nobody, except you. Damn it!' Then he thankfully turned his attention back to the road.

We drove for a while in silence, except for the sound of grinding teeth coming from Fitzroy. Eventually, I said, 'I feel I should apologise that you can trust only me.'

'Don't be stupid, Alice,' said Fitzroy. 'You're the one person I come closest to trusting completely in this world.' He spat this out in such a way that it made this sound like a vicious accusation.

We didn't speak for the rest of the journey. The main advantage of this was that Fitzroy's driving became much smoother for me and much less terrifying to other road users.

Chapter Fourteen

In which we embark on the first leg of the race

Although we were the last to arrive at the inn, we were in the first set of drivers to do the first leg. I had hardly time to swallow a hot drink (some peculiar coffee-tea hybrid), gulp down a sandwich, and stuff a few more in my pockets. Fitzroy, I saw, filled up our thermos while he stood eating and giving a frowning Gunther vaguely intelligible instructions.

However, when I climbed into the passenger seat, I found cushions waiting. I had barely a minute to arrange them around my person before Fitzroy jumped in. 'Goggles, Alan,' said Fitzroy in stern tones. I took the wretched things out of the glove compartment and put them on. They felt cold and awkward against my skin. Fitzroy reached over and pulled the strap tight. He slapped away my fingers when I immediately tried to loosen it. 'Has to be tight or they'll come off.' He moved the car into the line-up. We were starting in threes, twenty minutes apart. Alongside us were the Italian team, the voices of the two men could already be heard, loud and argumentative. The long nose of their green car gleamed in the afternoon light.

'How long till it gets dark?' I asked.

'Not long enough,' said Fitzroy. He was adjusting himself into a driving position, shifting left and right by inches trying to get exactly the right seating before the off. I stifled a laugh. It was a most undignified shuffle.

Markus and Peter, one of the German teams, were behind, hunched together in their exceptionally low-slung car. A peculiarly odd looking vehicle, it had panels of a variety of colours, and bolts sticking out. The engine took up an enormous length, much of it left open to the air – presumably for cooling. Markus, the driver, twiddled with the controls and the engine gave a sound not unlike that of a bull elephant (I saw one once in London Zoo. It made exactly the same noise when spooked by a dowager's parasol. I had agreed with it. The accessory was in very bad taste). I turned to share my memory with Fitzroy, but he stared straight ahead with the intensity of tiger stalking its prey. Even half-hidden by his goggles, driving cap and coat, an energy fizzed off him. He had said he had no intention of winning, but every fibre of him was taut with anticipation and intent. When the marshal took up his post with the chequered flag the spy was almost vibrating with excitement. I immediately began to rethink my part in the entire enterprise, but the flag went down and . . .

The first few seconds of the car accelerating were not unfamiliar, but instead of topping out at what I would consider a very fast, but quite usual, pace for Fitzroy, the acceleration kept on going. We pulled away from the others. Considering our opponents, I put this down to Fitzroy's reactions rather than the prowess of his car. They would catch us easily enough, but although we both knew this, Fitzroy kept his engine at full pelt, doing his best to put distance between them and us.

The wind whipped the breath away from me. Despite the windscreen, my seat felt as exposed as if I was sitting on a mountainside in a nightmarish storm. 'Is this safe?' I managed to say, but my voice sounded tiny as I struggled to find enough air to speak. My only answer was another upturn in speed. The road had a decent surface, but it was no more than a car and a half's width at most.

Despite this, roaring like a tiger, the Italian team came up behind us. Fitzroy swerved the car to the left, not to let them pass as I first thought, but to block them. The driver behind us gunned his vehicle harder. The sound of the huge engine made my ears ache. Again, Fitzroy moved to block him. We were on the open road, travelling through a rural landscape, but ahead I could see a village coming up. More importantly, the road would narrow further soon.

Fitzroy and the Italians continued to slew over the road, this way and that, they trying to pass and he trying to block. I had nothing to keep me in my chair except a low-slung side, my tightly gripped fingers, fumble-some in the gloves, and hope founded out of naked fear. My whole body jerked from side to side, and my head followed in a whiplash movement. I spared a brief glance behind and beyond the giant engine of the Italian car, which now appeared to be inches from our tail pipe, I spied the German car in the distance gamely attempting to catch us.

We raced along the open road with only snow-dressed trees lining the sides. The road itself had been cleared, but the branches around and above us were iced for winter. Tall, majestic trees, they blurred in front of me, but then somehow my brain compensated, and I saw them again clearly. On a slower drive I would have enjoyed this natural cathedral arching above us.

But it was the Italian team that worried me. Dressed like Fitzroy, little of either of the brothers' faces was visible, but both hunched forward, mouths slightly agape, showing gritted teeth. It gave them a wolfish look. Fitzroy was far from being a lamb, but the increased roaring of the engine behind us spoke clearly of their intention to pass us, no matter what the cost.

The road widened every so slightly. Here came the real danger. Fitzroy would lose his first place – or die trying to keep it. I cast a look askance. Coiled behind the wheel, he showed no sign of giving way.

The last thing I would do would be to shout at him when he was concentrating. At these speeds – at these incredibly unnatural speeds – the time between thought and deed was fractional. Unless I could come up with something short and useful to say, the best thing I could do to keep alive was keep my mouth shut and pray Fitzroy cared a little for my survival if not his own. Besides, I would be enormously angry with him if I had learnt the entire route and had yet to give a direction, and he crashed. As we approached the village, I recalled the map in my mind – and remembered that not only was there a sharp bend halfway through the village, but that before we reached it, the side of the hill fell away on both sides to scrambling scree slopes. It was almost as if those who had set the race were trying to kill us.

The Italian car pushed closer, then to my horror, the nose of the car attempted to nudge us out of the way.

A quick short push. A clear threat they would do more if Fitzroy didn't give way. But there was no room for two vehicles as far as I could see. The car behind us edged nearer again. I glanced at Fitzroy and saw he was speaking. Not to me. He was swearing under his breath. The Italians tried to nudge again, but this time he anticipated them and moved out of the way. They roared forward but were forced back by the lack of road beside us.

'Take the bloody hint,' said Fitzroy suddenly, 'there's no sodding road for you to pass on.'

I had paid so much attention to the drivers and their vehicles that I had failed to notice that we had come onto the stretch where the trees vanished, and the road fell away. Excellent navigator that I was. Apart from the severe bend in the village I would warn Fitzroy about, there was nothing for me to say. The first part of this leg was straight. Whoever got away first would be liable to finish first. Against the odds, this had been us, and the Italians seemed prepared to do anything to retake the advantage.

They edged closer once more. Again, Fitzroy avoided their touch, but a back wheel spun for a fraction of a moment over empty air, before Fitzroy pulled the car firmly back on track. I said nothing but wondered how white my hair would be by the end of this leg, let alone the rest of the rally.

The road narrowed again as we approached the village.

Hopefully everyone had been warned to stay inside. But no, there appeared to be people hanging out of windows and throwing . . . buckets of snow. They were throwing buckets of snow onto the road!

The narrow road leading towards the village descended at an increasingly sharp angle, but I could see that the road widened shortly before it entered the village itself and then narrowed again almost immediately. I wondered if, for this tiny settlement, this was a market area on the edge of the village. I prayed the Italians could not see the increased space. Certainly, when I had studied the map with Fitzroy neither of us had remarked on it. Neither of us had seen it as a possible passing place.

But the Italians had clearly earmarked it as such.

With a tremendous roar they caught up behind us and surged forward. Fitzroy had no choice but to attempt to avoid them. We veered to the other side of the road, our car tyres bumping along the edge. Involuntarily I lent towards the side away from the drop, as if my weight would make any difference to us turning over. Then I saw Fitzroy was doing the same. My mouth went dry. There was nothing else I could do. I closed my eyes.

It all happened so fast and yet so slowly, as if my brain, confused by speed, had lost all sense of natural rhythm. A blast of cold air shot past me. Fitzroy braked abruptly. The car slithered from side to side as, if wanting to dance. Then it spun, more times than I could count. The only music to this waltz was Fitzroy swearing. At least if he remained talking then we were both liable to be alive. I wondered if Fitzroy, in falling to his death, would scream. Probably not, I decided.

The spinning came to a halt.

'Are you all right?' asked Fitzroy.

'Are we still alive?'

'Very much so, but no thanks to those . . .' then he broke into another language, so I didn't have to listen to what profound obscenity he had thought up for the Italian drivers.

I opened my eyes. We were parked at an angle across the road at the widest point, which was covered in skid marks as if half a dozen cars had passed rather than two.

'I need to see if there is any damage before I try to move it,' said Fitzroy and sprung out of his seat. 'Stay there.' He crouched down and started checking underneath the car, working his way to the back. 'I'm not having another incident of broken steering rods or faulty brakes,' he said.

Behind us I heard the sound of an engine.

'The German team!' I said. 'We need to move now.'

'In a moment,' he said. 'I'm almost done.'

I stood up in my seat. 'There's no time!' I cried. As I did so, the German team bore down on us. Fitzroy, ever nimble, jumped aside. The German team, seeing the car, attempted to brake hard, but going at such a speed, it sent them into a skid. The driver fought valiantly to regain control of the car and almost did so. Except, as he passed, he clipped the edge of ours.

I have to presume that skidding on a road leaves behind slick tyre rubber of some sort. I cannot explain it any other way. There was no ice on the road, yet our car went into another spin. I sat down at once and avoided being thrown out. 'Pull on the brake,' I heard Fitzroy shout.

I fumbled, trying to find it. My head was spinning, and my vision blurred by the movement. I found it and pulled. To my enormous relief the car came to a complete stop.

'Euphemia,' said Fitzroy, 'stay very still.'

'Why?' I asked, putting a hand up to my forehead; my head still spun.

'It'll be fine. I'll get you out.'

I shook my head and stood up. Two things happened. Fitzroy screamed (and I mean screamed, a loud and manly scream, but it was a scream) 'No!' And I felt the car rock urgently beneath me. Without thinking I sat down at once – and this is what saved me.

Taking in my surroundings again, for the first time I realised the back half of the car was over the edge. The slope was such that it wasn't quite hanging in mid–air – well, technically it was, but it was only a couple of feet above the ground. The problem was that the ground fell away so steeply that once the car started tilting down enough, the front wheels would lift and descent would be in a increasingly rapid manner, which would be liable to include a couple of rolls at least.

'I'm going to come over and take your hands,' said Fitzroy. 'Then when I say jump, you jump to me.'

'No,' I said.

'Look, I know jumping out of the car last time didn't go well, but I'm here to catch you this time. You'll be fine.' He came across to the car. I folded my arms.

'No,' I repeated.

'For God's sake, girl, you can't be more scared of jumping out of this car than you are of staying in it?' As if to prove his point, a gust of wind rocked the car and made my stomach lurch. Fitz–roy grabbed hold of part of the bonnet and added his weight to it until the vehicle stopped rocking. 'Now come out.'

'If I do, we'll lose the car and be unable to complete the mission.'

'So,' said Fitzroy, 'unfortunate things happen. It's neither of our fault. We'll have to find another way. We can all squeeze into Gunther's car.'

'You know that won't work for exactly the reasons we estab–lished before, when we thought I wouldn't be able to come with you.'

'Damn it, Euphemia. Any minute now you're going to go off the side. Do you have a death wish?'

'Not at all, but you need to get the car back on the road. As soon as I get out, it's gone.'

'But what if I don't . . . what if can't get it back on the road. Or it goes over while I'm trying?'

'If it is truly impossible then I will jump – and I hate jumping out of cars – but only after you've tried.'

'Damn it, Euphemia, it's only a dratted car. This is your life.'

'No, it's the mission. You said if you had to, you'd put the mission before my life,' I said.

'As it turns out, I can't,' said Fitzroy. 'As your commanding officer I order you to jump.'

'You are wasting precious time,' I said. 'I could disappear any minute. I saw some rope in the back. I think if you sit on the bonnet, I might be able to get it.'

'Euphemia, no!'

'Can you jump on, please? I'm reaching for it now.' I put my hand out, only to demonstrate my intent, but the motor started to move. Fitzroy took a flying leap and landed on the bonnet. I didn't wait to see his reaction, but grabbed the rope and leaned forward again. I threw the rope onto the road. 'I'll make you a deal,' I said. 'I know we don't have long before another car comes, and I have no desire to die. I'll make sure I'm ready to jump if I feel the car about to go – if you give it your best to get it back on the road.

Cursing and swearing in some language that seemed to demand a lot of spitting, Fitzroy wasted no time in tying the rope off under the car. Fortunately, the rope was long enough, and the road narrow enough, that he could get it around a solitary, but sturdy, tree trunk on the other side, situated inches before the scree began. Once around it, he began to pull. The car inched forward at his effort. It wouldn't be enough. Once he had taken the strain on the car, I dropped lightly to the ground and took up the rope behind him. His head swivelled as he felt the tension change.

'Don't let go! We have a real chance to get the car up now.'

He gave me a look I couldn't fathom and got about pulling again with renewed vigour. My strength was of little help, but I merely curled the rope around me and leant back. My body weight was far more effective than my forearms. By the end of the next five minutes I was swearing in words I hadn't even thought I knew, but that I must have overheard from the spy in the past. I had rope burn to add to my bruises and in the distance I could hear the roar of another car.

133

However, and I put this down to sheer bloody-mindedness alone, we managed to get the car back on the road. Fitzroy didn't bother trying to check the undercarriage. He gestured to me to get in and we set off before the other car came racing through.

Common sense did prevail, and he pulled the car in just beyond the village entrance, into a small siding. Then he got out to check for damage.

'Is it bad?' I asked.

He shook his head. 'Not brilliant, but good enough to drive. Nothing Gunther can't fix.'

'Shall we move on then before anyone else passes us? We need to put up a good show, don't we?'

Fitzroy nodded and sighed. 'More people to kill,' he said getting in. I must have looked bemused, because he added, 'Whoever sabotaged our car previously, and now those bloody Italians who almost killed you . . . I mean us.'

'Let's hope the list stays that short,' I said.

'Oh, this is nothing compared to the list I keep at home,' he said with a smile. 'I have a positive ream of people who have done me an injustice that I wish to repay. Not, of course, that I will, but one can dream.'

'It's good to have aspirations,' I said lightly, then added with genuine concern, 'Are you able to continue? You're extremely pale.'

'You're not looking the picture of health yourself,' he said. 'Pass over that thermos and let's have something hot before we move on.'

'But the race!'

'Bugger the race,' said Fitzroy. 'Besides, the only decent drivers are ahead of us. I can easily out-drive the others.'

'Decent drivers!' I said, hearing my own voice come out hysterically high.

'I should have said decent cars,' amended Fitzroy. 'Eat one of those sandwiches in your pocket. Food will do you good. You're shaking.'

'I closed my eyes when the Italians overtook us,' I confessed. I bit into my sandwich.

'Me too,' said Fitzroy.

I choked as he dissolved into laughter. 'Your face,' he said, slapping me on the back, 'you must learn to take a joke, Alice.' (There are times when I fear Fitzroy truly does not understand what it means to be a gentleman, and never will.)

Chapter Fifteen

In which there are more deaths

Fully fuelled, we set off once more. Fitzroy drove as well as he boasted and easily caught up with two cars that had passed us after the German team had disappeared ahead. I'd got used to the speed and as long as we weren't slewing this way and that, I was reasonably content. I remembered the route and gave all the right directions at the right points. The speed made it quite nerve-wracking and intense, but I believe we were going as well as might be expected of us, when I spotted smoke in the distance. I touched Fitzroy lightly on the shoulder and pointed. He nodded grimly, presumably he had spotted it first. As we closed on the area the smoke came from, I found myself becoming more and more agitated. My heart beat faster and my palms were clammy inside my gloves. We had seen how easy it was to come close to disaster; what, or who, lay ahead?

'Who is ahead of us now,' asked Fitzroy as if he had read my thoughts.

'The Italians, one German team, the French, oh, and Amaranth.'

'Ah, yes, I remember Amaranth now. She waved in a spiteful manner,' said Fitzroy.

'Can one do that?' I asked.

'It's a difficult choice, but I'm rooting for the Italians to have gone off-piste. Preferably into nice little charcoal balls.'

'You don't mean that,' I said. (Though I found the thought

of Amaranth alive but ruffled, watching her car burn, quite heart-warming.)

Fitzroy studied a me a shade too long for comfort when he was driving at this speed. His look spoke volumes.

'Point taken,' I said. I sat back to scan the route for hazards. If someone had had an accident, who knew what had caused it, and whether there were traps or broken bits of things or people ahead. I disliked the thought of the latter, but I knew it was possible. I thought Fitzroy was liable to also be sweeping the horizon. Two pairs of eyes, as they say . . .

However, when we came closer to the smoke, the cause was unmistakable. First of all, there came a sickly sweet, yet at the same time savoury, aroma on the wind. I saw Fitzroy glance at me to see if I understood. I nodded. I kept my lips tightly together as I felt my bile rising with each breath.

We rounded a hilltop and there below us, before a sharp turn, we saw what remained of the Italian car. Fitzroy slowed. 'Sorry,' he said to me. 'We don't know what made them crash. There might be oil or some other hazard on the road. Look away if you want.'

But I couldn't. The once beautiful and graceful long–nosed car was now a smoking black and twisted shell. Inside that shell remained two man–sized charred objects. I looked away. As we got closer, I spied the Frenchmen's car, pulled onto the other side of the road to the wreck. Fitzroy pulled in behind them.

'You can come if you want,' he said. 'But you don't speak French.'

I shook my head. I knew he was trying to keep me away from the reality of the accident, and for once I was perfectly happy to be treated like an ordinary woman. We had hardly begun this race, and I was already beginning to lose count of the number of times someone had tried to kill one or both of us. Fitzroy had never described his missions as being this hazardous. In fact, what little he had told me had always made it seem as if he spent most of the time enjoying himself. On the other hand, he always said he never lied to me . . . Perhaps what counted for him as entertainment was . . . I stopped my thought there.

'What are you brooding about?' he said as he climbed back into the car.

'Are missions always as awful as this?'

'Not usually, but then things do tend to get more complicated around you.'

I gave him a look of speechless protest, which as usual he ignored. 'You're be glad to hear that Albert and Georges are fine – at least physically. Coming on the accident, they did what most decent human beings would do – in other words, what no other team did – and stopped to try and help. Apparently, the car was already fully on fire, and they kept being beaten back by the flames. Mentally, both of them are in a bit of a state. I said I'd tell the marshals as soon as I saw one and get them to send someone along. They weren't willing for us to take them to the inn, but neither are they prepared to drive, certainly not at racing speed. Possibly ever again. So, we're off.'

'What aren't you telling me?' I asked as we pulled away. Fitzroy waved to the Frenchman with the back of his hand.

'What I don't think you need to know,' said Fitzroy.

It said a lot that I didn't protest. I continued to navigate, but my mind kept going back to why Albert and Georges were too shaken to continue. They weren't racing drivers by profession, but they must have realised it was a dangerous sport. They had designed their own car! A car they had hoped to prove at the race. Surely, they had too much pride tied up in their design to quit . . .

'Stop thinking about it, Euphemia,' said Fitzroy. 'Or you'll work it out.'

'I wish you'd make up your mind about what name you're calling me. I'm getting confused.'

'It's easy,' said Fitzroy in his smug and annoying tone, 'Alice is my colleague, Euphemia is my friend, and Alan is a pain in my . . .'

'They were still alive when Albert and Georges got there, weren't they? They burnt alive in front of them. How awful.'

'Positively medieval,' said Fitzroy.

'How can you joke . . .?'

'About that? It's over, isn't it? A negative emotional response from me will only inhibit my driving. Besides, I wanted them dead for what they did.'

'Not like that!'

'Well, no,' said Fitzroy. 'Not like that, but even if I'm not enchanted by the method, I'm quite glad they're gone. They almost killed you and I find that unforgivable. So, apparently, does fate.'

'I don't know what to say.'

'Then don't. Navigate.'

We drove on with the silence only punctuated by my instructions. Maybe an hour later Fitzroy said, 'I know you think you've seen a lot of death, and perhaps that's true compared to most refined young women, but there will more, possibly more than you could ever have imagined. After a while, you become hardened to it – to losing people, to being helpless while good people are killed. You do what you can, but you know your abilities are far from infinite. It's when you truly understand that you either break down and weep for the world, or you become hardened to humanity's foolishness and never-ending desire to kill one another. I don't know which path you'll choose, but I would keep that time from you as long as I can.'

'Will I become useless as an agent then?'

Fitzroy shook his head. 'No, it will either demand more emotional energy from you that you ever thought you had, leaving you nothing for anyone else, or you'll simply grow accustomed to it all.'

'What about you?'

'Oh, I'm different. I have a terrible temper. I rage at everything and everyone – and I swear a lot in languages that really know how to curse. Arabic curses are quite wonderful. Would you like me to teach you a few?'

139

'No, thank you,' I said. I broke off to give him directions. 'The man on the boat I killed, you didn't seem particularly upset by that.'

'Well, I thought you'd made a mistake and I didn't want to you to dwell on it.'

'It would have been a big mistake,' I said. 'I don't think there is even a verdict of Murder by Mistake.'

'Death by misadventure,' said Fitzroy automatically. 'It's not like I knew the man, and I did understand you were trying to help me. Made me think I might need to keep a tighter watch on you in case you polished off anyone else you thought looked at me the wrong way.'

'Is that why you snubbed Amaranth?'

'Only partly. She really was the most awful bore. Quite a challenge to be both intelligent and utterly vapid, but she seems to be doing well.'

'You make me sound like a psychopathic protector!'

'I did wonder.'

'If you weren't driving, I'd hit you for that.'

'Not allowed,' said Fitzroy. 'And that includes stamping on my feet, as you do to your poor husband. I'm your senior in the service you're not allowed to mangle, bruise or abuse me in any way.'

I uttered a huff, which, in the cold, exploded into crystal-soaked air.

'Don't pout,' said the spy. 'Besides I'm beginning to think you might have been right. There's definitely something off about this damned rally. Where the hell are the marshals? I know it's an unofficial race, but with this kind of money at stake, you'd expect them to be at least checking we were all going the right way and not taking shortcuts.'

'Do you have a rank? Like in the army?'

'I'm a Captain,' said Fitzroy, sounding surprised. 'By rights I should be a higher rank, but I am known to be a little unorthodox in my methods.'

He gave me a quick look. I passed my acting test perfectly by neither snorting nor otherwise expressing derision.

The spy continued. 'We are in military intelligence.'

'I thought we worked for the King?'

'The army swears allegiance to the sovereign, not to parliament or politicians,' said Fitzroy. 'Did you read any of those books on the constitution I gave you?'

'What rank am I?'

'Somewhere below Private, I imagine.' He gave a chuckle.

'It is so difficult that I can't hit you,' I said. 'I feel that part should have been more fully explained.'

Fitzroy laughed, for once a genuine laugh. 'Not far now. Once we logged our arrival, we'll get hot baths and hot dinners. You'll feel much more the thing. Now tell me, am I allowed to talk to Amaranth again? She does have a way of picking up things about the group and their connections. I want to know if she knows anything I don't.'

'Do I have a choice?'

'As my trainee, not at all, but as my partner, of course. We need to agree on our plan of action.'

'I suppose you must, but what about being available for this mysterious contact to, er . . . contact us?'

'I'll think of something,' said Fitzroy. 'I'm so hungry now, I could eat a horse. Can't think of anything when I'm this hungry. Look! That's the stage point ahead. End of this leg.'

'Thank goodness.'

'Indeed,' said Fitzroy, 'but still so many stages to go! What fun!'

Chapter Sixteen

In which I meet a Griffin

As I alighted from the car, something touched the top of my head. I turned, but Fitzroy was fiddling with something on his side of the vehicle. It hadn't been him. I looked around and then I saw, very faintly against the darkening sky, tiny marks, as if someone was scratching the inky blackness with a quill. I put my hand to the crown of my head, and it came away wet.

'It's snowing,' I called to Fitzroy.

He looked up briefly, 'Grand,' he said. 'I wanted to test the tyres before we got into the mountains proper.'

I stood searching for the words. 'Is there anything about this trip that isn't delighting you?'

'The direction of the wind near the crash site.'

I thought for a moment and then shook my head. The deaths of the Italians had gone completely from my mind. How could I have forgotten?

'I am a terrible person,' I said as Fitzroy finally joined me.

'Don't be so hard on yourself. You're merely concerned that my unique style of driving will endanger us up in the mountains. It's natural that self-preservation would be foremost in your thoughts. Those who are gone are gone. It's normal to think thus. At least, I always do,' he said in a sudden unexpected moment of reflection. 'However, I would like to assure myself that the Italians died at their own hands rather than anyone else's.'

'You think someone might have murdered them because they had the best car?'

'There is a lot of prize money at stake,' said the spy, 'but you will learn that some people kill for far less. Desperation is a strong motive though, and many of the drivers on this rally are sorely in need of funds.'

We entered into the new inn, which looked uncannily like the previous one. So much so, I did a double-take to assure myself the scenery outside the window had changed and that I hadn't navigated us back to where we started. It wasn't so different, but there were undoubtedly more trees.

Fitzroy claimed our room at the desk. When he came back with the keys, I asked, 'Do you think we rank as possible winners?'

Fitzroy raised his eyebrows. 'I do handle the car extremely well, but I'm not a professional racing driver.'

'From what I can tell not everyone here is.'

'You make an uncomfortable point,' said the spy. He looked through the side doors behind me. 'I spy my lady friend. She's not looking too happy.'

'You're going to speak to her, despite the spiteful wave?'

'Hush, youngster, do not mock your elders. Come with me. You may be of use.'

I followed, with reluctance. Amaranth sat perched on a stool near a bar counter. She had a glass with a small amount of amber liquid in it. As we approached, she lifted it to her lips. I could see her hand shook slightly.

'So, wave and drive on by,' said Fitzroy. 'That is your attitude to a poor man in distress?'

Amaranth looked up. She considered him for a long moment. Long enough for even I to notice she had the most amazing violet eyes. The depth of their colour was both mysterious and soft. 'It's the nature of the game,' she said finally, 'the weak are left behind.'

'And yet here we are!' said Fitzroy throwing wide his coat and mounting a stool. 'Ready and willing to continue.' He raised one

143

eyebrow at her, turning his head slightly, so that he came across as mildly arch.

Amaranth shrugged slightly and went back to studying the bottom of her glass. She made it obvious that the drink was infinitely more interesting than him. I saw the corner of the spy's lips twitch. He wasn't in the least offended, as some gentlemen might have been. Neither was he perturbed. I noted the tenseness in Amaranth's shoulders. She'd changed her driving clothes for a wildly inappropriate evening gown. The inn's temperature remained high enough that she could manage with only a thin shawl, and it was through that shawl I saw how tightly her shoulders were set. Fitzroy was concentrating on both her face and somewhere below that the shawl didn't reach. Unusually for him, he'd missed her tenseness and had no idea he was about to have a drink thrown in his face. This surprised me, but I ascribed it to our harrowing drive, which gave me an idea.

'I do think it was a shame about the Italians,' I said.

Amaranth, not totally lost to social mores, tilted her head towards me and answered, 'A shame, but they did fight so much. I expect they were arguing when the car went out of control. So perish the unprofessional. A shame about the car too. It really was lovely.' Her voice was light, but the muscles around her eyes tightened. I was right. The accident had thrown her. She put up a good front, but not good enough. One hand went to the base of her throat, so clear a sign of agitation Fitzroy had to see it.

I could feel him watching me. 'But to burn alive?' I said. 'No one deserves such a fate.'

Extremely quietly, under his breath, I thought I heard Fitzroy say, 'I can think of a few.' But it may have been my mind playing tricks. I focused back on Amaranth. 'Can you imagine? And those poor Frenchmen, who stopped, trying to help, but unable to get close due to the flames. Listening—'

'Enough,' said Fitzroy firmly.

He stood and moved protectively close to Amaranth. 'My dear lady, allow me to buy you another brandy. You are looking pale.'

I heard Amaranth murmur something. Then the spy turned on me. 'Alan, you little ghoul, get up to the room and stay there. I shall instruct you on how one speaks to a lady later.' His back was now to Amaranth, so she couldn't see the cheery grin and wink he gave me.

I left them to it and went upstairs to wash and change. I didn't expect to see Fitzroy anytime soon, but he had damn well better send dinner to the room for me, I thought.

Once refreshed I went over to the window to look out. The wisps of snow continued to fall. On the ground below I saw them skitter along, blown by the wind. The ground was frozen; it wouldn't be long before the snow began to lie. I pulled on my heavy coat and wound a scarf carefully round my neck. I secured it under my coat in partial deference to Fitzroy's insistence one should never wear by choice anything which could be pulled tightly around the neck.

Downstairs there was no sign of the pair of them at the bar, so I slipped out the front door and headed to where I hoped the garages might be. The wind pinched at my face with a hundred vicious fingers. The temperature since we arrived had dropped like a stone. My boots, being most suited to a male, had a firm grip. While I had never been a fan of the corset, it was about then I began to understand how much women's fashions hampered them. I could cope with this weather so much better dressed as a man in my decent boots and thick trousers. I put my head down and battled forward against the wind.

I was in luck. Not only was the backyard where I had hoped, the various teams had again hung their flags outside their respect-ive doors. I opened the British one slightly and slipped in. I was less then three feet inside before I felt the keen edge of a blade against my throat and my arm was firmly pinned against my back, as I was pulled off balance towards by assailant.

'Give me a reason,' said Gunther's voice, harsh and threatening.

'It's me . . . err . . . Alan,' I managed to say. I could hardly speak, the blade was so firmly held against my throat. In fact, as I did so I felt it bite into my skin. I thought, I do hope he is on our side. But within a moment he had sprung back, and any sign of the knife had vanished.

'Oh, my goodness, I am so sorry ma'am.' This also had been a converted stable, with a small loft. The only illumination came from a lantern hung from the roof. In its pale yellow glow, Gunther had gone a very sickly colour. 'I had no warning you were to visit, ma'am. What with the Italians, and the sabotage the day before . . .'

I put my hand up to my neck and rubbed it with my thumb. It came away wet. I winced as the exposed nerves on the tiny nick stung as I touched it.

'Have I injured you?' asked Gunther, looking more and more as if he might throw up.

'It's no more than a paper cut, Gunther,' I said. 'Stings like the devil, but no real damage.'

At that moment Fitzroy's dog came running up, clearly woken by the noise we were making. He barrelled over to me and jumped up. All four legs came off the ground as he bounced up and down. He didn't bark once, but panted loudly with his long, soft pink tongue lolling uncontrolled from side to side.

I crouched down and petted him. 'Fine guard dog you make,' I said, rubbing his short wiry fur. 'Aren't you meant to warn your master of intruders?'

'He belongs to the Captain,' said Gunther. 'I don't think he likes me much.'

'Oh, dear,' I said standing. 'Sit, Jack,' I told the dog. He did and when I further requested he lie at my feet, he did so. Gunther's eyes widened. 'It appears even the dog has his orders.'

'Is there somewhere we can sit?' I asked

'This way, ma'am.' Gunther led me further in. He had set up a spirit burner near the back of the old stable, away from the draughts. It had a small kettle on it from which steam clouded the cold air. 'Oh, are you making tea? I would so much like a cup. I haven't had one since England.'

'I don't have any milk, ma'am.'

'I couldn't care less,' I said. 'And you really must stop calling me ma'am. As far as anyone else is concerned I'm a youth called Alan. The very fact you know suggests to me that you outrank me.'

Gunther shook his head. 'I wouldn't know, ma'am,' he said, passing me a tin cup full of hot tea. 'I only know I had my orders from the Captain to treat you as I would treat him. With full respect.'

'Gosh,' I said after savouring a mouthful of God's finest brew, 'that must have taken some swallowing.'

'Ma'am?'

'I mean you know I'm a woman and that I'm travelling in disguise with Fitzroy. You must have realised we are sharing a room and I am more than aware of his reputation. You must have thought of me as something quite . . . err . . . different from a lady.'

Gunther's gaze dropped to the floor. 'I confess my first thought on hearing about you was not . . .' He trailed off.

I nodded. 'Most reasonable,' I said. 'But I am not the Captain's mistress. I'm married to someone else. Not that I believe that would have stopped him in the past, but that isn't the way it is with us.'

'No ma'am, he explained it very clearly to me when I got the wrong end of the stick.'

'Ah,' I said. 'He does have a filthy temper.'

'Yes,' said Gunther. 'He is extremely defensive of you and your reputation, ma'am. He left me in no doubt there was no impropriety involved. Especially as you are an agent yourself.'

'No, there isn't. Though I won't be telling my husband the full details of this mission even if I am cleared to do so,' I said. 'I doubt many people would believe the innocence of our relationship if they knew my gender. Besides,' I added as an afterthought, 'having leapt out of the vehicle, I'm still too covered in bruises and generally stiff to contemplate anything, even if I found Fitzroy attractive, which I don't. He's not a bad-looking man, but he's certainly not my type.' I ended abruptly, realising it wasn't the done thing to discuss a Captain behind his back.

Gunther gave me a smile. 'I can see that, ma'am. I doubt you'd fall for any of his tricks.'

'Lovely tea,' I said. 'My agent moniker is Alice. Please use it when we are alone.'

'Griffin.'

'Ah, so Gunther was to suggest a possible German heritage?'

'I believe so.'

Jack wandered over and laid his head on my lap. I absent-mindedly fondled his ears. 'I came to ask you about this creature. Yesterday, Fitzroy said you were away from the car chasing the dog. Can I ask how he got out? I'm assuming from the way he greeted his master yesterday his attempts to escape are not infrequent, but this one got past you.'

'It was odd,' said Gunther. 'I give him the run of the garage, but whenever I have the doors open, I clip him to a long chain so he can get the smell and a sense of outside, but won't get run over or run away.'

'So he's learnt how to slip his collar?'

'No, that's the odd bit. It's as if he unclipped himself. Which shouldn't be possible.'

'Not for one with paws,' I agreed, examining the clip with my fingers. 'This is like a proper climbing – what do you call that thing – it screws shut.'

'The Captain reckoned I must have forgotten to shut it properly. He suggested my fingers might have been too cold for me to realise.'

'What do you think?'

'It's become quite a habit with me. I don't think I would have got it wrong.' He gestured with his hands, tilting the palms upwards, hopelessly. 'Nothing is impossible . . .'

'Except the dog unscrewing it himself. You didn't need to replace the collar or anything. It was fine when you recovered him?' Gunther nodded. 'How did you know the dog was gone?'

148

'It was pure chance,' said Gunther. 'I could have lost him for good. I looked up from working on the car and I saw he wasn't where he should have been. I ran out immediately, and because of his colour, I spotted him quickly.'

'Are you generally observant?' I asked. 'What colour are the Captain's eyes?'

'Blue, a light blue,' said Gunther. 'Except when he's angered, then they turn a steely grey.'

'I am convinced. I've never noticed that. So that makes me think it's likely whoever freed the dog was someone you know or was someone who wasn't out of place.'

Gunther nodded. 'You mean, I might have clocked them peripherally and thought they were petting the dog and assigned it mentally as not a threat.'

'Exactly.'

'So, it was planned,' said Gunther.

'It's not a clever plan. All they needed to know was you'd go after the dog. But why didn't Jack bark?'

'The Captain has trained him not to bark unless there is some kind of threat.'

'So he didn't bark at me because he'd seen me with Fitzroy and you? Who else has Fitzroy brought out here? Has he shown the car to anyone else?'

'The Italians asked to see it,' said Gunther.

'You heard about what happened to them?'

Gunther nodded. 'This rally driving business seems very dangerous to me.' I heard a disapproving tone in his voice. Whether of the whole business, or because Fitzroy was involving a woman, I don't know.

'Any other teams?'

Gunther frowned. 'No, I don't believe so.' He stopped and I got the impression he had something else to say.

'No one else at all?'

Gunther shook his head. 'No other drivers or navigators,' he said. Even in the gloom I saw pink creep across his cheeks.

'Amaranth,' I said. 'He brought her down here. A moonlit walk, with a stop by the garage to show off his engine?'

Gunther went firefly red at this. 'I wouldn't know what they did, ma'am. I took the dog for a walk as requested.'

I suppressed a sudden wave of nausea. 'I left him with her. Do you think he is in any danger?'

'She's no match for him hand-to-hand,' said Gunther. 'And he's always wary of his food and drink, no matter who gives it to him.'

I thought of the careless greed Fitzroy had displayed at White Orchards. 'I see. They say poison is a woman's weapon, but sabotaging the brakes, or whatever she did, proved to be almost as effective.'

'I'm not surprised,' said Gunther. 'I should have worked it out myself. I disliked her on sight – and generally I don't do that.'

'So did I,' I said with a smile. The dog in my lap gave a little gruffling snort. 'Oh, you disgusting thing,' I said, laughing. 'Pass me some straw, Gunther. This creature had fallen asleep and drooled all over my legs.' Gunther went to get some from the old stalls and passed me a handful. 'Not many ladies would wipe their clothing with straw,' he remarked.

I gave him a grin. 'But Alan would. Alan doesn't even care if he gets a hot bath every day. And I do. Very much. Mind you, it's much easier to be Alan on a mission like this. Skirts would be most hampering.'

'Indeed, ma'am,' said Gunther.

I had gone too far in my musing. I thanked him for the tea. 'I'll tell Fitzroy our thoughts,' I said.

'I appreciate that, Alice,' said Gunther.

I walked back to the room, taking the most advantage of the shadows that I could. It would be a difficult conversation to have with Fitzroy. If he had genuinely dismissed Amaranth as a threat, and wasn't playing some kind of long game he hadn't confided in either Gunther or me, it would be an uphill job to convince him of a threat he had already discarded. I already knew he had a weakness for women – a love of their company and a desire to protect them were written through him as clearly as Brighton was written through a piece of peppermint rock. But could one blindside him so badly on a mission? I'd always thought he applied a different level of judgement when it came to his work.

I opened the door to be greeted by the smell of steak and vegetables. He had ordered dinner for me. I sat down without even taking my boots off. I was so hungry and, somehow, he had persuaded the kitchen not to include sausage in my meal, or even any kind of exotic seasoning. This was almost as good as an English Sunday Roast.

When I had finished, I sat back and reflected. Fitzroy showed me more kindness that he would show a male partner, of that I was fairly certain, even if he would never admit it. He called me 'a friend'. He had worked, and did work, with others – like Gunther – but they weren't friends. Just how far could his weakness for women mislead him? Could Amaranth be our adversary, and could Fitzroy be too blind to see it?

Whatever the truth, I knew if I was to convince him of Amaranth's guilt, I would have to have some damn good proof.

Chapter Seventeen

Fitzroy gets in over his head

Over breakfast Fitzroy informed me that the general feeling was the Italians had indeed caused their own demise. 'I stayed drinking late last night to get the mood of the rally,' he said, reaching for the coffee pot. We were seated on a table to ourselves in a shadowed corner. 'I've got a devilish head today. Thank goodness we have a day's grace. I don't generally drink much, so when I do, I have the head of an angry bear in the morning.'

'Thank you for the warning,' I said, passing him the sugar. Inwardly, I cursed. I wasn't going to be able to even hint at Amaranth's possible misdeeds before we left tomorrow. At least Gunther was now on the alert.

'What about the Germans who clipped our car?' I asked.

Fitzroy scowled. 'Situation between our government and theirs is getting worse. We're lucky they didn't try and run us off the road entirely.'

'They did,' I said. 'You outwitted them.'

He gave me a thin smile. 'What happened to your neck?'

'Would you believe I cut it shaving?'

That earned me a small chuckle.

'Alan is scared of you.'

He grinned again. 'Ah, well, that's not something I have to worry about with you, Alice. You see me for the friendly chap I am.'

All too friendly, I thought. I didn't reply but passed him more toast. 'Am I allowed to know how it went with Amaranth?'

'What do you want to know?'

'Did you learn anything to our advantage? Other than what I have already told you?'

'No, I don't think so. I'm no closer to discovering who sabotaged the car, or if our contact is among the teams. I'm beginning to think not.'

'I'm confused.'

Fitzroy grinned. 'It's all part of the game. I thought there was an outside chance that the contact might be making contact with someone else, who would then pass the blueprints on to us. Hence the cover of the rally, but it seems unduly complicated.'

'My head is spinning trying to follow that, and I don't think I am dull-witted.'

'You're not. It's all about trust. Whoever is handing over these blueprints has our description, even the names we're using, but we'd be easy enough to replace. Due to our profession, we're not remarkable-looking people - no offence, but dressing you as a boy *has* disguised your natural beauty, and as you know, I dye my hair to a more common colour.'

'You mean if the details about us were intercepted, someone could impersonate us?'

Fitzroy nodded. 'It's not a difficult journey to get to Bremen from England, but it's long enough and secluded enough in parts for someone to have dealt with us before we got to the start and replaced with their own people.'

'But how can anyone tell?'

'Exactly, it's one of tricky things. Whoever is handing over the information has to observe us and be convinced we are who we say we are. You're doing a credible act as a boy, but I may have made a mistake giving them your alias, Alan. Maybe I should have given them Alice and told them you were in disguise.'

I opened my mouth to speak, but he held up his hand.

'Sorry, to be clearer, I told the case handler in England our details. I don't have the contact in Germany. They are only trusting this case handler, but he works in an office and there are so many ways mission details like this could be stolen. I don't think they have been. We run a tight ship, but the German end can't know that. They've been passing details to the case handler through their own channels. I don't have access to those.'

'Weren't we at least given a code word?'

'Yes, it's Dancing Maiden, if you can believe it. But honestly, I don't set much store by code words. Torture loosens lips easily enough.'

'And you didn't tell me this before?'

'I was afraid you'd make too much of what happened on the boat. The mechanic you thought was trying to kill me . . .'

'He was.' I was so indignant I splashed coffee from the pot into my saucer. Something my mother had trained me never to do.

'They are a British team. I have managed to check on the two that remain. Neither are known to the Service as people to watch. If I get an opportunity to ask C & C, I will, but it's too delicate to risk them picking up on why I am asking.'

I decided to change tack. 'Does Jack ever bark?'

'He's trained to only do so when there is a direct threat – well, as much as he can tell one.'

'How did you train him to do that?'

Fitzroy helped himself to an extra sausage from the platter that lay between us. He'd already consumed more than two-thirds of it. However, I didn't share the German propensity for eating large quantities of meat for breakfast, so I didn't object.

'I beat him into obedience, of course. Like I should have done with you.'

I dropped my fork. Fitzroy picked it up and gave it back to me. 'Honestly,' he said. 'You are far too eager to believe the worst of me. I trained him as you would train a dog to do anything, with rewards and affection. You've seen how he reacts to me. I am his main provider of sausages. If only female trainees were as easy to control. But then you don't like sausages, do you? Why this sudden interest in my dog?'

A waitress came by and exchanged my cup and saucer for

a clean one. Fitzroy, against protocol, poured me another coffee. 'Why this sudden interest in my dog?' he repeated.

'I was talking to Gunther—'

'Were you indeed, and what did you establish?'

'I think him insisting on calling me ma'am gave away a lot. He said you had been specific in instructing him how to treat me?'

'Sometimes I wonder why I ever involve anyone else, ever. Things are so much easier solo,' said Fitzroy, frowning. 'He wasn't meant to associate with you on this mission.'

'I think it fits with Alan's character that he would visit the mechanic. It's not as if his brother likes him much. In fact, I think he might even take Jack for a walk from time to time.'

'I take it you grew up with animals? Yes, you can walk my dog. He seems to like you.'

'Did he like Amaranth?'

Fitzroy frowned. 'I don't care to keep discussing her. But if you insist on knowing, Jack growled at her. He didn't like her at all. Probably her perfume. She wears a lot, and a dog's nose is very sensitive.'

'Oh,' I said. This put paid to my idea that Amaranth had secretly unclipped the dog to draw Gunther away from the car. I remembered that he'd said Amaranth didn't know what went on under the bonnet. This doubly ruled her out.

'You've gone very silent. You're usually quite talkative at breakfast.'

'I'm sorry. I was thinking.'

'About Amaranth?'

'In a way . . .' I was ready to explain, but again he interrupted me.

'I didn't think certain aspects of our missions would need to be open to general discussion. It appears I was wrong. For the record, I have no intention of bedding Amaranth. She has the morals of an alley-cat and I simply have no idea where she has been.'

'I don't understand,' I said.

Fitzroy rested his elbows on the table and buried his head in his hands. 'No, of course you don't,' he said more to himself than me. 'It's not something you have ever considered or will ever have to consider.' He lifted his head. 'Can we leave it at, I am not going to get intimately involved with Amaranth. I intend to flirt with her for a while. My refusal to go further will doubtless intrigue her, and while she still holds out hope, she will be easy to pump for information. She's excellent at picking up gossip even among men.'

'Could I not do that?'

'Not as Alan,' said Fitzroy. 'The best you can do is sit in corners and observe. You can't interact with anyone for too long. You're pulling off the youth character much better than I'd hoped, but your hair is growing too fast. Besides, whenever your face lights up with happiness, you become far too beautiful to be a boy.'

'Thank you,' I said.

'It's not a compliment,' said Fitzroy standing up. 'It's an inconvenience.'

The race continued over the next few days. The track was difficult enough that Fitzroy and I didn't have time for conversation. He needed to spend all his attention on driving, and I needed to ensure I paid attention to landmarks now encrusted with snow. Fitzroy kept our rating at a respectable middle of the pack. Having seen him deal with some extremely tricky moments, I knew he was better than that, but I confess I was relieved he didn't feel the need to push himself to extremes. I had no doubt he drove within his capabilities.

Every evening went a similar way. I retired to the room. Fitzroy booked hot baths ahead for us, his in a separate room. I tumbled out of my clothes into hot and steaming water. My bruises had blossomed from purple into a greenish yellow. It looked ghastly, but when I described them to the spy, he only commented that it showed I was healing and not continuing to bleed internally. After my bath, supper was delivered, I ate it by the fire while I dried and then I got into bed with a book, if there were any. Sometimes Fitzroy woke me up when he returned, but more often than not, I didn't see him again until I woke in the morning and saw him in the bed next to mine. He had ceased volunteering information about his night-time activities and I had ceased asking.

We had entered Cologne when things changed. I was reading a guidebook in bed about the Cathedral. It sounded magnificent and I was hoping I might get a chance to see it, though Fitzroy, as ever, was cagey about our schedule. I was reading about Albertus Magnus' - a hero of my father's - connection to the church when Fitzroy quietly opened the door. He scowled at me. 'I should have known you'd be still awake.'

'Is there a problem?'

He closed the door. 'No. Yes.' And fairly stomped across the room. He was carrying his boots, proof he had been trying not to wake me, but he now threw them under his bed before dropping down to sit on the mattress. The bed creaked alarmingly.

I sat up, more than decent in my wretched flannel pyjamas (I hated them, but they did keep me warm). 'Is there anything I can do?'

The spy made a grumbling, growling noise that I interpreted as him having been thwarted. 'What went wrong?'

'Amaranth,' he growled. 'Bloody woman. Wasn't going to take no for an answer. I've known some bold women in my days, but she takes the cherry.' He gave a bark of laughter at some personal joke, but he didn't appear any happier. If anything, his frown had deepened.

'What has she done?'

'She got me into her room and made it abundantly clear what she wanted. You don't want the details.'

'No, I don't. Do I have time to visit the Cathedral tomorrow?'

'Yes, probably,' said Fitzroy. 'Aren't you going to ask what happened?'

I shook my head.

157

'She only damn well tried to seduce me! Me!'

I pressed my lips together to suppress my smile. The spy wasn't fooled.

'I get the irony,' he snapped. 'So, I had to walk out on her. She wasn't taking no for an answer.' He threw himself back on his bed. 'Damn! Damn! Damn! She was just beginning to give me some useful information too. From what she's said, I'm fairly sure those Austrians have to be spies.'

I waited, not wanting to, as they say metaphorically, poke the bear.

'You don't need to tell me I played her too hard,' said Fitzroy. 'I should have taken it slower. With any other woman, I'd have got at least another week out of them before we came to the turning point. But, blow me, if she isn't the most forward, full-blooded woman I've ever encountered.'

'Some men might like that,' I suggested. 'She may have thought you one of those.'

'Then she misread me badly.'

'You prefer the demure, maidenly English rose?'

Fitzroy sat and scowled at me. 'Yes, Alice. After spending time with you, I can think of little as refreshing.'

I held up my hand in a 'peace' gesture. 'Do you think she realises you are a spy?'

'I doubt she's thinking about anything except my rejection at present. She's very self-obsessed.'

'But she is going to wonder why you turned her down after all your attentions.'

'Yes, damn it. Of course she is. Don't you get it? I'm telling you; I blew it. Haven't a clue how I'm going to handle her tomorrow.' He flopped back onto the bed.

'I suppose you could always tell her you were awaiting treatment for some . . . disease.'

Fitzroy rolled onto his side to look at me, his eyes wide. 'Do you want to utterly ruin my reputation? That devil-cat would tell everyone.'

'What, that you had a weak heart? Or that you need an operation for a fused disc in your back, or something of that ilk.'

Fitzroy sat up again. This time he looked less agitated. He wasn't smiling, but the frown had lifted. 'My apologies, Euphemia. I shouldn't have presumed what you meant. I thought . . . but, no. You didn't understand before so there's no reason why you should now. You are of an utterly different nature to her.'

'I'm very confused,' I said.

'So am I,' said Fitzroy. 'But that was a compliment, for once.'

'Thank you,' I said. 'Would you like to visit the cathedral with me tomorrow? It would give you a bit more time to think of how you might react to her.'

'Certainly. What's more, we can go out to breakfast. We might be able to find an Austrian-influenced café. Far less sausages. Bread, butter, jam, maybe cheese, and excellent coffee.'

'Oh, that sounds nice. Is there any chance of a decent cup of tea?'

'Less likely, I'm afraid, but the closest you'll get to sausage is speck.' He stood and leant over to ruffle my hair. 'Go to sleep. I'm going to undress now. We'll have a day away from all of this tomorrow. I think we've both more than earned it.'

I rolled over and closed my eyes. I was unsure exactly what was going on, but at least I would get to see the cathedral, and Fitzroy appeared to be in a more amendable mood. I reckoned this was as good as things could get.

Chapter Eighteen

Sightseeing in Cologne

The next morning found us both seated in a small bakery that was also a café. Our breakfast had been blissfully free of sausage. I sat back in my seat fully satiated. Fitzroy looked hungry.

'You could re-order,' I said.

He shook his head. 'I think we should get on with our day. I'll pick something else up along the way.'

I had studied the guidebook, but I was still not prepared for the size of Cologne Cathedral. I stopped in front of the entrance. Six large statues flanked the doors, above which there was another exotic pale yellow frieze. The archway progressed inward, where figures stood in their niches, and between the two doors stood the Virgin and baby Jesus. The facade above the arches was also intricately carved.

Fitzroy stood beside me considering the door. 'All that effort. All that skill,' he said.

'Did you know they started the cathedral and then stopped working on it for almost two hundred years?'

'I did,' said Fitzroy. 'It's based on the same idea as Amiens, but I believe the gothic vault inside is larger – if not the largest in the world. If you have doubts in your self-confidence, this building will steal it all. Inside a lesser man or woman might feel like a fly. I believe that was the general idea, to make one humble before God.'

'I shouldn't imagine you do humble,' I said.

'Not often. If we stroll around inside, you will find a great deal to admire if you like church architecture – the carved choir stalls survived the desecration of the French Revolutionary Army and on the south side there's the Bayernfenster, a quite lovely set of five stained-glass windows gifted by Ludwig I of Bavaria.'

'You've been here before?'

'A few times. It is an excellent place to meet someone. There are plenty of areas where it is difficult to be spied upon, and of course, there is an excellent reason for loitering.'

'You're hoping our contact might find us here.'

'I thought we'd spend a good hour and a half here. There is plenty to see.'

'Good, I'm keen to see inside,' I said, and started up the steps. When I entered through the doors, I immediately knew what Fitzroy had meant. The space was incredibly vast, and the roof soared in grand vaults above us. I felt less than two inches tall.

'Stop looking up,' said Fitzroy, 'it helps. Come and see the foundation stone. It's amazing to look at this and think this one piece of stone held so many ideas, dreams, and hopes, which we now see realised. None of the twelfth-century stone masons saw the cathedral built. I expect they thought it would never happen. It's a bit of a symbol of hope to me. We may not accomplish a great task, but there will always be others to pick up the pieces and take our hopes forward.'

He stood looking down at the stone, his face set and serious. For once I kept my mouth shut. He had gone into a strange mood that I had not beheld before. If such a thing were not impossible, I would have described his demeanour as forlorn. But a forlorn Fitzroy was too much of an oxymoron for me to consider it seriously.

He briefly reached out a hand to touch the stone. 'Do you ever think about what you will leave behind you?'

'Are you speaking to me?'

He stepped away from the stone. 'Well, I don't think the walls of this place are going to answer me.'

'I thought you might have been musing to yourself. You look – odd.'

'Thank you. I should hate to consider myself looking entirely ordinary, despite the necessity of hiding in plain sight. But my question?'

'No, I haven't considered it. My life has taken such unexpected turns, and been uprooted in ways I could not have imagined, that for now I am content to see what happens next. Although, of course, along the way I find it important to do what is right.'

'You mean your duty?'

'Yes,' I said. 'Both my moral duty and my duty to the Crown.'

'Hmm, that is an ambition in itself. We should wander around the aisles. Ensure we are seen.'

I almost made to take his arm before I remembered I was meant to be a boy. 'It feels wrong to dress in a disguise here,' I said.

Fitzroy looked down at me, the ends of his lips twitching, in obvious amusement. 'If God sees everything – which I do find a little uncomfortable – then he will be cognisant of your disguise already.'

'I suppose so,' I said.

'Sometimes you are such a typical vicar's daughter,' said the spy. 'Personally, I believe God is more interested in looking into our hearts than our deeds. But, either way, I'm doubtless in trouble come the afterlife.' With this parting remark he made off down an aisle with my trailing him.

We spent a good hour or so at the cathedral. We wandered both together and singly. I saw only a few other people come into the building. A mother and child, both very quiet and subdued. An old man in a shabby suit came and knelt down to pray. A black-robed priest emerged from a panel, which I only then realised was a door, and hurried away towards the back of the church to disappear into the panelling once more. (Rather like a giant church mouse bolting from one hiding-hole to another.) A young couple – she kept looking up at him and smiling, so I imagined

162

they were newly married – toured around the cathedral, stopping to look at all the particularly historic parts. Fitzroy caught me watching them, and came up beside me. Speaking softly he said, 'I had great hopes for them being our contacts, but they are clearly in thrall to one another. I doubt anyone could act that as well as they are doing.'

'You sound disapproving,' I said.

He shrugged. 'Given your upbringing I would have thought you found their actions more of the flesh than of the spirit.'

'You are in an odd mood,' I repeated. 'For what it's worth, I think God rather approves of love.'

'Hmm,' said Fitzroy. 'Not even sure I believe in it all anymore.' He rubbed his hands together. 'It's as cold as an ice cave in here. Clearly no one is meeting us. I need to go to the post office and see if I have any messages. We could also pick up some local papers to see what the common people in Germany are making of the state of play in the world. Or rather what their government is telling them to think.' He looked down at me. 'It would be very helpful if you could learn a language or two that is still spoken. It's all very well speaking Ancient Greek and Latin, but what use is that to you now?'

'I suppose Ancient Greek could be a language we could use to communicate, in dire straits.'

'Hmm,' said the spy once more and walked ahead to the main doors. I lingered behind, taking in one last view of the cathedral. I had no expectation of seeing it again. As a single man, Fitzroy could go where he wanted. As a married woman, I escorted my husband, who was not well enough to travel far, and as a spy I went where I was sent. In neither case were my wishes ever to be consulted. (Which if you think about it, is a bit rich.)

Accordingly, I was in a bit of a gloomy mood when I emerged from the cathedral. Because my eyes were downcast, I saw Fitzroy's cane lying on the ground, a little to one side.

I went at once to it and picked it up, looking around for the spy. I could see no sign. The area was not crowded, and I believed

163

I should have been able to pick him out easily. My thoughts raced. Had he been lifted up and taken off in a vehicle? Was this some kind of test? Had he picked up a trail and had no time to wait? No, more likely, I thought, was that he and an unknown person had disappeared into a side alley. The best hope was that this was our contact who had tugged him quickly into the shadows to pass on either a message or the blueprints we craved. The worst was that assailant, intent on his life, had dragged him off.

I spun on the spot, accessing options. I saw three. One, a tight, dark space, ideal for mugging a tourist. But it was a good twenty paces away. Two, a side alley directly beside the cathedral. Possibly someone could have come up behind their target and dragged them in quickly without anybody noticing. You would need to have a large amount of courage to choose this option, I realised, as the mouth of the lane was wide enough that you would remain in sight for several paces while dragging your quarry inside. Three was the furthest away, and I ruled it out as the target would have had to have been dragged across a busy roadway. Even if you could do it, by holding a gun to his back for example, traffic was too unpredictable to enter into the equation.

The thought of a gun made me feel slightly sick, but I knew Fitzroy to be more than competent in the fighting arts. I hoped that he had allowed himself to be taken, to move the scene away from the general public and not because he was in fear of his life. He was also an excellent cane-fighter, so why he should drop his confused me. He had trained me to assess the environment and to reason tactically. I would have thought of him assailed if I could not have found him, so he didn't need to leave his stick behind as if I was some kind of novice. My annoyance helped push down my fear. Fear for him and fear for me should I be left alone on this mission.

I chose the nearest alley. I approached from the side, carrying the cane as anyone might, but prepared to lift it as a weapon at the merest sign of a combatant.

Which is how, after seeing moving shadows, I came to be

waving a stick above the head of the young couple, who had seemed so much in love in the cathedral. Their attention was entirely on each other and the activity they were obviously enjoying. However, my sudden appearance, complete with a warrior cry (which was entirely involuntary) alarmed the woman so much she screamed and dropped her skirts, thus, discommoding her companion who was exposed in a most ungentlemanly manner. Before marriage I would have been truly shocked. Now, I threw the man a disgusted glance and looked behind them to check they weren't put there to distract me from looking further (this idea did seem extreme, but it is better to be thorough). I retreated on ascertaining there was no Fitzroy in that alley.

Out once more into the bright, but cold, sunshine, I ran across to my second choice. I cursed inwardly that I had chosen wrongly. Time is crucial in these situations. Running those several paces, a number of thoughts went through my head, but predominant of these were that only a gun in the back could have made the spy walk this far, unless he had a plan of which I was entirely unaware, or had taken leave of his senses. To be fair, I thought both might be possible.

The narrow slit of an alley was inky black in the sunlight. I circled round to the side. I was carrying the spy's cane, so it would be clear I was his aide, even if I resembled a slight teenage boy who looked incapable of hurting anyone. I stood to the side of the alley for a few moments with my eyes closed. I needed to accustom myself to the shadow in there. I knew it would not be as pitch dark as it appeared from afar, but I also knew going directly from bright sunlight into there would effectively blind me.

So it was, I turned and walked into the alley with my eyes shut. As I did so, I said in a high boy's voice. 'Brother, are you down here? I have found . . .'

I had more words prepared, but action was needed. I saw two assailants, both men, both wearing black masks. One continued his process of punching Fitzroy, who was backed up against a wall, repeatedly in the stomach. From the way the spy lurched

165

sideways on each punch it was clear this was far from the first. The second, and the reason why Fitzroy had allowed himself to get into this position, stood watching over them both, a gun trained on the spy.

On my words, the boxer looked up. 'Deal with him,' he said curtly. As the gunman turned away, Fitzroy recovered miraculously and leapt upon his opponent. I ran full tilt at the gunman. This startled him so much he involuntarily raised both his hands, and so the barrel of the gun swung skyward. I only got three strides before he recovered his composure, but it was enough. The vennel had widened sufficiently that I was able to wield Fitzroy's cane like a bat. I took a running jump, letting out a hideous cry, and swung the cane against his temple as hard as I could. He dropped like a stone.

Fitzroy and his combatant froze mid-fight for one moment. I threw the cane towards Fitzroy. Ducking down and grabbing it, he then lunged forward to deliver a hard blow against his opponent's sternum. The man's back arched and his arms went out. Fitzroy brought the cane up smartly, delivering a blow directly under his opponent's chin, flipping his head backwards. The spy stepped back and as the man's head lowered, Fitzroy brought the end of his cane down on the back of it. The man dropped to the floor. Without hesitation, Fitzroy stepped forward and repeatedly bashed at the man's head with his stick until he ceased to move. Even in the low light I could see fluid leaking from under his mask.

'Grab the other one's gun, will you? There's a good girl.'

I realised I had been frozen, watching him beat the boxer to death. I picked up the gun and passed it handle-wards towards him. Fitzroy tucked his cane over his arm and took it from me. He tested the lolling roll of the man's head on the ground with the toe of his foot. 'Think his neck's gone. How's yours?'

'I don't know,' I said. 'Do you want me to check.'

'I'll do it.' He stepped over the fallen boxer then squatted down and checked for a pulse on the neck of mine. 'Nothing.

Right, let's see who this villain is.' He pulled away the mask, revealing a blood–soaked face that was clearly Crawford, his eyes still open in a stone–cold stare.

'I say, Alice, I may well owe you an apology. It seems like that British team were a rotten lot after all. Must have German relatives and were siding with the enemy. Terrible thing.' He stood up and went across to the fallen boxer. I moved out of his way. It was only then I saw something glint as it fell out of the boxer's hand. Fitzroy squatted down next to the body, taking care not to get the edge of his trousers in the blood. 'And this, I assume, is Crabtree.'

He pulled off the mask to reveal a man neither of us had ever seen before.

'Well, I'll be blowed,' said Fitzroy. 'Now, how are we going to clean up this mess?'

'You're bleeding,' I said.

'It's nothing,' said Fitzroy taking out a handkerchief to wipe the edge of his cut lip.

'No, not that. There's a stab wound in your side.'

'Is there?' said Fitzroy, looking down in disbelief. 'The bugger of it.'

And then he collapsed in a dead faint.

Chapter Nineteen

Assassination

So, there I was, on my first mission in a foreign country where I had no knowledge of the language, standing in a dark alley with two dead men at my feet and Fitzroy slumped unconscious against a wall, possibly dying. I believe that to my credit I did not cry. I remember thinking, well, it can't get any worse than this. When I heard footsteps behind me. I swung around.

A tall silhouette stood there. '*Wo is die*?' he demanded.

'Do you speak English? I am in need of help.'

'Euphemia?' said a vaguely familiar voice.

'*Otto*?' I said.

'I heard they were dressing you as a boy. It's convincing. At least in this light.'

'Fitzroy has been injured. He may be dying.' I couldn't suppress the sob in my voice.

Otto immediately went to crouch over Fitzroy, turning his back on me and exposing the back of his head. The last time I had seen Otto, he had been unconscious himself, was bundled into a carpet (by me) and been taken away in the back of car. Being half-German, half-British, and of minor German nobility, the hope had been the British service could turn him into a double agent. That he was also known as a handsome playboy with no known dependents and a great deal of charm had not gone unnoticed by anyone. I had no idea if they had succeeded. For all I knew he could have been working with Crabtree, but where else might I get help? I decided not to hit him. I reasoned Fitzroy was too valuable a resource for the service to lose.

Otto, happily not privy to my thoughts, stood up. 'It's not good,' he said. 'He's lost a lot of blood. At least it hasn't hit the intestines. I'd have smelled that. But I can't see the damage properly in this light.'

'Who are you working for, Otto?'

'Pointless question, Euphemia. Whatever I say could be a lie. Better to ask if I'm prepared to help you two.'

'Are you?'

'Where are you based?'

I told him the name of the inn. He took a flask from his inside pocket. 'Try and get some of this down him while I get us a cab. It'll be less noticeable if we can get him to walk across. Do up his coat, and the public will think we are helping our drunk friend get home. What the devil does he mean leaving you in this predicament? I thought he was better than this.'

Before I could reply he left the alley. I could only pray he meant he was hailing a cab and not going for reinforcements. We weren't technically yet at war with Germany, but I suspected they'd take rather a dim view of foreign agents killing their people.

I crouched down next to my partner and put the flask to his lips. 'Please, Eric,' I said, using his real name, 'drink.' The whisky, or whatever it was, dribbled down his chin. 'Come on, Fitzroy,' I said trying a different tack, 'it's not like you to waste good whisky.' Something got through and he parted his lips enough to swallow a little. This produced a coughing fit and he opened his eyes.

'Euphemia,' he said in a thin voice. 'Get out of here. Run.'

'Otto's here. He's gone to hail a cab. If we can get you back to the inn, we can get you help.'

'Otto?' His eyes gazed with confusion.

'I don't know if he's on our side.'

'Run,' repeated Fitzroy.

'No, I'm not leaving you. And you can't order me to. I don't know enough about the mission to do it alone – and it has to be done, doesn't it?'

'You're more important.'

'No, I'm not. Drink some more.' I forced the flask to his lips.

'How bad is it?'

'Otto said you've lost a lot of blood, but the knife didn't puncture your intestines.'

'Thank God for that,' said Fitzroy. 'That's a death sentence. Speaking of which, you should go. We can't trust him.'

'Sit still. I need to do up your coat.'

'How wifely. I hope Bertram appreciates you the way he should. You're quite extraordinary, you know?'

'Because I know how to do up buttons?' I said, finishing the last.

'Because you are as brave as you are beautiful and I'm a damned cad for getting you into this business.'

'With notable exceptions, I do enjoy this work.'

Fitzroy opened his mouth to say more, but Otto appeared.

'Can you get up, old man? Euphemia and I will help you to the cab. It'll hurt like hell getting you back to the inn, but I daren't take you to a hospital. Once you're in I'll be able to apply decent pressure to the wound.'

Fitzroy lumbered to his feet, using the wall behind him as a crutch. 'Try not to enjoy that too much,' he said from between gritted teeth. Otto slung one of the spy's arms over his neck and in spite of Fitzroy's protests I took the other. It made us somewhat lop-sided, but we managed to get him into the cab.

'How will we find a doctor?' I asked.

'I have a man meeting us at the inn. He's discreet and good. Your beloved boss will get good care. Don't worry.'

'I am still here,' said Fitzroy.

'There, he sounds as irritated as usual. He must be feeling better,' said Otto.

'One day,' said Fitzroy in a quiet voice, 'I am going to kill you.'

'Perhaps,' said Otto, 'but not today.'

We managed to get Fitzroy into the room without being seen. The doctor arrived shortly afterwards. Otto wanted me to leave, but I argued with him long enough that the doctor threw us both out. We went downstairs and found a quiet corner. Otto ordered coffee for us both.

'What are you doing sharing Fitzroy's room?'

I blinked. 'I'm under cover as his younger brother, Alan,' I said.

'That's not reason for him to compromise you!'

'He hasn't. He's been a gentleman.'

Otto gave a snort. 'What would you know about it? He probably planned to wait until after the mission before he seduced you. Got you feeling safe from him, and you wouldn't know . . .'

'Otto, I married Bertram Stapleford.' I paused. 'So, I do know – what you think I don't know.'

'Congratulations. Where is your husband?'

'At home.'

'At home in England! If I had a wife—'

I held up my hand. 'Stop. We will attract attention if we continue to argue. Besides, no woman in her right mind would marry you.'

At this moment coffee arrived. Otto scowled at me but poured me a cup. He sipped the hot drink.

'I apologise. My last remark was uncalled for,' I said.

'Oh, you're doubtless correct,' said Otto. 'Besides, I have no desire to have a wife – especially one as outrageous as you. Tell me what happened to the German agents.'

I told him. He was noticeably paler by the end of the tale.

'What in particular causes you an issue?' I asked calmly.

'I don't know where to begin,' said Otto. 'I have seriously misread you. It seems you and Fitzroy are well matched.'

I shrugged, unsure if this was a compliment or not (I suspected the latter). 'What will happen when the police discover the bodies.'

171

'I sent some of my people to clean up,' said Otto. 'I'll file paperwork about a different mission going sideways. It will be difficult, but that's the job I signed up for. I'll have a few days' grace to think up something.'

'Why were you there at all?'

'Still suspicious? I was looking for you. I thought you might be the boy. It's not as if you can ever be yourself while spying. Anyway . . .'

'What do you mean?'

'How many female spies do you know?' said Otto.

'None, personally, but I believe there have been a few before me.'

'A very few and none of them remarkable in appearance. Fitzroy, for all the charm he can exude, looks like a regular chap. You will never look like a regular woman, so in the field you will always be put in one disguise or another. Or you will become known to all the foreign services.'

'Oh,' I said. Privately, I did not choose to take a double agent's word on anything, but I made a mental note to query Fitzroy later.

'I was looking for you,' said Otto, continuing to what he saw as the only worthwhile point to peruse, 'because our service, I mean the German service, has received information that someone will shortly try to assassinate one of the Kaiser's relatives.'

'Who?'

'I was wondering if it was you.'

'To what end?' I asked confused.

'To begin the war.'

I put my coffee cup down on my saucer with an unladylike chink. 'I think we need to establish some criteria here. Although I may have accidentally killed one or more German agents, I only did so in extreme circumstances where I was given no other choice. I am not trained to be an assassin. So far in my training I appear, it seems to me, to be headed towards intelligence retrieval, observation, and tactical situations. Fitzroy may know differently, but this is what I believe.'

'So you're not here on an assassination mission. I had been told you were coming through, but not why.'

'Definitely not,' I said firmly.

'Well, in that case I need to ask you to help me save the Kaiser's relative. Or rather ask Fitzroy's permission to borrow you. I doubt he's up to much.'

'I think I should go and see him,' I said. Inside I felt completely at sea. I knew about Germany's naval build-up, and their antagonism against other powers. I even remembered vaguely my father commenting on some society scandal back in 1908, but I thought that Wilhelm II was a warmonger, and we were trying to stop him. I did not want to voice my ignorance to Otto and expose my naivety.

Otto stood and bowed to me. 'I shall request a room here. I will speak to you both in the morning.'

If Fitzroy is still alive, I thought, but I merely nodded and headed upstairs.

In our room I found a bandaged Fitzroy, sitting up in his bed and looking more than usually grumpy. I had barely closed the door before he said, 'I hear Otto is snooping around.'

'He helped me get you back here and arranged the doctor,' I said. 'I couldn't have managed things without him. You owe him your life.'

Fitzroy made a noise between a tiger's growl and a snort.

I came over and sat carefully on the edge of his bed. 'I can't say I like him much either.'

The spy raised an eyebrow. 'You've changed your tune. Last time you saw him you ended up in a passionate embrace, if I recall correctly.'

'I was trying to chloroform him,' I said. 'It all went a bit sideways – as you well know.'

This earned me another growling snort.

'Can we trust Otto?'

'About as much as a two-headed snake,' said Fitzroy.

'Oh good,' I said. 'So his fears may be a ruse for separating us while you are injured.'

Fitzroy blinked at me. 'We're on a mission,' he said. 'You're not going anywhere, even if what he says is true. We are still to collect the info.'

'There seems to me to be several pressing issues that need our attention. But firstly, how badly injured are you?'

He opened his mouth to speak.

'I want the clear, unvarnished truth. No jokes or evasions,' I said.

He frowned. 'Very well, I have been lucky. Nothing of great significance inside me has been injured. However, I have lost a great deal of blood. I am not even sure when he stabbed me. I was too intent on delivering my retribution. I never saw the knife. My temper almost undid us both. I must apologise for that.'

I shook my head. 'No apology is necessary for what passed in the alley. However, there is another apology I will be demanding of you shortly, as well as enlisting a promise.'

Fitzroy sat up a little straighter and immediately winced as his wound smarted. 'Do I need to remind you I am the senior officer here?'

'You are. You are also injured and not necessarily capable of continuing in charge. If I believe that to be so, I am to take over myself, am I not?'

This time the growl was low, long, and deep. 'If you were a fully trained agent, possibly. But you are still in training.'

'As you have often told me, in the field rank can become immaterial,' I countered.

By this time the frown and stern gaze had become quite thunderous. I shifted very slightly further away from him, though I thought it most unlikely Fitzroy would ever harm me.'

'If you are considering giving me a good shake,' I said, 'remember if will only open your wound again.'

'I would never shake a lady,' said Fitzroy. 'You, on the other hand . . .'

'Listen, Otto says his office received intelligence that someone

174

is about to assassinate one of the Kaiser's relatives. He thought it might be us – trying to start the war, if you please. When I said I was aware of no such plan, he asked for my help – he has assumed you are too ill to continue whatever we are doing. He may even believe we are here to do the rally, nothing more.'

'Did he say who?'

'No,' I said. 'That was when I decided to be offended and end the conversation. I am confused about the political situation and I didn't want to let him know that.'

'Did you tell about our mission?'

'Of course not. Nothing at all.'

The frown faded to be replaced with a look I knew all too well; Fitzroy was curious. 'Good girl,' he said. 'Not surprised you're confused. I haven't exactly kept up to date with the day-to-day goings-on myself since we've been in the field. Collecting the papers and any messages from the post office was to be my errand after the Cathedral, before we were so rudely interrupted.'

'Do you think Otto is telling the truth?'

'I won't be able to tell until I see him for myself. What did you think?'

'I have no insight. I am too confused. I thought the Kaiser was the war-like party in all this?'

Fitzroy nodded. 'Wilhelm II is a highly intelligent man, with a chip on his shoulder. He can't decide if he wants to be British, as his mother was, or if he wants the German Empire to be better than the British. He loathes his mother, although she is dead, and is deeply torn between his loyalties. Many in Britain have pointed out he was extremely fond of his grandmother, Queen Victoria. She certainly took a great interest in him as her first grandchild by her eldest daughter. However, when he was born, his mother would only be attended by British doctors and his arm was damaged by one of them during the difficult birth. He blames her and them for his not being able to be a full man. His masculinity is very important to him – he felt his father was not masculine enough and a weak man. He is, or was, strongly influenced by

Chancellor Bismarck, turning his back on his parents. He ascended suddenly to the Kaisership when his father died after only months of being in charge. He is extremely temperamental and undiplomatic. He turned his back on Bismarck before the old chancellor died, but is, if anything, more under the influence of the army than ever before.'

'He's married, isn't he?'

Fitzroy nodded. 'Yes, she's always stood by him despite his affairs. Princess Augusta Victoria of Schleswig-Holstein. Known in the family as Dona.'

'Six children?'

'Six legitimate children,' said Fitzroy.

'Do you believe he wants war?'

Fitzroy ran a hand through his head. 'Everything I've read and heard suggests to me that he is torn – again – between two fantasies: that of being the Peacemaker of Europe and that of being the extreme victor with an Empire that rivals if not exceeds the British one. Either, or even both, may be true.'

'But the navy?'

'The German war machine is not aimed exclusively at Britain. Russia could equally be its main target and is thought by many to be so. The particular clash with Britain is if he moves into France.'

'What do you think will happen?'

'I don't know. I don't think the Kaiser knows himself. I think his generals would like a war, but even they aren't terribly concerned as to who it is with as long as it enhances the new German Empire.'

'That's rather sickening,' I said.

'Some day you should try reading about the establishment of our Empire. It has some pretty sticky bits in it too. Of course, ours is all history. Our King is a great man, ruling a great Empire. I cannot say the same of Germany.'

'Does this mean I should help Otto? If this would indeed prevent hostilities?'

'No, I need you.'

I leant back to look him over. 'You cannot be seriously considering continuing in the rally?'

I swear Fitzroy's lower lip jutted slightly, like that of a child being told he cannot have another helping of pudding. 'I don't see why not. We don't have to win. We only need to get the information. By the way, has Otto dealt with Crabtree?'

My hand flew to my mouth. 'I had completely forgotten . . . you think he is also against us?'

'The rest of his team were, so it seems likely. Never mind. One of us can deal with him when he makes his move. I take it Otto is playing off our detritus as something done by the agents out to kill this relative. Who is it?'

'He wouldn't say.'

Fitzroy sucked his teeth. 'Now that is very interesting. I wonder . . . Before you ask I know of no British plan to assassinate anyone in the Kaiser's family. At my level I should know if it had been set in motion before we left England.'

'Ah,' I said. 'But we've been out of contact.'

'To be fair, I think it more likely it would be sympathisers of Bismarck. The Kaiser treated his old mentor quite abominably.'

'Would he have wanted a war?'

'The Kaiser or Bismarck? Only he's a bit dead to ask. His sympathisers would want Germany to remain great – there's an undercurrent of greed coming across in German international relations at present. But exactly where it springs from no one is clear,' said Fitzroy. 'On the edge of conflict things do tend to get a bit muddled. That's why its such a dangerous time. One side makes a mistake and . . .'

'I see,' I said. 'How disconcerting.'

Fitzroy laughed. 'Only you could describe an impending global catastrophe as disconcerting.'

'Would it be that bad?'

'Worse than you could imagine,' said Fitzroy, his tone suddenly serious. 'I've seen enough fighting to hate it, and the potential scale of this is . . .' he searched for a word, 'staggering.'

177

'Which is why we need to know about this weapon? Something to cut short the insanity?'

'I'm glad you can see it like that,' said Fitzroy. 'Some people get very foolish over weapons. They want to save everyone, and you can't - ever.' He face closed in on this. He looked past me, obviously remembering another time. I waited, but he did not speak.

I broke the silence. 'In that case, I should move to my next point.'

'Were you ever a secretary?' asked the spy. 'You are a model of efficiency tonight.'

I ignored this attempt to rile me. 'When you were attacked, I can understand that you did not want a fracas that included a gun to take place in a public place.' He nodded. 'However, dropping your cane, I presume as a warning to me, was extremely foolish. It deprived you of the very weapon you could have made most use of in disarming the gunman. You could have already had the upper hand before I arrived if you have not discarded your weapon.'

Fitzroy began to snort again. This time in a defensive way.

'Can you tell me why you did it?'

'I left it pointing in the direction I was taken,' he said.

'That is a lie, and as you have given your word never to lie to me, I presume you are lying to yourself,' I said. He tried to speak but I overrode him. 'Even if you had, it would have been useless - possibly kicked aside by another pedestrian or even taken. The area was busy. In fact, you might even have been able to walk away if the Germans spies were also unwilling to shoot in a public place – which I suspect they were. But you chose to walk into an alley alone and unarmed. Why?'

'I'm tired,' said Fitzroy. 'I need to sleep if we are to get back on the road again in two days.'

'Perhaps I should send Amaranth up to tend to you?' I said. 'I expect she will have heard, if not the details, that you are indisposed. She might take it as a chance to start again. To display her charms.'

'I am clearly not in the situation to take advantage of anyone's charms,' snapped Fitzroy, 'and certainly not those of that poisonous harpy.'

'That is a little cruel. Maybe I should tell her how out of sorts you are . . .'

Fitzroy's hand flashed out to catch me, but I had already risen. 'Euphemia, don't you dare let that woman in here.'

'When you're defenceless?'

'I'm never defenceless,' growled the spy.

'You're certainly at a disadvantage and I am sure she would appreciate how well your blue silk pyjamas go with your eyes. Not to mention how they must currently be unbuttoned due to your injury.'

'Euphemia, don't you dare,' growled the spy, more fiercely than ever.

'Then tell me truthfully why you dropped your cane.'

'You're not going to believe it was an accident, are you?' said the spy.

'No,' I said, 'but I will fetch Amaranth to nurse you. Being a mere boy, I wouldn't know how.'

'Dammit, girl, I dropped the bloody cane because I wanted you to get out of there.'

'That did occur to me, but I hoped you wouldn't consider me that green,' said gently. I came back to sit on the side of the bed. 'You have to stop protecting me, Eric. You almost got yourself killed. You are more important to the service than I. Besides, I am meant to be here as your partner. I did well enough when I found you, didn't I?'

Fitzroy looked past me. 'Too well. And you saw . . .'

'You at your worst, beating a man to death.'

Fitzroy's gaze came up to meet mine. He looked as startled as I had ever seen him. 'You cannot say you approve of what I did.'

'I believe it to have been necessary.'

Fitzroy's eyes widened in horror. 'Dear God,' he said. 'What have I done to you?'

'It's not the first time I have seen you kill. Merely the first time I have seen you do so in a rage. You had told me that—'

'I know. I have never killed a man in anger before, but I was frightened for your safety.'

'Well, you have to stop that,' I said in a tone I used to my little brother Joe when he was being foolish. 'If I am to work with you, please pay me the courtesy of treating me like a spy, even a trainee spy, and not some young lady you must protect from the world. You say you want to see more female spies in the service. If you attempt to behave like a gentleman towards them then you render yourself hampered, don't you?'

'Yes,' said Fitzroy. 'But I don't like—'

'I'm afraid it doesn't matter what you like. I am set upon this path now, and my view of life has been challenged and changed. There is no going back after what I have seen.'

Fitzroy dropped his head. 'You must loathe me.'

'On occasion,' I said, 'but only when you are being extremely annoying, like now. For goodness' sake, buck up. You offered me a position in the service. I chose to take it. That is where we are and there is no changing it.'

'No,' said Fitzroy in a low voice.

I reached out and laid my hand on his, very briefly. He looked up even more startled than before. 'This is not your fault. I like this world. I also love my husband and the peaceful world I can retreat to on occasion. I have the best of it all. Please stop endangering us by trying to protect me.'

'I'll try,' said Fitzroy. 'Though it goes against my instinct.'

'I am aware that you have tried to save every woman you have ever come across because you were unable to save your mother . . .'

I stopped. A muscle twitched in the spy's cheek, his eyes bored into mine, but he also leant away from me. 'I'm sorry,' I said. 'I have gone too far.'

'No, you are acute. I will consider what you have said. But for now I must sleep.' He lay down and turned away from me. It was clear our conversation would not be continued tonight. I got into my own bed wondering what was to happen next. Much of what I had said was fair, but at the end I had overstepped the mark, and I was unsure Fitzroy would ever forgive me.

Chapter Twenty

Crabtree

When I awoke the next morning, it was to an empty room. Considering that Fitzroy had looked as if he was at death's door last night, I rose and dressed quickly in something of an alarm. All sorts of thought echoed through my mind, from him being rushed away to hospital to Crabtree spiriting him off in the night. However, I am not a heavy sleeper, but I had become used to the spy coming and going at night, and his movements did not always rouse me. As I hurried down the stairs to breakfast I consoled myself with the thought that despite his state he would have resisted forcible removal and even I could count on not sleeping through that.

I entered the eating area to see Fitzroy, Otto and Crabtree breakfasting together. All three men sat with their backs ramrod straight (My mother would have approved) and, as I approached, I could see each of them seemed to be smiling through their teeth.

'I could not in good conscience ask you to do that,' Crabtree was saying. 'I am sure he will return before we are due to depart.'

Fitzroy muttered something like, 'I wouldn't count on it,' under his breath. He must have caught sight of my approach from the corner of his eye as he kicked out at chair from the table. I hesitated, unsure if this was a sign I should go or stay. Beneath the table he flicked a finger at the seat, so I sat.

'I don't know,' Otto said, 'I think it sounds like rather good fun. If my old friend here can manage I am sure I could too.' He smiled at Fitzroy in a cold and adversarial manner, all teeth and cold eyes. Crabtree appeared oblivious.

'In all modesty I have to say I was always the better driver,' said Fitzroy.

A girl appeared at my side and laid a plate of cooked breakfast in front of me. This time it resembled more of an English repast, with scrambled eggs, tiny roasted pieces of potato with onion, sliced cold ham, toast, and the inevitable sausage. With only a cursory glance the spy scooped the potato and onion off my plate and onto his with several quick passes of his fork. His eyes flicked to mine. 'Too much garlic,' he said. 'I don't want your breath smelling disgusting in the car.'

'But yours . . .'

'I won't smell that,' he said and turned his attention back to the conversation with the others. As he knew I was particularly fond of potatoes I was now certain I remained in the doghouse.

Doghouse. In all that had happened since, I had forgotten we had yet to ascertain who had let Jack out of the garage in order to tamper with our car. I could not mention this is present company, but it seemed unlikely this was anything to do with the Germans we had encountered in Cologne. This meant another, as yet unidentified, enemy.

'Did you hear the Russians have left?' said Crabtree. 'It is one of the reasons I am tempted to accept your offer. The field is reducing.'

'Really?' said Otto and Fitzroy as one. They both then exchanged annoyed looks at the other. I took the joint comment to signify professional interest.

'Did they say why?' I asked. Crabtree started slightly as if he had forgotten I could speak.

'No,' he said. 'The innkeeper remarked on it when I came down. Said the heavily bearded men had paid their bill and left. He wanted to know if the race was still continuing.'

'Doubtless trouble back home,' said Otto. I could see by the

183

twitch in Fitzroy's left cheek and his sudden attention towards his plate that he wanted to ask more but didn't want to show his ignorance.

'I don't believe I've seen a newspaper for days,' I said, and I gave my approximation of a youth's laugh. This was bad enough Fitzroy grunted to help cover the sound. 'Not that it would do me any good,' I continued, 'I don't speak or read a word of German. So I am afraid I am completely ignorant of what is happening in the world at present.'

Crabtree gave me a slight smile. 'I feel much the same,' he said.

'*Sie keine Deutsch gesprechen*?' said Otto. Crabtree passed him the salt. Otto accepted and used it. Then he said, 'Well, there's a lot of bad feeling towards the Tsar and the Royal Family. Peasants are getting rather stirred up. It's one of those moments when people fear the worst . . .'

'And hope for the best,' I said with a bright smile.

Otto shook his head. 'No. I was going to say the worst that they fear is likely to be the least of it.'

'But they're all related, aren't they?' said Crabtree. 'Through Queen Victoria? Seems to me like most of the world's royalty are now an extension of the House of Saxe-Coburg-Gotha.'

Fitzroy lifted his head at this. 'Would there be a problem with that?'

'Not at all,' said Crabtree. 'I was only hoping it would make them all get on better.'

Fitzroy actually smiled at this. 'How quaint,' he said. Poor Crabtree blushed.

'So what is next?' I said.

'That's what we were discussing,' said Crabtree. 'Your friend here,' he indicated Otto, 'has offered to be my navigator. Crawford seems to have gone missing.'

'Really,' I said, opening my eyes very wide for a moment and forgetting I was not a girl, 'have you told the police?'

Crabtree shifted in his seat. Otto, in contrast, became very still. 'The problem is,' said Crabtree. 'I don't actually know the chap. For all I know he's gone off on legitimate business. We don't go off again until tomorrow. I'd have liked to have gone through the ice notes with him – although I don't even know if the chap we picked up in France knows how to do 'em. We went shares on the car, Crawford and I. For all I know he's called a halt to the whole thing and gone off home. He tends to be clam-mouthed about things, and I – I am grateful to get a chance to drive again.'

'Difficult,' said Fitzroy through a mouth of ham. I thought he'd finished, but looking down at my plate I found I suddenly had no ham left. I signalled a waitress and asked for more of everything to be brought to the table.

'Oh, I say, I don't know if I could eat any more,' said Crabtree.

'It's for my brother,' I said. 'He has an almost unhealthy appetite.' This earned me a glower, but no vocal rebuke.

'Who's left in the race?' asked Otto.

'There's a rather lovely woman called Amaranth, with her young dog of a husband,' said Crabtree. 'I think she's American and he's a British noble.'

'An insignificant one,' said Fitzroy. 'And not her husband.'

Crabtree gave him a confused look, but went on, 'There's the weird German prototype. All bits. Like some kind of jigsaw system.'

'Wimble and Housmann,' said Fitzroy.

'Muller and Mann have a fairly standard vehicle, suits their ability. They're German too,' said Crabtree. 'And Braun and Milche, also German.'

'Austrian,' corrected Fitzroy.

'Is there much of a difference?' said Crabtree, naively offending everyone at the table except me.

'I imagine they are more nervous,' said Otto enigmatically.

'And the last lot, other than the Fitzroys and possibly myself,' he nodded to us, 'are the Belgians. I haven't taken much notice of them. They tend to rise very early and retire before I'm even out of my bath for dinner.'

185

'So of all the teams that began we have only five left?' said Otto. 'It sounds as if it is anyone's race.'

Crabtree shook his head. 'Unless I can pull something out of the bag with my driving skills, it's between the Germans and the Fitzroys. There is only so much the rest of us can do when they have such superior vehicles and excellent driving skills. You seem to be a top notch navigator, young man,' he said to me. 'Have you been doing it long?'

'Not long,' I said. 'But I had a good teacher – my father,' I added for clarity, just as Fitzroy began to smile. The smile turned into a frown.

'If you excuse me, I'm off to have a word with my mechanic. If you're serious about navigating for me, Otto, I'll be in the garage for the next hour. After that we'll have to get a look at the ice for tomorrow night.' He rose, bowed and left.

'So you agree the Austrians are most likely spies,' said Fitzroy to Otto.

'Of course. They are naturally eager to understand what is happening in the German Empire and this is an excellent way of scoping us out.'

'Us?'

Otto shrugged. 'Your *brother* says you are not here to assassinate a member of the Kaiser's family, but I have not yet heard that from you. My sympathies may lie with the British, but there are some lines I will not cross. My blood is equally split between the two empires.'

'Are you sure you don't have some Russian in you too?' said Fitzroy.

'I do not believe so. Why?'

'That's the only way I think the situation could be made more morally complex for you. Otto, my dear chap, I do believe you have positioned yourself firmly in the untrustable camp.'

'He did save our lives,' I said.

'And his own neck. If we had been taken alive either of us could have sold him out for leverage.'

186

Otto's lips thinned. 'This is no time for joking.'

'It's certainly not a good place for this discussion,' said Fitzroy. 'Catch me later when I go out to look over my car, shortly before lunch. If you're aren't up the side of a mountain by then. For now, I need to rest.'

'Of course,' said Otto. Fitzroy rose, and picking up the large bowl of potatoes and onions, along with a clean fork, he headed upstairs. I followed.

Once in the room I asked, 'Are the Austrians definitely spies?'

'Seems likely,' said Fitzroy. He'd propped himself up on his bed and was attacking the bowl of food with vigour. This made what he was telling me slightly muffled. 'Not to worry. They're not spying on us. Much as our friend Otto said.'

'You don't trust him, do you?'

He stuck his fork upright in the bowl and placed it down beside him. 'Think about it. A double agent is a man who betrays his primary loyalty for a secondary one. No matter what the motive, it makes him an untrustworthy sort by nature. Can you imagine being a double agent?'

'I can imagine being undercover for the Crown.'

'Quite different. You see my point, don't you? What do you make of Otto? After all, you've known him much more intimately than I ever will.'

I felt myself blushing furiously. 'It was only a kiss and it was necessary at the time.'

'You should hear how Otto describes it,' continued Fitzroy. 'Deep, long, passionate, like a beauty awakening after a long sleep . . .'

'Shut up,' I said rudely. 'I doubt he said anything of the sort to you. Besides, I think he doesn't know what side his heart is on yet. He obviously feels loyalty to the Kaiser's family – but perhaps he doesn't like the idea of war. He could have let the others finish us off. I think he is a man who dislikes violence in all its forms. Probably sees himself as more lover than fighter.'

'I suppose,' said Fitzroy picking up his bowl again. 'Personally,

187

I consider myself equally split between the two. But that aside, you did say he thought we might be the assassins. It does seem as if he is more likely to try and talk us out of it than shoot us.'

'Just to be clear . . . *Are* we the assassins?' I asked.

'What do you think?'

'I think you would have sent Cole or someone like him.'

'Exactly,' said Fitzroy. 'I've been thinking about this relative. I should ask Otto about it privately. I suspect he won't mention it in front of you. Gentlemen aren't used to ladies being spies.'

'I'm not sure he thinks I am much of a lady after what happened yesterday, and he's appalled that I am sharing a room with you. He thinks I am totally lacking in morals.'

'Then he's an idiot,' said Fitzroy shortly. 'We're professionals. Being anything other than comrades would totally wreck our mission. I might have to have a little chat with him about that. It wouldn't do if he mentioned anything unnecessary about you and me to others in the trade.'

'Don't forget your injury,' I said. 'You don't want to open the wound again.'

'Careful, now you're almost sounding wifely,' said the spy with his first genuine grin of the day.

I ignored him. 'Is it true I will always been in disguise when I am working?' I asked.

'Otto said that, did he? Well, you are extremely beautiful, and as I think I have mentioned more than once that is rather an inconvenience.'

'I am sorry,' I said, not meaning it in the slightest.

Fitzroy waved my comment away. 'But then I am a very handsome man, and I successfully down–play that. Spies can't look remarkable when they're working. I suggest you ensure when you're not on a mission you make every effort to look your best. It will not only separate you further from Alice, but it will doubtless make Bertram a very happy man.'

'He loves me for my mind,' I said, sniffing haughtily.

'Of course he does,' said Fitzroy. 'But he's also a red-blooded male, isn't he?'

'We never did discover who let the dog out,' I said, changing the subject.

Fitzroy's eyebrows rose briefly, but he followed my lead. 'No, and I am not sure we ever will. Seems likely to me it was Crawford or someone he paid. Seems you were right about that mechanic trying to off me on the boat.' He shovelled yet more food in his mouth. 'Don't look smug,' he said. 'Beginner's luck.'

'I didn't say a word,' I said.

'No, but you thought some very loudly,' said the spy. He put the empty bowl down beside his bed and leaned back. 'I'm going to take it easy today. I need food and recovery time before I drive again. The two next legs are Frankfurt and Stuttgart. Easy enough driving. But it's the night drive over real mountain roads that is going to be the real challenge. Gunther sent up some ice notes last night and we need to spend some time going through them and the maps. I don't want to take the risk of driving again until my wound has formed some semblance of healing.'

'So you're determined to continue?'

He nodded. 'Sounds like the world is going to hell as usual. We still have a chance to do something to minimise the devastation. Can't turn our backs on that, can we?'

'Not if you put it like that. But what about Otto's assassination attempt theory?'

'We'll deal with that when we must. For now I'm betting he will tag along with Crabtree because he doesn't trust us.'

'And as we don't trust Crabtree . . .'

'It leaves us to get on with the job.'

189

Chapter Twenty-one
The Night Rally

The drive to Frankfurt was overnight, but it was hardly challenging compared to the snowy heights we had previously overcome. I rather enjoyed seeing the cottages and quaint small villages all lit up at night. The buildings were so unlike British architecture with their coloured facades, plaster-covered brickwork, and ornate stone along walls and roofs. It wasn't ornate like our Great Houses were, but resembled more than anything as if someone's grandmother had learnt how to knit in stone. I found it friendly and inviting.

Otto, Crabtree, Fitzroy and I continued to eat together at the inns in an atmosphere of politeness and suspicion that for the most part went right over Crabtree's head. He knew he was missing something, but like a dog who doesn't know how to open an ice-box, he couldn't get at the source of his concern.

Stuttgart was equally undemanding. The most surprising aspect of these two stretches and the accompanying inn stays was Amaranth's lack of pursuit of Fitzroy. She smiled and waved occasionally when we were at the inns, but did not approach us. She still wore her utterly unsuitable gowns, so it wasn't long before Otto was paying her court. She gave every indication of being delighted by his attention. Even Jack seemed to be behaving, although I did make time to visit him, both to take him treats and to walk him. He was the most affectionate thing. I even deliberately walked him past other team members to see if he ran up to them or showed some partisanship. He was uninterested in Otto, Crabtree, and the Austrians – although he perked up a bit when they fed him some sausage. The only result I got was that when I came across Amaranth with her very young man, he barked and pulled at the lead as if he wanted to take a chunk out of her. She was all horrified and aflutter, so I stopped taking him around the others after that in case she made trouble for him, and accused him of being vicious, instead of simply having good taste.

But at last we came to the first leg I had been really dreading. Tonight we would head over the mountains. Yet again, the reliable Gunther had provided ice-notes, covering road conditions, expected weather, and what tyres he thought were best on the car. He even brought a new shovel to put in the boot. Fitzroy had laughed.

'If we need that,' he said, 'I will have done something very wrong.'

To make matters worse, when we went out to the car it was already snowing lightly. The night sky shone a deep, dark blue, doubtless effected by the lights of the town. The inn stood on the edge of the valley, so as I looked down I could see a scattering of butter yellow-lit windows and snowy roofs. Cold tapped lightly against my skin, but under my multiple layers I felt warm enough – verging on too warm. However, I was grateful not to be wearing a skirt. I clambered up and took a last look at Stuttgart.

'Like a Christmas card, isn't it?' said Fitzroy from beside me.

'I'm imagining all the people tucked up by their fires reading.'

'And drinking whisky,' said Fitzroy sadly. 'Don't be fooled. It's mild down here with the snow falling. It will get much colder as we go up.'

I looked past him at the rise of the land. 'It seems impossible to think we'll be up there tomorrow.'

He gave me an odd look. 'Let's try for some optimism, shall we?'

'How's your wound?'

'I won't be going dancing any time soon, but driving should

be fine. I hope you're well wrapped up. I'm going to be taking this slowly, for both our sakes.'

I nodded. I didn't bother suggesting dropping out. We still didn't have that vital piece of information. I found myself looking over repeatedly at the inn, hoping beyond hope that someone would appear with a vital envelope. Fitzroy busied himself with getting the car ready, but I saw him watching me. He gave me a wry smile as if he could read my thoughts.

The engine burst into life, shattering the bucolic scene. If he hadn't still be injured, if – if a host of other things, I would have been excited for the night drive. Especially now I knew he wasn't going to drive like the devil. Bertram, I thought, would have loved it, but his driving skills would definitely have ended us up in a ditch, or stuck halfway down a mountain. Much as I loved him, I did not love the way he drove. (What is it about gentlemen drivers? Stick them behind a wheel, and be they ever so intelligence, they suddenly lose all their wits and become six-year-old boys in their toy carts again. Only these carts can go damned fast.)

Crabtree, who was on a later start, came over to wish us well. He added, 'I say, old man, I know this is a competition and everything, but would you mind if I gave you a little advice as an ex-professional driver?'

I could see all Fitzroy's metaphysical fur stand on end, but he only nodded and gave the thinnest smile.

'It's going to be ruddy awful in those mountains and ruddy cold. Don't be tempted to put the foot down. We're getting light snow on top of compacted ice, and that's a deadly combination for the best of tyres.'

'I've been thinking the same,' said Fitzroy to my surprise. 'It's clear the rally organisers don't care about our lives. It would suit them if we all failed.' He gave a bark of laughter. 'I assume they have some other fish to fry apart from a simple race.'

'I've wondered,' said Crabtree. 'If they had any humanity they'd delay tonight's leg. But I hear they've been setting up stage points and selling seats!'

'Ah,' said Fitzroy, 'all about the money. The more of us that crash the more they can charge at the next leg.'

'That's immoral!' I said.

Both men smiled so patronisingly at me I feared Crabtree had seen through my disguise. 'Ah the ideals of the young,' said Crabtree. 'It's the way of the world I'm afraid, Fitzroy minor. After all, aren't the rest of us here for the prize money?'

'Your reputation?' I countered.

'Yes, but having that reinstated would regain me a lucrative career.' He patted the bonnet of the car. 'Stewards getting ready to start you. *Bonne chance*!'

'We're in Germany,' muttered Fitzroy. 'What an idiot.'

I didn't have time to reply before we were waved off. A small crowd of people, all scarves, hats, and big coats from my point of view, had suddenly appeared to wave us off. They must have been waiting inside the inn.

Our car and Amaranth's were started together. Amaranth put her foot down at once. Flurries of snow and ice shot into the air obscuring our vision. But through it all we could see her car fish-tailing in front of us.

Fitzroy braked. Too hard. The engine stalled and the car started to spin. Everything blurred. The snow became tangled lines of white against the darkness. He fought the wheel, steering into the spin. It took us terrifyingly near the edge of the road and a drop I knew to be more than twenty feet. The only force remained the car's momentum, but Fitzroy managed to bring us to a halt safely in the centre of the road, albeit we were now facing the other way.

The spy swore, describing Amaranth in terms I strongly felt she deserved, but which I will not repeat. 'Are you injured?' he said.

I shook my head. 'Only dizzy and feeling as I have been on the worst carousel in the world.'

'Don't be sick in my car!' He jumped down and restarted the car. He turned it on the ice with surprising ease. Then he looked at me, 'I know I said I wasn't going to go fast, but I'll be damned if I let that – that *woman* beat me.'

'Go for it,' I said, gripping the sides of my seat.

'Besides,' said Fitzroy flooring it, 'we'll have tyre tracks to go over.'

'Is that good?' I managed to say. The speed at which he had taken off had stolen my breath, and now as he tore up the wooded hillside road, I could feel my fingers already beginning to ache with the effort of holding onto the seat. 'Right, ten feet!'

Fitzroy fishtailed the car, or whatever the proper manoeuvre is, and neatly rounded the corner.

'No idea,' said the spy. 'But I'm damned well going to overtake her.'

'Run her off the road?'

'Don't tempt me,' he said from between gritted teeth.

Now I had to concentrate harder than ever, shouting out directions to him as powdery snow flew up in sheets from both sides. It wasn't until we emerged from the first section of woodland that I realised it had actually stopped snowing and that all of the stuff coming into the car was caused by us.

I looked over at Fitzroy. If I had expected to see him hunched over the wheel, gripping it tightly, head jutting out against the wind, I was disappointed. Instead he sat much at his ease, handling the wheel with a surprisingly light touch and a slight smile on his face. I winced inwardly. I had seen this expression before. It was when he was at his most restless.

I chose not to distract him with idle chatter. Although we had not taken long to turn the car, Amaranth must have put on a super turn of speed. There was no sign of her at all, except the tyre tracks.

After we had travelled another mile or so, across open country, the fields quiet and blanketed with snow, the tracks began to disappear; it was snowing again. The road climbed still, but at a gentle inclination. I knew from my studies this was the easier part of the leg, so I wasn't caught out when Fitzroy revved the engine to new heights.

The light from our lamps barely broke through the night and the snow. Without being asked I began to give Fitzroy distances to bends, angles, and all the other information I could about our slowly vanishing road. Back at the inn I had thought I could never learn it all – and even Fitzroy hadn't thought I needed to learn all the road measurements. Fortunately, I have always found sheer terror an excellent aid to my memory, so even if he had been completely unable to see I would have been able to direct him.

What I could not do was divine if there were sheep, deer, or even wandering villagers on the road. Ours wasn't the kind of a car to survive a crash. As the spy had kindly explained to me on our journey, whatever we hit would likely bounce up over the bonnet and into our laps, killing us both if the ensuing crash did not. At the time he was stressing how important it was for me to navigate properly.

I cast a sideways look at him, and saw that a serene expression not only remained on his face, if anything he was even more relaxed. His shoulders had slumped down, and if I didn't have the evidence of my eyes and my ever-numbing fingers and toes, I might have thought him driving along a clear country lane in summer. For all I knew, in his mind that was where he was.

I uttered a few silent prayers and carried on shouting directions. I had to shout louder and louder as the road took us further and further up. The wind howled like a giant, ravenous beast, the snow and ice crunched, flurries spewed up from under the tyres and the engine had become deep-throated and straining. Every time I opened my mouth, the cold caught the back of my throat, making me cough, but I kept on calling. I knew we were getting to the beginning of a long series of bends, and at this speed, Fitzroy had to hear my directions if he was to keep us alive.

I seriously considered trying to get the spy to slow down. Amaranth must be long gone, I could only hope in the wrong direction. There were two hairpin bends coming up with bad drops and I didn't want to go round them at this speed. Also, as if

195

the journey wasn't perilous enough, I could see thick fog below us. I could only hope we would stay above it.

I was wracking my brains with a way of signalling my desire and my fear to him, without distracting his ability to drive, when a light appeared in the middle of the road ahead of us. By appeared I mean, one minute it wasn't there and the next it was. It took my poor befuddled brain a moment to realise it was a man standing with a lantern in the road. I noted that already the lamp had a faint halo; fog.

Fitzroy slammed on the brakes, and pulled the car as far into the side as he dared. We knew there would be other cars behind us. The Germans with their prototype were probably the only ones with a hope of overtaking us, but then their vehicle was more like a rocket on wheels, and it would be unwise to even get clipped by it.

Everything stopped. Fitzroy had us tucked into the side, near a steep slope, but with our wheels still on the flat. The light bobbed towards us, revealing Amaranth's driver, Luke. 'Thank God you stopped,' he yelled over the wind. 'Amaranth's been taken ill and I don't drive.'

The expression on Fitzroy's face was a mixture of delight and deep irritation. 'Wait here,' he said to me, 'I'll see what's up.'

'She's got herself wedged in the car. It will need the three of us to get her out.'

'What on earth?' said Fitzroy.

'I think she's hurt. Please hurry,' said Luke.

I looked to Fitzroy. He shrugged, so I jumped down and followed Luke across to the other car. As soon as I stepped out of the car my feet appeared not to want to obey me. This was the moment I realised how deadly the road beneath actually was, and how magnificently Fitzroy had been driving. I would have even complimented him, but I had to concentrate hard to stop myself slithering and sliding all over the place. Fitzroy either had an excellent sense of balance or good crampons, as he appeared to have no such trouble.

We arrived at the car to find Amaranth slumped over the driving wheel. Fitzroy jumped up on the running board and felt for a pulse at her neck. I hung back. Something wasn't right. Amaranth moaned as the spy pulled her into an upright position. At the same time I went to check the front of the car. Yet, when I saw the front of the car it was without a mark.

'Something is wrong,' I yelled to Fitzroy. He looked up from the woman who was half slumped and half out of the car. 'The car is too well parked.'

Fitzroy dropped Amaranth as if she was a sack of potatoes. Her eyes flew open. Neither of us paid her much attention. Behind her we both saw the absence of our car. Luke was running back towards us, clutching a shovel.

'Sir! Sir!' he called. 'I saw it starting to go, but I didn't get there in time. She's gone over.'

Fitzroy swore and pelted past him with me hot on his heels. However, the spy managed to stay upright, I completed half the distance on my bottom. When we reached the spot where the car had been parked, we saw tyre tracks leading off down the slope. Without hesitation Fitzroy plunged after them and I followed. I slipped again and started tumbling down the hill. This time I remembered to tuck my head in and protect it, so while I had no idea if I was up or down, at least I would avoid concussion. It lasted perhaps few minutes, before the spy caught me, and brushed the snow from around me. I sat up, dizzy, confused, and determined to keep my dinner inside. On top of everything else I couldn't bear to revisit those sausages.

I heard an engine in the distance. The next group catching up with us. 'Are you injured?' he asked.

'Whose engine is that?'

The spy's expression became most grim, his eyebrows lowered and his lip went so thin they almost vanished. He still wore his driving goggles and so appeared more demonic than man. 'Amaranth's. Your instincts were correct, if a mite slow. It was a trap.'

'The . . .' I repeated what he had called her.

He smiled. 'Never say that in front of Bertram. He'd drop dead on the spot.'

'What do we do?'

'There's some snow caught around the front wheels, but if we dig her out I think we should be able to do a controlled roll down to a lower road I remember from the map. It meets up with the proper leg not too far on. We shouldn't lose too much time.'

'He took our shovel,' I said.

Fitzroy went to the boot. I followed. The boot was empty. He said, 'No shovel, no rope, no thermos, no blankets, no food. How the hell did he get it all out in that short time.'

'I expect he dumped it on the road.'

'That's unconscionable,' said Fitzroy. 'People die out on these mountains.'

'We could go back . . .' But only then did I look at the slope I had fallen down. 'Oh,' I said. 'It's rather steep.'

Fitzroy nodded. 'On a good day it would be hard, but with my wound, and you still recovering, I don't think it's going to be possible. I say we clear the wheels then do as I suggested.'

'A controlled roll downwards? It's steep.' The spy shrugged, as if to say he didn't see another option. 'Oh, damn and blast those stewards,' I said, 'and the car-wreck-loving public. Where are they when you need them?'

'Not on the side of this freezing cold mountain. Come on. You'll have to help me shift the snow.'

'With what?'

'Our hands,' said the spy. 'Aren't gloves a marvellous invention? Besides, it'll warm you up. Like chopping firewood. Heats you twice.'

I followed him to the front of our car. Fitzroy double-checked the handbrake Luke had loosened, and then we began digging like dogs in the snow.

He had one thing right. It did warm you up. I finished my front tyre and went to check the back one on my side. A branch had caught under the hub, but amazingly the tyre was undamaged. I removed it with a combination of care, difficulty, and swearing.

Finishing, I looked up to see Fitzroy already back in the driver's seat. He was sitting awkwardly, listing to one side. However, when I appeared he straightened up and re-buttoned his coat.

'Are you bleeding?' I asked.

He nodded. 'No point lying about it,' he said. 'The effort of shifting the snow has caused the wound to open a bit. I'll be fine, but we need to get out of here even if we don't finish the leg, and find a farmhouse somewhere . . .'

'That bad?' I said. 'You wouldn't suggest that unless . . .'

'Get in, Alice. Let's slide this baby down the hill.'

Chapter Twenty-two
The Last Hoorah?

Fitzroy released the handbrake and the car began to slide downwards. We'd managed to clear the tyres for a few feet and it was enough so that when the car met the drift on the field it ploughed through and on. We travelled slowly with Fitzroy controlling the brakes. At the bottom of the field, we managed to turn into an icy little patch of land.

By this point the spy was grunting with effort. 'Perhaps I should drive,' I said as we manoeuvred out on the lane.

'I'd let you, but you don't remember this bit.'

'You could call directions for once,' I said.

Fitzroy gave me a quick grin. 'I don't think I have the knack of that like you. I get too caught up in my own head.'

'Should we turn back, then?'

'I've been thinking about that. We could. I don't give a damn about the race at present. There's no point the pair of us dying on this mountain. We can still try for the intelligence, but only if one of us is still alive.'

'So turn back?' I said.

'Do you know the way?'

'No, but we're on a road. If we turn about it must lead to somewhere.'

'Actually, now we're down I don't think it is the road I had hoped. I think we're still higher and this is more of a – ledge?'

'Great.'

'My sense of direction can take us so far. I think we're now closer to the end of the leg than the beginning. I'm hoping that also means closer to stewards or paying guests. Anyone we can get to help.'

'What about the cars following us?'

'Even if they were willing to stop, they may not stop us down here. We didn't go off the road. We were parked at the side when that paramour of Amaranth's sent the car down.'

'I don't have enough information to give a good answer,' I said. 'There are too many unknowns.'

'That's no uncommon on a mission,' said Fitzroy.

'I think we should head back.'

'But those last big bends were the finale, weren't they? Surely that makes us nearer the end?'

'There's fog below,' I countered. 'Who's to say this ledge won't run out and we'll disappear off the side of the mountain in the mist.'

'Happy thought,' said Fitzroy. 'But that could happen either way, couldn't it? If there's less road isn't there less risk?'

'I appreciate you listening to me, but you're the one with the experience, you decide,' I said. 'If it doesn't play out and we end up in dire straits I won't blame you.'

'But I would,' said the spy. He put the car into gear and moved off in the direction of what was most likely to be towards the end of the race. Inwardly I kicked myself for not making more of a fuss. Every fibre of me felt this was the wrong way, but I had nothing but instinct to offer, so I kept quiet.

'You're very tense,' said the spy.

'It doesn't feel as if this mission is going well?'

'And you blame yourself?'

This time it was my turn to scowl. 'I'm not aware of having done anything wrong.'

'I should rephrase that. I've been thinking that dressing you as a boy, as much as anything to preserve your reputation, has added a level of complication to the mission. If our contact has been told to look out for a man and a woman then they'd miss us.'

'Why would that happen?' I asked. 'And how might my reputation be harmed? No one knows who I am?'

Fitzroy slowed the car's progress. 'This fog is a damned nuisance. 'Fraid I'll have to crawl along as we don't know the terrain.'

'Fine by me.'

'Yes, but fog is damp. You're going to get wet as well as cold and the wet air you're breathing in won't help either.'

I pulled my scarf up over my mouth and nose. He nodded approvingly. I flapped a hand impatiently.

'Oh, your questions. As if a mouthful of wool could quieten you! Our descriptions could have got muddled simply because someone was cack-handed or not up to their job. Happens all the time. Even in the service never trust anyone to do what they say they will. They may intend well, but still be a bovine-faced imbecile recruited because Papa did something important in India. I imagine you're heard the phrase "plans never survive contact with the enemy"?'

I shook my head, but he didn't seem to notice.

'Well, when it comes to desk jockeys, as opposed to field agents like ourselves, you can bloody well count on their end going wrong somewhere.'

He lapsed back into silence. He kept having to wipe his goggles with his hand as mist formed on them. I thought of helping, but decided that would be distracting. Minutes later, he seemed to recall my other question.

'I'm confused about your comment on your reputation. I wasn't suggesting Euphemia Stapleford would come into disrepute. We'd really have messed up badly for that, but honestly, dear girl, you can't believe that sharing a room with me is the done thing? I admit from a mission perspective splitting us up when there may be enemy agents on the look-out does not make sense. But unless you had taken on the role of being my wife, which in these little rustic outposts would likely have meant only one bed, you would have been regarded by the other racers as a . . .' He coughed. 'You know what I mean. I can't imagine you're going to tell Bertram about our nocturnal arrangements.'

I pulled down my scarf. 'He'd be very shocked, but he would trust me. Of course, he wouldn't trust you. He'd want to punch you.'

'And quite rightly,' said Fitzroy. 'As a spy I found this the best arrangement for the mission, but if you were my husband I'd be livid.'

'I didn't know you were the possessive type.'

'Oh, I am, terribly, with anything that is mine. Luckily, I'm not intending to ever marry. I'd make a dreadful husband. Far too selfish and obsessed with my own interests and entertainments. Did it not occur to you it was a lot to ask of you?'

I shrugged. 'I've said it before. I don't always like you, but I always trust you.'

'Thank you,' said Fitzroy. 'That is almost enough to humble me. Almost.'

I opened my mouth to reply, but before I could there came a loud bang. A sharp, fierce shudder radiated out from the front wheel nearest me. I flew forward and only avoided going over the bonnet as Fitzroy flung an arm in front of me, pinning me back. The car grumbled to a halt.

'What did we hit?' I asked.

'I rather fear it was a rock,' said Fitzroy. 'Let me go look.' He climbed out. Even inches from the car his outline became ghost-like in the fog. I could just make out he held onto the car as he made his way round to the wheel and then knelt down, disappearing from sight. What seemed like a very long time later, but in reality could only have been minutes, he returned and climbed back into the car. I watched him with concern.

'Your side is hurting a lot, isn't it?' I said.

'The good news is we're no longer on a ledge. In fact, we appear to have dipped down into a small valley. The bang was us finding one side. We're in no danger of sliding or falling or being run off the mountainside.'

'Well, that's good,' I said, but even as I watched him, I saw the edge of his face blur. 'The fog's too heavy for driving further, isn't it?'

'Rather a moot point, I'm afraid. We've thrown the old girl around rather a lot and she's come through. However, this time I've mashed the wheel arch. This car isn't moving without serious outside help.'

'Oh,' I said. 'That's not good.' I thought a moment. 'And you said we're in a valley? Are you sure?'

'You didn't notice, but I brushed the edge of the other side just before we hit your side. I over-compensated. But you see the problem?'

'Not only will rescuers not know where we are, but there is no visibility to find us and the temperature is still dropping.'

He nodded. 'Yes, and what with that toe-rag lover of Amaranth's stealing our supplies, I don't have the gear that would have helped us . . . well, you know.'

'I wonder if it was him that let out Jack and sabotaged our car? Jealousy is an excellent motive.'

'Before today,' said Fitzroy, 'I would have said the spineless jackass didn't have the gonads to do anything like that. However, I am rethinking that position.' He sighed. 'The best we can do, is climb in the back of the car, and stay close. I don't like to ask, but you're slender and I'm losing blood again. Unless we huddle up – well, let's not think about that yet.'

We got into the back of the car together. 'Normally, I would never cuddle up to you,' I said. 'But I'm cold.'

'We're not cuddling,' said Fitzroy putting his arms round me. 'We are huddling – for warmth.'

'Should I try and tighten your bandage?' I asked.

'I don't fancy exposing my skin to the air,' said the spy, his breath warm against my ear. 'Besides, I think there is only slight bleeding when I exert myself. If I stay still, I'll be fine.'

'I take we're waiting for the fog to lift?'

'Yes, when it does, we can take the lie of the land, and see whether it's worth setting off on foot or waiting for rescue.'

'In all the stories I've read of expeditions it's the wandering off in the snow that generally gets people.'

Fitzroy chuckled. 'That because they are in the middle of Antarctica or somewhere equally remote. It might seem as if we're in the middle of desolation here, but we're between Stuttgart and Zurich. Both of which are major cities. Civilisation – and help – is close by.'

'Doesn't feel like it at the moment,' I said.

'I know. Have you forgiven me yet for getting you into this business?'

'I've already answered that. I'd never have been happy as a respectable married lady.'

'Even with Bertram?'

'Oh, I would have made the best of it with him, but there would have always been something missing. It's funny to think that my father spent his life avoiding the world after his one adventure . . .'

'But you got one sniff of a murdered body and that was it. Is it true that you dragged the poor man out of a corridor by the leg?'

I laughed. The cold caught at the back of my throat and gave way to a coughing fit. When I had myself under control again, I said, 'I think we should avoid humour for now. It was a servants' corridor, and I offer the excuse that I was in all likelihood on the verge of exposure, having been soaked to the skin by cold English rain and unable to change into dry clothes for a long time thanks to that horror of a housekeeper Mrs Wilson. I take it there's a file on me?'

'Of course. I wrote most of it, but there's a reasonable amount of information that has been extracted from police reports too. I believe one of my arguments for recruiting you was that you were a disaster magnet and it was safer for the whole country if I trained you and kept you on a tight leash.'

This time I laughed into his shoulder, so the cold air didn't hit me so hard. 'What's next? A bell round my neck?'

'Excellent idea. Although I'm going to have to rethink the idea of us working so closely in the field.'

'This isn't to do with my reputation again, is it?'

'No. For once it's entirely my fault – actually, that's not as unique an experience as I would like. You were spot on when you said I kept trying to protect you to the detriment of our work. Don't think I haven't noticed how when planning we finish each other's sentences or how much alike we think when considering options. You, Euphemia, have a sang-froid when it comes to killing that almost equals my own. You are always prepared to do what is necessary, and you don't trouble yourself with guilt afterwards when it is neither needed nor appropriate.'

'That makes me sound – callous.'

'It makes you remarkable. One in a hundred men, maybe fewer, are able to reason like this – maybe far fewer. I've never met a woman who could do so, who was also as intelligent and sensitive in other matters as you.'

I reached up a hand to his forehead. 'Are you growing delirious?' I asked, touching his skin. His was cold, but also clammy in a way that didn't seem right.

'No, I don't think so. I'm simply telling you some of things I would normally keep inside my head.'

'Why?'

'It's difficult – at least for me – to praise you without it sounding . . .'

'Improper?' I said.

'I suppose that will do.'

'But I meant, why tell me now?'

After a lengthy pause, he said with some effort 'I thought you would have guessed.'

'No,' I said, though many possibilities were running through my mind. However, I did suspect what he would say next.

'My dear girl, if the fog doesn't lift soon this may be our last hoorah.'

'You mean, we'll die here?'

Chapter Twenty-three

In which I acquire another husband

'If we had the blankets, the thermos, and other stuff I packed, we'd stand a much better chance, but without them . . .' He trailed off.

'I'm not ready to give up yet.'

'Good girl. Neither am I, but you need to understand the stakes. If it lifts enough for you not to fall off the side of a cliff, you'll have to think about leaving me. I'd give you my coat and if you kept moving, and there is a village near here, you'd stand a chance.'

'But you wouldn't.'

'It would be rather a waste for us both to die. I'm not up to it, besides it would let me go out with a noble ending. Something I hadn't dared hope for.'

'No,' I said, tugging on the collar of his coat, 'that isn't going to happen. You were born to be shot and I won't stand in the way of your destiny.'

'Euphemia,' he said kindly, 'I applaud your loyalty, but you must learn to be pragmatic about this as well. Spies die all the time. Ours is a risky job. I have never expected to live into my old age, and I have ensured no one will grieve or suffer when I am gone. I've had a rare old time in the service. If I'd had the time, I would have told you some tales you'd barely believe – and a few you'd have doubt-less given me a row over. I wouldn't change anything I have done in my life. I don't think, even at my age, there are many men who could say that.'

'No,' I said. 'I won't leave you to die.'

'I'd suggest you could shoot me – like an old horse – but I fear it would bring down an avalanche on you.'

I found myself choking back tears. 'Don't joke like that. For all you're an arrogant, smug, infuriating pig of a man at times, I don't want to lose you.'

'And there's me singing your praises at our farewell, while you . . .' He reached out a hand and placed it gently against my cheek. He wiped away a tear with his thumb. 'Ah, if I've affected you so deeply, maybe there's hope for me in the afterlife yet.'

I looked up at him in despair. He kept his hand lightly on my cheek and moved his face very close to mine. 'Ah, Euphemia,' he said in a soft voice, 'if only things could have . . .' Then his voice changed entirely, back to the crisp efficiency I knew. 'Hang on a minute. I can see your eyes are brown.'

'They've always been brown,' I said confused.

'I can see you,' he said.

'I can see you too,' I said, wondering if there was some deeper meaning I was missing.

He pulled away from me. 'The fog's lifted.' He bent down under and reached under the driver's seat. He pulled out an oddly shaped gun. 'Euphemia, I need you to get out of the car, point this at the sky, turn your face away, and pull the trigger.'

'I said I wouldn't leave you.'

'You're not,' said the spy. 'This gives us both a chance. Now hop to it.'

I did as he asked. The gun went off with a bang, and a bright red light appeared in the sky arching above us. A little shaken I got back into the car. Fitzroy pulled me back into the 'huddle'. 'That, my dear girl, was a flare. We have a member of the US Navy, Edward Very, to thank for that rather short-barrelled pistol you just fired. If Gunther wants to be paid, he should be out looking for us. The light will hang up there for a short while, and it goes high enough to be seen from quite a distance. Never understood why most people think they are only useful at sea. Thank goodness I kept it inside the car and not in the boot for that wretched crap-stain to find.'

I put my hand up to his forehead again. 'I think you're coming down with a fever. You're sounding delirious.'

'Nonsense. I never get ill. Besides, I have to look after you. I can't do that if I'm ill. No, I don't mean look after, that's patronising. I mean train you. Train you so you can look after yourself without me hanging around in the background. Not sure I'll ever be able to think straight when you're around, Euphemia. Damnedest thing you said about me not being able to save my mother and wanting to save every other woman instead. Never would have thought of that. But it makes a weird kind of sense. She was thrown from her horse. Broke her neck. I wasn't there. Always thought I'd have been able to stop the creature bolting if I'd be riding with her. Quite a horseman even then. Always felt guilty I'd chosen not to go out that morning.'

'You were nine. You'd never have been able to hold two horses.'

'The desire to protect, defend, preserve, all those sorts of words, something you love, like your mother or your country or . . .'

'Shhh,' I said. 'I can hear a car.'

'Don't interrupt,' said Fitzroy. I could feel him starting to burn up beside me. 'I was about to tell you something important. Now what was it. It had something to do with us . . .' He rambled on, becoming more and more incoherent. I held on to him and prayed hope would arrive soon.

When it did arrive, it was in the unlikely form of Otto, propelling himself down the side of the valley on a rope. He held on to the rope and sort of bounced off the rock. Obviously, someone above was playing out the rope.

He came over to the car grinning. 'Not as good a driver as . . .'

'He's sick,' I said. 'He needs a doctor.'

Otto took one look at the delirious Fitzroy and said, 'Let's get him out the car. He'll have to go up by rope, but I've got both Crabtree and Gunther with me.'

'You can't,' I said. 'He's bleeding – from the wound again.'

'There's no other way to get you both out of here. God only knows how you got down here in the first place. Once he's up we can get a doctor quickly. Help me with him as much as you can, will you?'

It was Otto's muscle, but my coaxing, that helped us get Fitzroy into a rope sling. By the time they winched him up, his eyelids had fluttered closed and he was unconscious.

'You next,' said Otto, holding out the sling. 'Nothing to be scared of. Be over in a trice.'

'I'm not scared,' I snapped. 'Let's get this done.'

Without another word, he tied the sling around me and gave the rope a tug. The rope dug into various soft parts of my anatomy, and it was sore enough to make me bite my lip. But the view, as I rose up above what was more of a gully than a valley we'd ended up in, was quite breathtaking. It would have been a beautiful place to die, but I was delighted I wasn't to be called to do that today. Once at the top, I scrambled out of the ropes and ran to where Fitzroy lay in the back of Gunther's car. Jack was licking his face and whining.

'Can you manage?' I yelled to Crabtree. 'We need to get him to a doctor now.'

He gave me a thumbs up and threw the sling back down for Otto.

'Gunther, we'll have to go fast. Do you need me to drive?'

'That will not be necessary, ma'am.'

Subsequently, it transpired that Gunther must have gone to the same driving instructor as Fitzroy. He tore along the now visible road, such that my hat, though pinned to my head, blew away. My hair, longer now, spread out defying the brilliantine as Gunther pushed his car to its limits. Even Jack barked with excitement. I looked over, afraid he would try and jump out. Instead, he dropped down into the footwell beside Fitzroy and continued washing his master's hand with this tongue. I offered no conversation as the wind stole my breath, and Gunther's driving took all

210

my attention. I believe I prayed us around every point. We flew along so fast I was unconvinced our tyres still touched the ground. He braked before the hairpin bends, but once halfway through accelerated, making the engine screech as he forced it into a lower gear and climbed.

Without fog and snow falling, the distance seemed so short. That we could have died so close to help made a huge impact on me. One I have never forgotten.

We drove into an inn courtyard, barely slowing. '*Hie! Hie!* We need help!' shouted Gunther. '*Hilf uns!*'

People ran towards us. Finally, we were safe.

Later, in the room, I asked Gunther why Fitzroy hadn't used him in the race.

'Bit of a problem with my rights and lefts, ma'am,' was all he said as he went away to arrange the speedy arrival of a doctor. I stayed with Fitzroy, who by now was making little sense. I washed and changed into loose trousers and a top. I left my hair free, as I felt the charade had run its course. Fortunately, we had been missing so long that a doctor was already on the premises and I was barely dressed before Gunther was knocking at the door with him.

'Mrs Alice Fitzroy,' said Gunther without blinking. 'The sick gentleman's wife.'

I quickly put my left hand behind my back, before the doctor saw my lack of ring. To my relief he was a younger man with bright blue eyes that sparkled with intelligence and humour. 'You can stay if you wish, ma'am,' he said.

'You're English!'

'Sent from the Embassy, ma'am. Apparently, your husband is an important man. We might have to whisk him into hospital. Would Germany or Switzerland be your preference?'

'Switzerland,' I replied promptly.

'Good choice. Now, I think I'd better get on with it. If you do choose to stay, you might mention to your husband that I'm a

211

doctor and not trying to attack. I've been told he has a fearsome left hook.'

'I'd better stay then,' I said. As I crossed the room, Gunther pushed something into my hand. I felt my wedding ring and slipped it on my finger.

'Perhaps you could undress him for me?' said the doctor. I glanced at Gunther, who slipped cowardly out of the door. 'Just down to his underthings.'

'There's a wound on the side of his chest you'll need to see.'

'Oh well, top off too. I don't think we need go further than that.'

Fitzroy was extremely restless. His eyes flickered. He muttered in low indecipherable tones, but he chuckled suddenly at the doctor's speech.

In the end the doctor cleaned and replaced the bandage. He wrapped Fitzroy up in covers and gave me powders to make up with strict instructions on how to dose the spy. 'Don't keep the fire so high. We want him to warm through, not be scorched on the outside. We need to keep the blood down close to the internal organs. I'll be staying on at the inn till tomorrow. Reception can get hold of me at any time.'

'Do you think he will get worse?'

'No, he's clearly fit and healthy, but the wound is slightly infected. I've cleaned it out as best I can and put iodine on it. He's also still low on blood. I don't believe he will get worse, but unless he's made a miraculous recovery by morning, I think I will be taking him off to hospital.'

'But he'll live?'

'Well, you know, Mrs Fitzroy, doctors hate to make promises like that. Life is so uncertain, but I wouldn't say you have anything to worry about.' He patted me on the shoulder and went out.

Only now did I realise we had been given a lovely suite of rooms, with a bathroom and one big double bed. However, there was also a plump-looking sofa, and being not overly tall I was sure it would suit me. I certainly wasn't leaving him alone and unprotected.

I was sitting by the fire, dozing and thinking wistfully of supper, when Gunther entered, but instead of food he was carrying clothes. He offered these to me. 'I thought these might be more appropriate. But I'd keep the boots you have. It's still slippery underfoot. What did the doctor say?'

'It seems likely he'll be off to hospital tomorrow.'

'Well, that's a rum do and no mistake,' said Gunther, lapsing into what I assume was his native accent. 'Sorry about the ring, ma'am. I don't know where he put yours. I hope he's not too angry about it. Blame it on me.'

Puzzled, I examined the ring on my finger. I'd been too tired to previously care, but now I could see it wasn't mine. It fitted well enough, but it was thicker and somehow the jeweller had embedded strands of red gold running through the yellow. 'It's all right, Gunther. He's given me this one to wear before.' I might as well have stated my intention to fly out of the window for the look of shock that crossed Gunther's face. He covered it quickly. And frankly, I was too tired to care.

'Mr Crabtree and the German gentleman have invited you down to dinner, ma'am. I'll stay with the captain. I'll give you a minute to change first, shall I?' Gunther, it appeared could be as conniving as his master, but I agreed. If I was going to watch Fitzroy for most of the night, it would be good to eat and relax first.

I found the two men, sitting at a table, waiting for me. They both stood when I came over. 'Really,' I said. 'You didn't do this for Alan.'

Both of them looked confused, so I took pity on them and sat down. I lost Alan's voice and mannerisms and became simply myself. It was rather a relief. I hadn't realised how much I had changed my behaviour to inhabit the role. I thanked them profoundly for rescuing us. There was much gentlemanly muttering and grunting about only doing one's duty. 'How is the old bu – man?'

'Fitzroy? Gunther's watching him, but you got him here in time. I suspect it's the end of the race for us, but after a few days in bed he'll be up and about. Doubtless cursing our fortune.'

'That's too bad,' said Crabtree. 'He's a fine driver. I don't believe I ever saw him on the circuit. Do you know where he trained?'

'Here and there,' I said. 'With others who also drove far too fast.' I gave a light, ladylike laugh. 'He's a fiend for speed. Likes the excitement.'

'He's very lucky to have such a game lady to act as his navigator. For him to be doing so well you must be pretty top-notch too.'

'It's all quite new to me,' I said. 'I'm too terrified to forget anything.'

'Does Fitzroy get very cross when you do?' asked Otto, an undertone of actual concern in his voice.

I smiled and shrugged. 'I haven't got it wrong yet.'

Drinks arrived and Otto fell back into his old ways and began to flirt. Crabtree remained a little off until I carefully displayed my wedding ring. I saw him eye it several times. I decided to wait and see what he said. By the time our soup had arrived he had struck upon an idea.

'Pardon my saying so, but I did become used to calling you Alan. Otto obviously knows you from before, but I do not feel it appropriate for me to address you by your Christian name. Should I call you Mrs . . .?' He looked at my hopefully, like a dog who has performed a trick.

'Fitzroy,' I said. 'Mrs Fitzroy.'

Otto choked.

After much back-slapping, red-faced and panting, he sur-faced for air, gulped a few times, and said, 'So you did marry him? I wondered.'

I raised an eyebrow in the vague hope of signally him to stop. 'Who else could it have been?' I said.

'Yes. Yes. It makes a kind of sense. But after the death of his previous fiancée—'

'All before my time,' I said cutting him off. 'We're happy

214

together.' I desperately wanted to ask him what he was talking about. The dead woman must be the one the ring was made for, but the last thing I could do was expose Fitzroy's past to a civilian like Crabtree.

Otto finally saw sense and dropped the topic. I asked Crabtree to call me Alice as he had saved my life. He and I chatted happily about cars for the rest of the meal. I'd found I'd learned more than I realised and actually quite enjoyed the topic. Otto piped up occasionally, as if to remind us he was still present, but offered very little in the way of conversation.

We were on the coffee when a waiter presented me with a message. I read it.

'Gentlemen, it seems that my husband has proved medical science wrong yet again. He is sitting up in bed and would like to see us, after our meal.'

'Shouldn't he be resting?' said Crabtree.

'Indeed, but I'm sure a quick visit will do no harm. He doubtless wants to thank you both.'

'Hardly in character,' muttered Otto, but I decided not to hear.

When we did go up, we found Fitzroy sitting up and looking attentive. However, I could see a flush remained in his cheeks and the glitter of his eyes was too bright. Jack was curled up at his feet on top of the covers. From somewhere the marvellous Gunther had found him more pyjamas; this time of scarlet silk with black piping. With his hair brushed, he looked quite the thing, and I could tell by his slightly smug expression that he knew it. I only hoped someone had bothered to tell him we were now married.

'Gentlemen, wife,' he said, allaying my immediate fears. 'Do come in.' He motioned to me to sit beside him. I sat on the edge of the bed, and he put one arm possessively around me. I watched Otto's eyes widen at this, and of course the double bed. I bit my lip as I realised he might actually think Fitzroy and I were married, and that the truth I'd told him earlier was my cover story. The poor man was dreadfully confused. I turned and dropped a kiss on Fitzroy's head. 'I'm so glad to see you looking better, darling.' Under my breath I added. 'You shouldn't flinch when I kiss you.'

'Otto, Crabtree, please sit down. I need to relay my deepest thanks to you for our rescue. You both went above and beyond what could be expected of you and we are very grateful.'

He tightened his grip around my waist, making me jump in surprise. I gave a little laugh to cover it and said, 'He is definitely feeling better.'

Otto blushed and Crabtree seemed to find something of interest to look at outside our window. Fitzroy laughed, following my lead. 'Not quite as good as that, my dear, but on the way. On the way.'

Crabtree rose at this. 'No need to thank us. I have no doubt you would have done the same for us. But I think we should leave you to your rest, now.' Otto also rose and nodded. Gunther opened the door for them. At the last moment Fitzroy said, 'Oh, Otto, one moment, if you don't mind.' Crabtree, already through the door, murmured something and Otto returned.

'I believe congratulations are in order,' he said. 'Euphemia told me some story about her marrying a country gent, but I should have known. . . .'

He noticed I had risen and that Fitzroy had leaned back. Jack wiggled his way up the bed and onto his master's lap. The spy began stroking his ears. 'I wondered if we should take Crabtree into our confidence.'

'Bring him on board as an asset?' I said.

Fitzroy nodded. 'But I wanted to ask Otto first. Did you become his navigator as an opportunity to keep an eye on us or for another reason.'

Otto sat back down in a chair. 'Can we speak frankly?' he said.

'I rather wish you would,' said Fitzroy. 'I feel terrible and I want to go to sleep. I do not want to end up in a hospital in Zurich, nice though they are. Alice and I have work to do.'

'Is she your wife?'

'I'm in the room,' I objected. 'You can ask me.'

'I'd rather ask you both together,' said Otto. 'You're both unreliable when it comes to the truth.'

Fitzroy gave me a smile. 'Naturally. But no, Alice is not my wife. She told you the truth when she said she is married to a country gentleman.'

'Of obviously enormous understanding,' said Otto. Before either of us could comment he continued, 'I took the opportunity because I need your help with the assassination plot and because I don't trust the pair of you or Crabtree.'

'He's not one of ours,' said Fitzroy.

'I realise,' said Otto. 'He's not one of ours either, from what I can discover. At least he didn't pick up on any of the code words I dropped in conversation. He's either a very cool customer or he's playing a deep game.'

'You've spent more time with him than either of us now,' said Fitzroy. 'What exactly do you suspect?'

'You're after something and so is he.'

'We're here for an information drop,' said Fitzroy. 'Nothing to do with any assassination attempt.'

'Can I ask for your word as a gentleman on that?' said Otto. 'I know I'm technically on your side now, but I draw the line at murdering any of the Kaiser's relatives.'

'That isn't in your terms of agreement,' said Fitzroy. 'But as it happens, I can give you the word of a spy, which is worth far more, that I know nothing about any plots against the Kaiser's family. Personally, I would have thought such an action would incentivise him to go to war. Not something the service is especially keen on. Remember, we don't serve the government.'

'Then I think Crabtree may be involved. The other two with him, the man who disappeared on the boat and Crawford, they were both agents – our agents – but Crabtree is not known to us. He was supposed to be the one honest part of the team, but I think he is playing his own game.'

217

'It would be pointless to hope that the Kaiser and his ministers, chancellor, et cetera, are all playing for the same team, I suppose?' said Fitzroy.

'They don't advertise, but there are factions. Between us, the Kaiser grows more temperamental by the day. It is little more than a toss of a coin each day whether England is his loathed enemy or Russia.'

'That's a bit unpredictable,' I said.

'He cannot, I believe, bring himself to commit to war with his beloved grandmother Victoria's country.'

'He's doing a damn fine impression then,' said Fitzroy. 'Is insanity a question? I ask that respectfully,' he added as he saw Otto stiffen. 'Even in Victoria's immediate family there have been certain incidences.'

Otto bowed his head in acknowledgement of this admission. I determined to prise the details out of Fitzroy later. 'He is a passionate and quick-tempered man. But once the temper is past, he can be reasoned with as sanely as any man.'

'Who do you believe is going to be killed?' I asked.

'We don't know,' said Otto.

'If it's not us,' I said, 'then do you think it is another faction's influence? And what might they want to achieve?'

Fitzroy smiled at me and nodded. Jack opened his eyes and his pink tongue lolled out. Of all of us in the room he was the most contented creature.

'Your capture would make it look like it was arranged by the English,' said Otto.

'Our capture and demise, you mean,' corrected Fitzroy.

Otto glanced to see my reaction, but I gave him none. 'Yes,' he said, 'but I think England, although ready for war, is not seeking it. Is that not right?'

'There will always be people seeking to make money from war,' I said. 'Arms dealers and the like.' I was remembering my late employer, Richard Stapleford, who had once seemed more demon than man to me.

'I agree,' said Otto, 'but would any of them be unscrupulous enough to initiate war?'

I laughed at that. Fitzroy snorted and shook his head at me. 'Possibly,' he said. 'But I think it is more likely a German faction. They would have the right information to track the family and get them into a disadvantageous position.'

'I agree, and all I can think is this may be a form of a threat to get the Kaiser to rein in his temper – and unpredictability.'

Fitzroy frowned heavily. 'There's something to that.'

'So, it would have to be not too important a member of the family—' said Otto.

'No,' I interrupted. 'It would have to be someone who mattered to the Kaiser.'

'Any significant person's assassination would start the war,' said Fitzroy. 'It would be attributed to us.'

'Not,' I said, 'if that person was only significant to the Kaiser.'

Now, Otto was frowning. 'I don't follow.'

'I do,' said Fitzroy. 'She means one of his illegitimate children.'

Chapter Twenty-four

In which I prove to my own satisfaction men's boots are far superior

'Fitzroy, do you need me for this discussion?' I asked. 'Only there was a great deal of muttering going on not quite behind my back. If our contact is a member of another team, they may now recognise us.' This was more than I wanted to say, but I couldn't help noticing the high colour remaining in the spy's face. I didn't think he was at his best. I did worry about leaving him with Otto, but what else could I do?

'What?' said Fitzroy looking at me. 'Could you get me some iced water, if you would? I have a burning thirst.'

'Of course,' I said. I could relay this task to Gunther and then set about patrolling the inn in the hope of being accosted. It was a slim chance, but with Fitzroy more ill than he realised I could feel this mission slipping away from us.

As it was, I encountered Gunther on the stairs. 'He wants iced water,' I told him.

'Send a waiter up, would you, ma'am. I don't like leaving him with that German fellow.'

'You don't trust Otto either.'

'Ma'am, no one ever trusts a double agent.'

I nodded and left him hurrying up the stairs.

This inn was bigger than the others. It had a cage-style lift in the centre stairwell, but it creaked alarmingly, and I wasn't predisposed to trust it. I trotted down the steps, almost going head over heels once as my skirt tangled with my boots. I had forgotten how cumbersome long skirts were. There might be women who climbed mountains in this attire, but having enjoyed wearing trousers I was already planning having my seamstress come up with some designs for more practical wear that nonetheless wouldn't offend the population of the Fens.

I was about to turn onto the last landing when I heard Crabtree's voice. 'Look, I know it must have been difficult with the girl in disguise, but we had our reasons. You can trust me with it now.' I stopped frozen to the spot. My heart thundered in my chest, but I could barely breathe. The all-round good egg, Crabtree, was not on our side after all.

A man's voice answered. I knew the voice and yet didn't recognise it. I was certain I had heard it before in the dining hall of one of the inns. I thought the accent was German, or could it be Austrian? 'I need the code word.'

'Dancing Maiden,' said Crabtree.

'All right, meet me by my car in half an hour,' said the other. I stood on tiptoe, but I couldn't see around the corner without moving forward in a manner that would completely expose me. I held my breath, hoping Crabtree would leave first and I would see the other man. But it was Crabtree who remained. I saw him stroll into the bar across the lobby. Fortunately, he did not turn round and see me. The pair of them must have been standing in the recess at the foot of the stairs. I was unimpressed that neither of them had checked the stairs.

I ran lightly back up the levels to our room. I tumbled through the door to find all three men about to broach a whisky. 'You can't have that!' I exclaimed.

'Who? Why?' said Gunther, standing in the middle of the room holding the decanter.

'Fitzroy is too ill, and I need either you or Otto to come and catch Crabtree with me. He's a villain.' A chorus of eyebrows lifted at that. A few years ago, the stern look of so many gentlemen would have daunted me. Now, I simply described what I had heard quickly and efficiently.

'I'll come,' said Otto. 'Then you'll owe me.'

'Excellent,' I said. 'Gunther can keep Fitzroy in bed.' Gunther spun round to see his commander indeed trying to climb out from under the covers. We left him remonstrating with Fitzroy and set off with a smart step down the stairs. I explained about the odd accent.

'Austrian?' asked Otto.

'I wouldn't know,' I said. 'You need Fitzroy for languages.'

'Who of the teams we have left could it be? And why now?'

'We're on the border with Switzerland,' I said. 'Beside the difficulty in identifying us, wouldn't it feel safer to do it here?'

'Perhaps,' said Otto. 'So, your plan is that we lie in wait by the cars?'

'If we get there in time.'

'And if anyone else sees us, what are we doing?'

I shook my head and ran quickly towards the front door. 'We'll have to think of something.'

A blast of cold air hit me and reminded me I was dressed for dinner, not for driving. Otto took off his jacket and wrapped it around me. 'I suggest we pretend we are on a tryst away from your tyrannical husband, who is so jealous, he made you dress as a boy.'

'If we must,' I said. 'But I am not kissing you again.'

He took my hand and led me through the shadows to a vantage point that looked across the courtyard. Some of the garage doors were open and light flooded out, but it was no match for the pitch dark of the mountainside. There remained plenty of dark shadows. Otto drew me into the deeper shadows and into a firm embrace. 'Are you sure?' he whispered in my ear. 'I bet I am a better kisser than Fitzroy.'

I slid my left leg between his. He tightened his hold on my waist. He bent his head towards mine. I avoided his lips and whispered in his ear. 'If I bring up my knee in one quick motion, you will be speaking in a different register for a week.'

He laughed softly.

'Keep your mind on your job,' I hissed.

I felt him stiffen. I twisted my neck to look round. I saw Crabtree striding brazenly towards the garage of the Germans, Mann and Muller. Crabtree had stopped in front of a lit garage. He had his hand up to his eyes. Then came loud voices. 'We should intervene before this gets any worse.'

'Not yet,' said Otto. 'They've twigged he's not right.'

His grip on me was firm enough I could not escape without fighting. Reluctantly, I waited. Otto had been a German spy long before he became a British one. He might understand these situations better than I. 'I'll wait two minutes. Then I'm going in,' I said curtly.

I didn't have to wait. Crabtree pulled a gun from his pocket and shot twice. The sound echoed around the courtyard. He dashed forward and then back out. All around us we could hear the sounds of men shouting, alarmed by the noise.

Otto said something in German. It didn't sound polite.

'He'll be going for his car,' I said. 'We have to get there first.'

'He's got a gun,' said Otto.

I scraped the outside of my foot down his shin and stamped on his foot. He released me uttering another string of German. I took off across the courtyard. But it appeared I was not the only one who wanted to catch Crabtree. Two men staggered out of the garage. One clutched a bleeding arm, but still managed to support his fellow, who raised a rifle and fired in Crabtree's direction.

The sound of the gun firing inside the garage had been loud enough, but now with the percussion echoing around the courtyard, it could no longer be thought to be the backfiring of a car. People rushed out in all directions.

'Get him,' cried the man with a gun. 'He is a mad man. He shot at us!'

As ever, the English language remained the common denominator, and people poured out from the garages to give chase. In front of all of them, I heard a thump behind me and a curse in German. Evening shoes, I thought. Otto always did like dressing up too fancily. I ran on with a gathering crowd at my back.

The others were passing the word, and soon people were coming from all sides. Even a few hardy souls who had been out for an evening walk joined in the hue and cry. At this point Crabtree stopped, turned and fired into the crowd. Behind me dissolved into chaos as people dived for cover. I didn't. Not for reasons of bravery, but because it had never occurred to me that Crabtree, who in my mind I was still struggling to cast as a villain, or even anyone, would ever do something so ungentlemanly as to fire into a crowd of innocent civilians. Luck stood by me as I ran on. He shot once more before turning to run again. We were closer to the hotel, and I caught sight of his face, white with panic, but also grimacing in rage. The crowd had blocked him from getting to his own car in the garage. He ran up to the hotel, looked right and left. He saw me gaining on him, and this time raised his gun to fire directly at me. This time my danger sense did kick in and I threw myself sideways into a damned good roll. Unfortunately, I ended up in a rose bush.

Frantically, I fought my way out. Depending on the gun, he could have up to four shots left. If I was him, it would be very tempting to shoot me while I was trapped in the foliage. While not his ultimate goal, I feared it would give him a degree of satisfaction.

The cursed thing scratched and tore at my hair and skirts, but I pulled myself free. Behind me I heard people shouting about calling the police. The desire to follow a mad man with a gun had waned. As I pulled free, I cast about for sight of him. We were on the top of a hill. There were few trees to provide cover and running down the hill would leave him totally exposed. As I hesitated, Muller and Mann came up beside me, both of them sporting shotgun wounds.

'Where did he go?' Muller asked.

'I don't know,' I said. 'There is nowhere for him to go.'

'We will check he is not running down the hill. If he is, we will shoot him.'

'He has to try and get back to the car,' I said.

'We must intercept him before then,' said Mann. 'He has the papers.'

'Papers?' I said. Although I almost certainly knew what they were, I wanted confirmation before I risked my life further.

'The ones given to me by my brother-in-law, the inventor in Bremen. He made me promise I would not hand them on till we reached Zurich. He is fleeing into France.'

'Dancing Maiden—' I said.

Muller interrupted. 'It is a terrible thing that cannot be loosed upon the world by anyone. If both sides have it,' he paused, 'we can talk later. We must retrieve them before the police arrive. We will check the hill. We can find a vantage point. Claus is an excellent sniper. If he is outside, we will get him. You must search the hotel.'

'It would make no sense for him to go there,' I said.

'There are hostages to be taken,' said Mann curtly.

'Damn it!' I said and left them. As I reached the doors of the hotel I was thinking furiously. Where would I go if I were him? I would try to find another exit. I had a sudden flash of memory of my first night on the road with Fitzroy. The kitchen!

I ran through the dining room, aware that I would draw attention to myself, but I had little choice. A waiter carrying a tray of soup was emerging from a door. Reasoning this must be the way I needed to go, I ran full tilt towards him, yelling at him to get out of my way. He stopped, still staring at me, his mouth open. I continued forward, making 'move aside!' motions with my arms. To no avail. I had no choice but to push past him. I thrust him to one side and bolted through the door. Behind me I heard the sounds of crockery shattering and the shrieking of guests.

I found myself in a narrow passage. I ran along it until I came to a cross way. I chose the passage that led towards the rear of the hotel, assuming this was the best chance of finding an exit, so this would be where Crabtree had run.

My hope that the network of staff corridors would be small and simple ended quickly. Clearly the hotel had been expanded over time, and while I did find one kitchen, it appeared to have no exit. At least the chef who was chasing me with a ladle didn't shoo me out of a back door, but back the way I had come. I wondered if Crabtree had had the same reception, but the scattering of junior chefs accompanied with the inevitable dropping of foodstuffs and upsetting of pots suggested either I was their first intruder, or they were remarkably slow learners.

There must be a rear entrance, but time was moving on and I was no closer. I could hope the Austrians had got him, alive or dead, at this point I didn't much care, but I needed to cease running in and out of larders. It was time for me to find Otto, Gunther, and even Fitzroy. If nothing else, the latter would offer his pithy advice or, more likely, remonstrations. I clearly wasn't handling this situation well alone.

I changed my tack and headed back to the lobby, intending to return upstairs. There were probably servants' stairs, but I knew all too well how easy it is to get lost in those, and the occasional boarding up of an exit door is all too liable to confound one completely. At least I could use that wretched lift system. By now, despite being the fittest I had ever been in my life, I was considerably short of breath.

I emerged into the lobby and marched quickly towards the lift. My untidy appearance would only be enhanced if I ran. I could also hear Fitzroy saying in my head, 'Not so much a member of the secret service, but an agent of the obvious, ineffective, and extremely loud service.' I was cursing myself for getting it all wrong, when I saw him - Crabtree. He must have entered the lift moments before I arrived and was now gracefully ascending. I ran to the control panel, but no amount of pressing recalled the lift. There being nothing else for it, I began to run up the stairs.

226

Round and round the stairs went. All the while Crabtree ascended smoothly beside me. I noted the odd-shaped bulge in his pocket. He still had the pistol. He'd lost his hat, but on spying me he lifted an imaginary one, saluting me. I didn't waste time responding. I knew I was on my last reserves of energy. My one heart-stopping fear was as soon as he reached the top, he would press the button to descend. I could only hope he feared the mob had pursued him into the inn. But where the hell was he headed? He'd had the opportunity to catch his breath, but where could he possibly go from here?

As he continued higher and higher, I realised there was only one possibility. He was going for the roof. There had to be a fire escape he had spotted. It made sense. I knew Fitzroy would curse me for not checking the location of the exits when we arrived. If he hadn't been so ill, he would have done so, and so should I.

My chest was burning now. My legs almost jelly-like. Sweat coursed down my face and into my eyes. With one hand I swept my hair back, taking most of the burning drops away from my face. Could I go further? Should I go to the room and seek help? What if I lost him? He had the plans for the Dancing Maiden. I had no idea what that was. All I knew was that they had to be retrieved and taken to Britain.

Of course, the lift reached the top before I did, and Crabtree dived through the door of the fifth floor. I followed, as fast on his heels as I could manage. This time I could see him ahead of me. I called for Gunther as I ran, but I had no idea if he would hear me through the thick hotel doors. Crabtree got to the end of the floor, opened a side window, and stepped out. This act caused me to stop in shock, gasping for breath. Had he taken his own life? I had to know. I carried on and saw that the window opened out into what first looked like the night sky, but closer inspection showed there was a ledge that ran along the side of the building.

I poked my head out. Crabtree shot at me. I managed to duck back as I saw him raise his arm. What was that, five? Six shots? I couldn't remember, but at least I had seen he was working his way along the edge. Unless he had lost his wits, he must have a plan. Taking a deep breath, I stepped out onto the ledge, flattening myself as close to the wall as possible, but facing outwards. At once I realised my mistake. The wind whipped at my long skirt. I scrambled for a handhold behind me as I heard the window close. I could only go forward. By a supreme effort of will I did not look down. Instead I held myself there for a few moments, waiting for my heart to slow enough that breath again was possible. During this time Crabtree did not shoot me. I looked to my side and saw he had vanished. If he had gone back in through a window and closed it, I was in real trouble. I couldn't go back, and our room was at the extreme other end of the building. The wind lashed a little light snow in my face. This, I told myself, would make an excellent fireside story, if I survived.

Having no option but to freeze and fall to my death, or to edge along this what I now perceived as slippery and narrow ledge, I edged.

After a couple of paces, it widened slightly, and I attempted to turn around. For a heart-stopping moment I thought I was about to fall – and then I decided that facing outwards was perfectly fine. I wondered if anyone would spot me and think to open their window. I heard voices from up ahead and managed to cry out. The wind whipped away my words, and as I passed the window, I heard it firmly click shut.

I continued out. Voices rose up from below. I could not bear to look over and see what was happening. Even if vertigo didn't overcome me (and my sense of balance), I knew the wind would take me. On I went. My life not precisely flashing before my eyes, but certainly I came up with a good few ideas of what I'd like to do to Crabtree should I be lucky enough to capture him.

Then, without warning, the wall behind me gave way. I fell backwards.

Landing on a small section of roof that lay between two protruding windows. I scrabbled up and backwards to find myself in a corner area with no Crabtree but with an iron staircase winding down the side of the building.

I gave up a small prayer of thanks and stood up. I peered over the edge and I saw Crabtree working his way down the spiral staircase as fast as he could. I would never catch him.

I cast around looking for something to throw at him – anything to stop his progress, but the section of roof was bare of anything except a small chimneypot and I doubted my ability to uproot it. I could untie a boot and attempt to drop it on his head. But my feet were small. Even with perfect aim I would achieve little except possibly drawing fire.

Now, I could hear Bertram's voice in my head. All these wretched men telling me what to do! He was saying that I'd done all that could be expected of me, and that I should stop and wait for Otto to bring reinforcements. There was nothing I could do.

Otto! He must be en route. Maybe even bringing reinforcements. It was imperative I stopped Crabtree.

At this point I remembered my mother cautioning me as a child against frivolity and playing in a manner unsuitable for a lady. Usually I regret recalling such times, but for once it gave me a good idea. Offering up several very fast prayers, I flung one leg over the side of the railing and, hoping the banister wasn't too wet to slow me, I set off down the railings much as I had done on the Vicarage staircase as a child.

My skirt with its heavy material soaked up the water nicely, and I fairly flew along. The turns were so tight I was quickly as dizzy as I was terrified, and I was truly terrified. As I closed in on Crabtree he turned, sensing something but unable to comprehend what. His eyes widened as he saw me. I had no way of slowing myself, so instinct took over and I and rammed my forearm against him as I went past.

The uniqueness of my attack, as well as its suddenness, was of enormous help. As I whooshed past, the harsh impact on my arm promised a bruise of truly enormous proportions, but it affected

Crabtree more. He span, his feet going out from under him, and down the stairs he went.

As I watched his legs fly over his head, and his weight increase his momentum to speeds greater than mine – I still continued down the railing like a witch on an unconventional broomstick – I saw clearly that he was taking quite a battering. With luck his neck would be broken before he reached the bottom.

Then, still astride my metal ride, I saw Otto coming up from the bottom of the stairs. I shouted a warning, but there was nothing else I could do.

Otto, seeing Crabtree hurtling towards him, launched himself over the side to allow the traitor's body to pass. He hung on with his hands and started to swing himself back over to the stairs – only he clearly hadn't understood how I was descending. We collided and I found myself thrown off into space. I hung there for a moment thinking about how time did really slow down when you were about to die, before I felt a strong tug on my skirt and Otto pulled me back onto the staircase.

Chapter Twenty-five

In which Amaranth reveals all and I acquire yet another husband

Otto and I descended together and managed to retrieve the papers from the broken body of the ex-racing car driver before the police arrived. Otto slipped them to me and told me to go back to the room. He said he would tell the police we had both being trying to stop Crabtree, who had been suffering from a dangerous depression after losing his team, and with it the last chance of resurrecting his career, and that we had both being heroically trying to stop him committing suicide. He asked me to get Mann and Muller to play along, and that he would make out that in his madness Crabtree had been thinking they were fighting a duel.

I had no idea if he could pull this story off, but I wearily slunk back into the hotel. I encountered Amaranth on the way, who followed me into the lift, babbling about how she had never told Luke to remove the equipment from the car – and could I ever forgive her – and she was so sorry Luke had let Fitzroy's dog out.

'If you will send bath salts, scented soap, new clothing and the softest fluffy towel to my room, I will forgive you everything,' I said. She seemed surprised, but I didn't stay to discuss it. Mentally, I attributed the sabotage of our car to Luke's jealousy, but now was not the time to tell Fitzroy. He'd only try to kill Luke and open his wound yet again.

I opened the door to the room to find Gunther redoing Fitzroy's bandage. 'He tried to follow you,' he said.

Fitzroy gave me a sheepish look. I passed the papers to him. 'I am going to run a bath. Supplies should be arriving shortly. I will leave the door open and tell you everything I know, on the condition no one enters, because right now I am extremely weary, but I am also extremely fed up. Intrude upon me and I will not be answerable for my actions.'

Gunther, and even Fitzroy, gave me startled looks. 'I can run that for you, ma'am,' said Gunther.

'No, continue patching up our gallant Captain,' I said, flinging Fitzroy an angry look. He had the grace to blush. 'I know perfectly well how to run a bath myself.'

Amaranth was as good as her word, and the necessary items along with a new silk nightdress were delivered. Gunther left them where I could whip them inside the bathroom without exposing myself. During my long and luxurious bath, I told them both baldly what had happened. Fitzroy tried to interrupt, but I bit his head off and said I was too tired to do this more than once. Did he want to hear it or not?

I must have hit the right tone, because after that I only heard the occasional gasp, chuckle, and once even a snigger, which I think must have been Gunther. I knew with the papers in his hand, Fitzroy wasn't going to be angry, and with Otto's cover story we should be able to get out of this with little difficulty.

Finally, I came back into the room, smelling of roses and lavender. My hair might be curling damply, but my scarlet nightdress was very much the thing. Or so I assumed seeing the faces of the three men when I entered the room. I flung myself down on the sofa where I intended to sleep and demanded blanket and pillow. Gunther passed me a hot, sweet tea with brandy, and I listened to them tidy up the end of it all. Well, half-listened. After everything I was having difficulty keeping my eyes open. Otto seemed to have managed things with the police. Mann and Muller had headed off to have their wounds tended to somewhere, and the hotel was offering free brandy in the bar. Interestingly, the Austrian team of Braun and Milche had also taken off, which added credence to Fitzroy's belief they were spies, who had taken the opportunity to leave and report back to their masters. (I didn't mention this at the time, as Fitzroy would have gone all smug again.)

'Thank God, that's all over,' I said, laying my cup on the floor beside me. 'I'm going to sleep. Don't worry about disturbing me. I doubt the last trumpet could.'

I pulled the blanket down, and as my head hit the pillow, I heard Otto say, 'So now we have to save the Kaiser's son.

I gave a cry halfway between a whimper and a wail and pulled the blanket over my head.

The early afternoon sun was already sliding towards dusk though we had only finished luncheon an hour ago. We had waited for Otto to receive delivery of a new car while the old one was taken away to be examined. By whom I wasn't entirely sure. For the discretion of the delivery driver he could have been police, German secret service, or from our service. Whoever he was, he'd left a highly expensive and luxurious car for Otto. That, coupled with the delivery of my clothing for this mission, left me feeling somewhat spoilt. If all went well it could be positively enjoyable. I felt bad at leaving Fitzroy behind. He would be, by now, on his way to hospital in Zurich, with the loyal Gunther and Jack accompanying the service doctor.

He had been perfectly furious that I was completing this mission with Otto. His eyes glittered as much from anger as fever, but he knew it was the only option. He didn't like Otto getting the credit, but he appeared to be even more put out that I was going with Otto at all. However, it had been the only plan that made sense, and he had had to give way.

Around me the mountains, no longer a threat to life and limb, glowed with the first touches of sunset. The air smelled of firs and pines. The cold caught at the back of one's throat, and even inside this luxurious motor it was hard to feel warm. But the countryside around me was truly breathtaking. The snowy tops of the mountains now touched with pinks and yellows of the fading sun, the slopes so white they seemed blue, dotted with dark green trees, and below in the valleys the cosy lights of small settlements, were all reminiscent of a Christmas scene – only this was real and so beautiful. When one is yelling directions and praying that one's race partner will not drive one off a cliff there is little time to admire the scenery. Now, cruising towards Zurich with the double agent, dressed to the nines, and having nothing to do except sit back in my very comfortable seat, I finally got to appreciate how stunning this part of the world truly was. I said as much to Otto, who took this almost as a personal compliment and became quite chatty.

He filled in some of the blanks of the previous mission that I had missed. 'It turns out Crabtree had left his car on the other side of the hotel. He'd expected he wouldn't be able to get it out of the garage after meeting with the carriers. Whether he expected to have to shoot them or not, we don't know, but he went armed.'

I snuggled down further in my new fur coat, deciding there were some luxuries associated with female clothing that I could live with. 'Do we know how he knew the code word? Fitzroy only told me what it was when we crossed into Germany.'

'No,' said Otto. 'We don't and it's a worry. Fitzroy thinks there must be a leak back in London, but how he's going to track that down with the whole of Crabtree's team dead I have no idea.'

'How long did Mann and Muller have the information?' Even as I asked, I could see the pocket I'd sewn into the inside of my corset burning. Fitzroy had insisted I take the papers as he was in no position to look after them, he'd said. He'd also told me not to even tell Otto that I had them with me.

'You did sleep through almost the entire debrief, didn't you?'

'I find being shot at and falling off staircases awfully tiring.'

Otto turned briefly to smile at me. Unlike Fitzroy he didn't take his eyes off the road for any length of time. He drove efficiently, and with a reasonable turn of speed, but he was by no means as flashy a driver as my partner. 'Mann's brother-in-law was the German-born inventor that created whatever "Dancing Maiden" actually is.'

His eyes flicked towards me again. I shook my head. 'I haven't seen it,' I said. 'I suspect it's, as they say, above my pay grade.'

Otto let out a tiny hiss from between his lips. 'So like Fitzroy to keep everyone out of the loop, even when he can barely stand.'

'The brother-in-law?' I prompted.

'He passed the information to Mann in Bremen but insisted he didn't pass it on to the British until they were on the border with Zurich. Apparently, he fled through France to the Channel. We've no idea if he made it. He expected to be persuaded. He said from the day he had completed the plan he was under watch twenty-four hours a day.'

'So, we had double the chance of getting it,' I said. 'Either in paper form or from him directly. But if he was being so closely guarded, how did we get through to him?'

Otto shrugged. 'That is, as you said earlier, above my pay grade. Either Britain has other double agents of whom I am not aware, or he was even cleverer than we believe him to be.' He paused to negotiate a sharp mountain turn. Fitzroy would have continued to talk, but I kept my silence allowing Otto his concentration. 'The same could not be said of Mann. He spent a long time thinking that Amaranth and her companion were his contacts. The said lady being somewhat free with her manner, it appears he mistook her flirting as her trying to subtly make contact.'

I laughed. 'As if Amaranth could be subtle about anything.'

'You seem quite light-hearted about the woman, considering she tried to kill you.'

'She only tried to get us out of the race. It was Luke who removed all the survival gear. I don't think Amaranth thought for a moment we would go down the hill after the car. She was in it for the money. She's living on Luke's allowance at present and I would imagine, should he bring her back to Britain, that will quickly be withdrawn.'

'One assumes the boy also has to return to school,' said Otto.

'He's not that young. He's at college.'

'Still far too young for her,' said Otto, giving a slight snort. 'I'm surprised you two have become, dare I say it, friends.'

'I talked to her after breakfast this morning. She's had a rough time. More or less sold off by her father to an American industrialist, who showed, shall we say, a darker side after marriage. Now she's divorced her family have disowned her.'

'Then she should not have married in the first place,' said Otto.

'I've known what it is like to be wholly without income, have you?'

'Of course not. I manage my finances well.'

'Women, ladies, rarely get that option,' I said. 'Until you have been without income you cannot understand how she feels. I thought it was bad enough when my mother, little brother, and I verged on destitution, but at least I had family. Amaranth is alone.'

'You? How?' Otto spluttered his confusion.

'How did we manage? I went into service – not *the* service, but service, and my mother, the daughter of an Earl by the way, gave piano lessons.'

Otto drove on in silence for some time.

We began to descend from the mountain top towards Zurich. 'Are you married to Fitzroy?' said Otto suddenly.

'Of course not,' I said. 'The ring is part of my cover. Besides, aren't I meant to be married to you now?'

'I don't suppose you'd like to be, would you?' said Otto. 'A new Anglo-German pact? You are even more remarkable than I had previously thought. I think we would make a good team. You have a sense of adventure most women lack. Together we could achieve much.'

I looked at his profile. 'I assume you are speaking in jest?' I said.

'Why so?' said Otto. 'I am a well-educated, rich, cultured man, who is not wholly unattractive. You could do worse.'

Otto, as he knew very well, was extremely handsome. I didn't

236

bother to bolster his ego. 'I am fairly certain that I have mentioned I am already married – to an Englishman, back home.'

Otto shrugged. 'It is not difficult to arrange things. There are few men who would be as good an option as myself. Is he rich? Is he titled? Is he an agent?'

'No to all,' I said. 'But I happen to love him very much and I would take it strongly amiss if anything were to happen to him.'

Otto shrugged. 'Well, in that case, although we will have little enough time, I suppose we could fit in a brief affair. If you are willing?' He turned to look at me full in the face for longer than was safe by anyone's definition. 'I still remember that kiss you gave me. It was the third best kiss I have ever received and if Fitzroy is to be believed, you were still a virgin at that point.'

'Otto, stop it,' I said. 'I am about to put myself in mortal danger to save a member of your royal family. Fitzroy and I agreed to help you because we fear that an assassination might cause your Kaiser to make ill-advised and overly emotional decisions, but I have not been ordered by either Fitzroy or London to help you. If you keep baiting me like this I damn well won't.'

Otto glanced over at me, frowning. 'But you agreed to act as my wife. We must make it realistic or people will not believe the charade. We must appear to be intimate with one another and I only know of one way to achieve that.'

'Believe me, I am a far better actress than you imagine.'

Otto shrugged. 'And I thought it was meant to be us Germans who were all work and no play.'

'Will I be expected to speak German?' I asked. 'Because I haven't a word.'

'No, the ball is in Switzerland. Most present will speak in English. It is a neutral country, and no one outside its borders speaks Swiss.'

'And you are sure you and Fitzroy have correctly identified which of the Kaiser's children are to be assassinated?'

'There is no certainty, but the killing of one of the Kaiser's illegitimate children would be a harsh blow that he would not

237

acknowledge in public. The son in question is a respected noble-man, but few knew of his true parentage. The ball is an excellent opportunity for someone to kill him. It makes him the most likely target out the illegitimate children who are known to us. The others are currently in places we would consider secure.'

I wondered which 'us' he was talking about but decided to refrain from asking. When I had first met Otto he had appeared no more than an Englishman About Town. Now, the longer I spent with him the more German he appeared. I could not help remembering Fitzroy's comment that any double agent was fundamentally untrustworthy.

'Besides, if I am wrong, then all that has happened is you have had a nice time at a ball. The passport you have names you as my wife, so you will need to play that part. But otherwise all you need to do is talk and dance with the gentleman in question, while I take out the assassin. There is no reason why you should not even enjoy the champagne. It should all be easy enough. Afterwards, we could even enjoy another bottle together.'

It appeared that Otto had no intention of ceasing trying to persuade me into his bed. As an Englishman I had known him as a playboy, but not a person who would force himself on a woman. I wondered if the German side of his was the same. The service had, I knew, forced him to turn to our side. I did not know what inducement they had used, and how much reason he might have to hate anyone willingly serving the British Crown.

It was not much longer before we pulled up before a strange combination of hotel and inn. Wooden, with a high, pointed roof and several balconies, the Swiss chalet where we were to stay sparkled with lights. Ladies and gentlemen in smart clothing, but not yet evening dress, stood out on the balconies to watch the sunset. The air filled with chatter and laughter.

Otto left the valet to park the car, and the porter to bring the luggage. He signed us in, ordered a bottle of champagne to the room, and let the pageboy lead us to our room. The room, like the rest of the building, was luxury at its height. Although there were two comfortable seats by the window, and balcony door, the majority of the room was taken up by an enormous bed. Closets were fitted away, and we had our own discreet small bathroom hidden behind a final closet door. Otto flung himself down on the bed and stretched out. 'Finally, somewhere comfortable to lie! Come join me, wife. I promise to behave. The softness of this mattress is a miracle after those nasty little inns.'

I eyed him warily. 'Honestly, Euphemia, you know me. I very much want to make love to you, and I will continue to suggest it throughout the evening. However, I would never hurt you.'

'I'm holding you to that,' I said. I took off my shoes and lay down on the other side of the bed – out of arm's reach. 'Oh, you were right,' I said. 'This is super.'

'I am right about many things,' said Otto. I heard him vaguely moving, but my head had not been on the pillow for more than a few moments before I fell fast asleep.

Chapter Twenty-six

Dancing

I awoke to the sound of singing. It took me several moments to remember where I was. Someone had placed a coverlet over me. I checked – I remained dressed. From the bathroom Otto's tenor echoed in something vaguely operatic. Wagner, I guessed.

I assessed myself in the mirror and decided I was clean enough for tonight. During my travels across Europe my standard of hygiene had been challenged from time to time, but I had only bathed this morning. I took my opportunity and changed while Otto wallowed.

He reappeared with only a towel around his waist. His upper body was remarkably well toned. I did my best not to look at it. This was made all the easier by my inability to finish pinning up my hair. I had been provided with a diamond, or possibly paste, pin for my hair, but although it had grown it had not grown enough for me to arrange my hair as I had done previously.

'Let me,' said Otto. 'I am rather an expert at helping women fix their hair.'

He said this is such a cheeky way I could not help but laugh. Picking up a brush, his quick fingers rearranged my hair, pinned it in place, and fixed the pin in. 'There, you look lovely,' he said.

I was about to compliment him on his skill, when out of the corner of my eye I caught sight of his towel on the floor. Of course he had needed to use both hands, but I now cast my eyes carefully down. 'Perhaps I should await you downstairs,' I said.

Otto, realising my discomfort, chuckled. 'No, that would look unusual. I am not embarrassed. Germans are proud of their bodies. We are not as hide–bound as the English.'

'You do refer to yourself as German all the time. In England I would never have guessed,' I said, my eyes still firmly fixed to the comb on the dressing table.

'I have to,' said Otto. 'My life depends on being German. It is a state of mind I can not afford to let slip. My dual heritage is known, and as such my loyalties are always in question. If I save the Kaiser's child tonight, my place will be confirmed. It is of the utmost importance. I assume this is the only reason Fitzroy let me have you.'

'I'm not his to give,' I snapped.

'As an agent, I meant,' said Otto. 'Only as an agent. I am aware you are otherwise very much your own woman. Any woman who could keep Fitzroy at bay for weeks on end must be formidable in her own right. I assume you did keep him at bay?'

'As it transpires Fitzroy knows only too well how to be a perfect gentleman.'

'Ah, now suitably abashed, let me gather my clothes and retire to the tiny washroom to change.'

I stayed staring at the comb until I heard the bathroom door close. I was annoyed enough I considered wedging something in the door and locking him in. Unfortunately, I had no idea what the Kaiser's son looked like, so instead I sat down on the edge of the bed to wait.

Otto appeared looking every bit as handsome as he thought he was. He offered me his arm, which as I was pretending to be his wife, I took. I could have insisted we waited until we were outside, but I felt there was no need to be petty. Besides, we were now working and there was no time for any more of his games. I only hoped he realised that.

We took a cab to the ball, which was in a *schloss* – a castle. The cab took us to a gated entrance, much like a lodge back home. But once we were through this, having shown our invitations, a horse and carriage awaited to take us to the summit where the *schloss* stood. Unlike a British castle, it was a bright white that shone in the moonlight. Mostly square it had short tubby turrets. We driven through yet another opening and into a grand courtyard, lined with marble statuary. On one side the doors were flung open. Two braziers lit the entrance and beside them were yet more guards, who checked our invitations again. Moving through a highly polished hallway, where we were relieved of our outer garments, we then entered into a huge ballroom. For a moment I felt completely overwhelmed. A full string orchestra took up a corner, a buffet and drinks were laid along one side, and the ballroom floor was already filled with dancing couples, all of whom were dressed exquisitely. The women dripped with diamonds and the gentlemen wore tuxedos so well-fitted they could have been painted on. I stumbled slightly as without pause Otto led me onto the floor and took me in his arms.

'It is quite a sight, is it not?' said Otto

'I don't think I have seen anything quite like it,' I said. 'My previous experience has been of smaller balls.'

Otto's lips twitched at this for some reason. 'We shall dance and circulate for a while until we spot our quarry.'

'Will no one recognise you for who you really are?' I asked quietly.

'Even for me this ball is normally – how would you say – beyond my touch. The people present represent much of the wealth in Europe, and many of the royal families. After all, through Victoria so many of them are related.'

'How will we know him?'

'He is blond, blue-eyed, late twenties, and has spent time in the military, so his figure should be good, but mostly we will know him because he is too young to have normally achieved the number of medals he is wearing. I am told from a distance it can look as if he is wearing plate armour.'

'Well, that is an excellent defence,' I said, trying to be light-hearted. Now we were here the enormity of the mission sank in. This would not be easy.

'Yes, unless he is shot in the back,' said Otto. 'You will need to shield him from that.'

'Of course,' I said, as if this was something I did every day.

We spent twenty minutes spinning around the floor, before Otto relented and we went to the refreshment area. By now the room had become even more crowded and the heat given off by so many people was quite overwhelming. More windows and doors had been flung open, but after I unwisely allowed Otto to give me a glass of champagne, the temperature became too much to bare.

'Can you excuse me one minute while I . . .' Otto looked down at me. 'Do not be long, we have not located him yet, and with the opening of so many windows I fear it will be all too easy for someone to slip past the guard.'

Of course I should have stayed, but I felt ready to faint. I'd fainted before and I knew all too well the strange woozy feeling that came over me beforehand. I slipped away, having no idea where the ladies' room would be, so instead, as all I needed was air, I picked a door at random and stepped out into the night. The singular most amazing event of that night, despite what was to come, remains for me the night sky. I wandered a little way a way from the door, and the night dropped like a blanket around me. Looking up I saw not an inky blackness, but a sky that made all the diamonds in the world look tawdry. The stars were not only beyond number, but so numerous that the very night was crowded out by their glory.

'It is magnificent, is it not?' came a male voice at my side.

I turned to see a handsome young man in his twenties, with ears ever so slightly too big for his head, also looking up at the sky.

'Oh,' I said in a deliberately surprised voice, 'I did not realise there was anyone else out here. I did not mean to disturb you, sir.'

He stepped closer and offered me his arm. 'Even in the moon-light I can see you are a little flushed – if you forgive me! The

243

ballroom is insufferably hot and they only offer champagne to drink. What I would give for a decent cold beer!'

It was only at this point I noticed his uniform and the array of medals. He must have seen me looking, 'Ignore all those,' he said. 'They are no more meaningful than the diamonds worn inside.' He smiled. 'Except for one or two. It is not a misname to call them decorations.'

I laughed. 'I am sure you are being modest, sir.'

'Perhaps a little. Tell me, are you a student of astronomy?'

I shook my head. 'I cannot claim to be. I was merely enjoying the sight of the sky. It is so clear up here.'

'Undoubtedly we are closer to God,' he said. 'You should learn of the stories man has cast among the stars. They say more about us than you might imagine.' He began to point out constellations and tell me of the legends that had begat their names. He talked fluently and with the knowledge of a scholar. It was only when I gave a little shudder of cold that he stopped. 'I am a fool! From being too hot I have made you too cold. Come back in with me – and if I may be so bold, will you honour me with a dance?'

As Otto had made no attempt to find me, I assumed he must be seeking the assassin. I would have preferred to keep the Kaiser's son outside – if this was indeed him – but I could not deny I was shivering with cold.

We re-entered the room. He took me in his arms, and we began to dance. He was an excellent dancer, and he held me lightly in a most gentlemanly way. As we waltzed, I kept thinking how in the future this man might turn out to be my country's enemy. I realised I had not listened to what he was saying. I excused myself, saying I found the room distracting.

'But not as nice as the stars?' he asked with a smile.

I gazed up to return the smile and saw a violinist, who should have been playing, reach into his instrument case. It might have been nothing, but I couldn't take the chance. Much to my partner's surprise I suddenly took the lead, keeping my back to the orchestra and moving us further into the crowd.

My partner almost tripped but caught himself in time. 'Is this a new thing?' he asked.

'Oh yes,' I said. 'From England. Ladies take the lead there all the time.'

'The English are so strange,' he said. 'I take it from your accent you are Swiss?'

I agreed and was trying for a witty reply, when I again caught sight of the violinist walking down the side of the room. He had one hand behind his back. Again, I executed a neat turn. This time my partner was ready, and retook control, swinging me round the other way. As this took us further into the crowds I did not object. 'But this is most entertaining!' he said. 'Why has this not been done before? I await your next surprise, my dear.'

I did my best to look over his shoulder and spot Otto, but all I kept seeing was the violinist sneaking around the edges of the room like a prowling cat. How did he hope to get away with this? I wondered. Or was he prepared to die for his cause? Perhaps he hoped to get away in the ensuing chaos. I swung my poor partner this way and that, until even if he still found it amusing, I was getting breathless and giddy.

Finally, I spotted Otto. He stood between a champagne fountain and a lovely young woman in a very low-cut gown, with whom he was chatting avidly. When the violinist was the furthest away from us I could hope for I swung us both past Otto. If my dance partner had been less experienced, I might have been able to swing us into him, but he righted my course before any collision could happen. 'This has been fun,' he said, 'but we both grow a little weary. Let us have a small drink and continue to get acquainted.'

I almost wept with relief when he swung us to a stop by the champagne fountain. As he did so I heard the lovely young woman say, 'You are a cad, sir. You left me to pick up the bill.'

I would have liked to have heard Otto's response, but I broke in. 'Sir,' I said to my partner, 'may I introduce my husband, Nicoli Straussbergen. Nicoli, this charming gentleman brought me inside when he saw I had become too cold. We have been dancing delightfully, despite the fact one of the violinists has not tuned his instrument correctly.'

My partner snapped his heels together and introduced himself. The lovely lady disappeared into the crowds looking confused. 'So your wife also has a musical ear,' said the Kaiser's son. The look on Otto's face had confirmed it for me. 'I too detected something amiss with the orchestra, but I could not quite put my finger on it. Only that they sounded unbalanced.'

'Indeed,' I said, looking at Otto, 'I believe one of the instruments to be very unbalanced.' I opened my eyes wide at him, trying to convey my message.

It was then I spotted the violinist, who had edged around the side of the room and through the crowd to be only a mere fifteen feet or so away. Couples danced between us, but I saw the resolve in his eyes. I stepped backwards onto the Kaiser's son's feet, treading as heavily as I ever had on Bertram's. As he stepped back, trying to smooth an unmasculine 'ouch', I put myself between him and the gunman. His eyes met mine, and he saw that I had uncovered his intent. This was the point at which I hoped he would flee.

Instead he removed the gun he had held under the folds of his jacket and fired into the air. Immediately there was pandemonium. Screams from the women, oaths from the men, rent the air. The noise had ricocheted so for a few moments the exact location of the gunman was unclear to most present.

I turned and pushed the Kaiser's son as hard as I could. Surprised, he fell backwards into a tray of refreshments. He grabbed me as he did so – whether to regain his balance or because he had seen the gunman, I didn't know. The table broke beneath our weight and we tumbled into a heap onto the floor. Meanwhile, Otto put his head down and charged the gunman.

It all happened very fast. I had barely lifted my head, let alone sat up, before I saw the gunman fire once more. The shot clipped Otto's arm, but he kept going, reaching the man and slapping the pistol from his hand, before he used his other hand to deliver the most enormous punch to the man's head.

By the time I sat up, it was over, and Otto had slumped to a sitting position clutching his arm. Four men ran over to us and grabbed the Kaiser's son. He seemed less startled by this than everything else, so I had to assume they were his security detail. As he was manhandled out of the building, I saw him look at Otto and give a slight nod. Otto nodded back. Some gentlemanly understanding had been exchanged.

Otto's wound was exactly what we needed to get us out. While servants cleared the mess, and guards searched the *schloss*, pointlessly as it was all over then, as soon as we saw our gunman being taken away, I escorted my husband to a carriage to take us to the local hospital.

In the carriage, Otto remarked, 'He saw me. He will recognise me when I report to the service what I have done.'

'How will you explain me?'

'One of my many girlfriends. It will not occur to anyone that a pretty girl could be anything more.'

'Excellent,' I said. I tied the makeshift bandage I had torn from the tablecloth tighter around his arm. Otto winced. 'If you'd kept your eyes on me, we could have managed everything much more easily.'

For once Otto didn't argue.

I left him in the hands of the doctors and went off to find Fitzroy. He was in a private room with Jack under his bed, and Gunther taking notes. Presumably a report or merely a sheet of orders. He looked pale and his hair was madly curly, but he was sitting upright, and I could see no sign of the fever in his eyes.

'Did you?' He asked the moment I opened the door.

I came and sat down on the bed. Jack crept closer underneath and began to lick my ankles. I reached down and fondled his ears. 'You know, if your dog could purr, I think he would.'

'Oh, forget Jack,' said Fitzroy. 'Did you save the Kaiser's son?'

'Otto dove heroically across the room, taking a bullet in the arm, but flooring the gunman. He's a bit of a hero.'

Fitzroy growled. 'I suppose it's too much to hope for that it was more than a flesh wound?'

'I'm afraid so. I imagine his place in the secret service is now thoroughly cemented.'

'Well, that's something I suppose.' He looked me up and down in my evening wear. 'Must have been a very posh party.'

'It was. In a *schloss*. I hated every moment of it.'

Fitzroy laughed. 'No doubt you much prefer falling down mountainsides or dropping off roofs.'

'You know, I think I do,' I said. 'It's much more fun than being in a stuffy ballroom.'

'You're just in time,' said the spy. 'I'm giving Gunther his orders for the trip back. You'll be back with Bertram before you know it.'

'Oh no,' I said. 'I am tired, and bruised, and exhausted – and I have learnt that there are spas here. I fully intend to be well rested before I return.'

'You can't possibly travel alone,' said Fitzroy.

'No,' I said. 'I'm going to drive you back. That way, by the time we get back to England I will be a most competent driver – and you won't have to wait until you are entirely healed. No twisting the steering wheel for you.'

Fitzroy looked at Gunther.

'It solves a lot of problems, sir.'

'Damn and blast it,' said the spy. 'You know she'll only drive me into a ditch.'

'Oh, I doubt that,' I said. 'I'm more likely to drive you to madness first.'

Fitzroy moaned and lay back in the bed. Jack jumped up on top of the clothes and began to tongue-wash his face.

'Oh, for heaven's sake, dog, not you too. Why is everyone out to get me?' said Fitzroy.

'I'm not,' I said. 'I'm going to take care of you all the way home.'

'Saints preserve me,' said Fitzroy. 'The things I do for my country.'

The Unofficial Monte Carlo Rally